Caught Running

Madeleine Urban

Abigail Roux

Dreamspinner Press

Published by
Dreamspinner Press
4760 Preston Road
Suite 244-149
Frisco, TX 75034
http://www.dreamspinnerpress.com/

Cover Design by Mara McKennen

ISBN: 978-0-9801018-8-1

Printed in the United States of America
First Edition
December, 2007

eBook edition available
eBook ISBN: 978-0-9801018-9-8

"Caught Running" is for everyone who didn't become what they thought they would, but still found happiness.

To my soul sister, Willow, for her love and encouragement. I would never have gotten this far without her. – Madeleine

To my darling husband, who married me even after he knew I was crazy.

- Abigail

Chapter I

"HEY, Coach! Where are the basketballs?"

Jake Campbell looked up from his clipboard and narrowed his eyes at Jeremy: junior, running back. He took a moment to find it amusing that he categorized the kids he knew on sight by first name, class, and position if they played one of the sports that he coached.

"We're not playing basketball today," he answered as he checked Jeremy off his attendance sheet.

"Aww, man! We're running?"

"You betcha," Jake drawled with a pleased grin. "Outside," he added with relish. "In the coooold."

The kid's shoulders slumped, and he turned to head for the gym exits that led out to the football field and the track that circled it. Jake chuckled and shook his head, checking off more kids as they straggled out of the locker rooms.

Jake enjoyed his job at Parkview High. The kids liked him, and he liked them, for the most part. He coached year-round: football, wrestling, and baseball. And he won. Here in Georgia, winning was a big deal.

P.E. classes were just the five or so hours of warm up before he got to do his real job. That hadn't changed at all since he'd walked these very halls as a student himself years ago, and no one cared enough about high school phys ed to try and change it. Jake huffed and ticked off the last name on his list. Baseball tryouts started today. Just two more hours of this mind-numbing repetition, and he'd be able to get to the good stuff.

"NO, Carolyn, you can't petition PETA to get a waiver from dissecting the frog. The frog's already dead. It donated itself to science. Don't let its sacrifice be in vain," Brandon Bartlett said, shaking his head as he walked toward the front of the lab, watching the students pull on their latex gloves and cloth masks.

"Jimmy, no fire today. Off with the Bunsen," he said distractedly, hearing a huff from his side, and the slight whoosh of gas-fed flame shut off. He pointed out the correct instrument for Callie to use and moved to the whiteboard.

Brandon pulled his glasses from his shirt pocket and slid them on as he looked at the teaching materials. "You all have the directions for the dissection, and trust me, they haven't changed from yesterday when we went over them. Yes, Kelly?"

"Mr. Bartlett? What if I get guts on my uniform?" the cheerleader asked.

"There are aprons in the closet. That would be an intelligent security measure," Brandon answered. "Drake?"

"Can I cut off its head first?"

"Is cutting its head off first in the directions?"

"No, Mr. Bartlett."

"Are we going to tempt fate by not following the directions?"

"What fate?"

"Scrubbing out the dissection pans every afternoon for a week."

"Sir! No cutting off the head, sir!"

Brandon rolled his eyes. Sophomores. No longer wide-eyed and scared, not yet mature enough to be trusted to their own good sense. "Good choice."

As the students got to work, Brandon notated their presence in his attendance book and also marked who had been given what equipment on the two-person teams. He glanced up, a half-smile on his face. This was his lab. After almost ten years of teaching, twenty-five grant applications and a good wrangling with the principal and the school board, they'd agreed to build the large facility.

He was proud of his work at Parkview High. Even more so because it was *his* high school – he'd walked these same halls for four years – and he felt quite at home, although the students looked younger and younger each year. He frowned, glancing over at the gaggle of cheerleaders. He didn't feel that old, but...

Checking his schedule, Brandon remembered he had planning period during his next block, before the last class. He'd skipped lunch and left his meal in the fridge in the lounge, so he'd escape there to stop the drain of his mental faculties. He glanced up to see Drake and Aaron flinging frog guts at each other and sighed. Some days he could just feel his brain dribbling out of his ears.

AN hour before his last class of the day, Jake sat in the corner table of the teachers' lounge, sipping his water and eating his sandwich as he read. He had camouflaged a paperback in the Sports page of the morning paper, and whenever someone came in, he would curl the newsprint around the book protectively and follow the person with hard black eyes. It wasn't worth the jokes from these prisses about his reading ability to do otherwise.

He sat with his back to the wall, feet up on the table, waiting for one of the other coaches to come in and hoping no one else made the effort to try and talk to him. In high school, a lifetime ago, he'd been the leader of the pack; popular, athletic, good-looking. Now, as a coach in the same high school years later, he was dealing with a herd of teachers who had all been nerds in school and resented him on principle. Jake had quickly learned how the outcasts felt. The only difference, he mused with a small smile, was that now he didn't give a flying fuck what the others thought of him.

Having met Rhonda in the hall, Brandon walked with her, talking shop. As the chemistry teacher, she'd petitioned the administration to get an Advanced Placement class, and Brandon had asked for one, too, so they were discussing plans for the next nine weeks. They talked all the way to the lounge, where Brandon glanced around and saw Jake Campbell sitting by himself, reading.

They were and always had been complete and total opposites. Jake had been the Homecoming King their senior year – and the Prom King, too. Mr. Popular. Brandon had been Valedictorian and the captain of the Academic Team. A nerd – and even amongst the nerds, not so popular because he hadn't come through the same system of schools they did. Still musing while grabbing his lunch, he sat at a round table in the middle of the room where he could keep talking with Rhonda.

Jake slowly slid lower in his chair and lifted the paper higher, his eyes at a level where he could still see the room but quickly divert them before contact was made.

Brandon tried to make eye contact, to at least give Jake a nod, but the other man deliberately wouldn't look at him. The science teacher sighed. He'd tried to be friendly to Jake, and to Misty and Troy as well – other students from their class who had come back to teach – but none of the three would even acknowledge him. They obviously held their high-school opinions close to their hearts. He wondered why he tried. Shaking his head to something Rhonda asked, Brandon started on his lunch.

Some people Jake could just *feel* in a room. Brandon Bartlett was one of them. Jake didn't know why. He supposed it was because he remembered the guy from high school, and the memory weighed heavily on him. No matter how old you got, high school was always yesterday. Jake had never been the type of guy who'd gotten his rocks off on making other people miserable, but some of his teammates and 'friends' had, and he remembered the way they'd treated Brandon and his type. It was a painful memory for Jake; he had never joined in, but he had never tried to step up and stop it, either.

Jake shifted in his seat and sniffed as he read the same line over again in his book. The door to the lounge opened again, and Jake looked up to see Gerald and Lena walk in together. He almost sighed in relief – his fellow outcast phys ed teachers to the rescue. They were a dying breed – the real coaches. The other coaches in the school were either decent part-timers, like Troy; off-campus hires; or teachers who had once touched a piece of sporting equipment, like Misty. Those were worse than the people who only taught; they thought they were at the top of the food chain, straddling the academic and athletic worlds. But only a precious few did either job well, and those were the ones smart enough to disregard the invisible class barriers.

"Well, hello, beautiful," Jake drawled in greeting as he folded over the newspaper. His eyes purposefully went from Gerald's hulking form and his perfectly shaved mocha-colored head to the athletic blonde beside him. "And hello to you, too, Lena," he added with a smirk.

Brandon's eyes shifted up to see the newcomers, but he carried on his conversation as the two made a beeline to Jake, not even a smile or a glance in his and Rhonda's direction. Resigned, he popped open his Gladware bowl of grapes and nudged it toward the other teacher so she could share.

"You're such a pervert," Lena laughed softly as she headed for the fridge.

"'sup, Coach?" Gerald asked in his deep bass voice as he sat down. "Who won last night?" he gestured to the paper Jake was holding. "Or can you even tell when you hold the paper upside down?" he asked pointedly as he flicked the corner of the page with a laugh.

Jake cleared his throat and blushed a little, smiling sheepishly as he slowly put his book in his lap and turned the paper right side up.

Rhonda snickered in the middle of a sentence, and Brandon frowned, turning to look over his shoulder at Jake and Gerald, one of the other football coaches. It looked like Gerald was teasing Jake about something. Brandon looked back to Rhonda. "What?" he asked.

She leaned forward to whisper. "Jake was holding the paper upside down. You know, the one he was reading so intently that he couldn't even acknowledge our presence?"

Brandon's brows flew up, and he grinned widely. "Really?" he said in a hushed voice, barely resisting the urge to turn around and look again. "That's pretty funny that Gerald caught him."

Jake kicked Gerald's shin under the table and blushed harder, sliding down further in his seat as Lena tossed Gerald a bottle of water and giggled. "I hate you both," he declared with a small smile, tossing his book onto the table and laughing along with them.

Snickering again, Rhonda leaned forward. "Don't you think he's handsome? I think he's really handsome."

Brandon boggled. "Gerald?"

"No, silly. Jake!" she whispered excitedly.

Brandon wondered where the cool and collected chemistry teacher had gone. She had to be ten years older than he was. "Ah ... I went to school with Jake," he said uncomfortably.

"You didn't tell me you were friends! Maybe you could tell him a little about me," Rhonda wheedled quietly, smoothing her red hair behind her ear.

Now Brandon was really getting wigged. "I said I went to school with him. Not that we were friends. And, Rhonda, if you want to approach him, I'm thinking that's something you should do yourself. He never really liked me then. Doesn't now, for that matter," he added quietly as Rhonda tossed flirting looks over his shoulder.

"How's the team looking this year?" Lena asked as she sat down. She coached fast-pitch softball, and they always had a little bit of a competition between the two teams.

Jake shrugged and sat up straighter. "Couldn't really say," he answered ambiguously, smirking at the woman as Gerald gave a booming laugh. Jake caught snatches of conversation from the other table and glanced over there. The chemistry teacher peered at him, batting her eyelashes in an alarming manner, and Jake's eyes widened. He automatically looked over at Brandon questioningly, trying to gauge whether he should retreat or if this was something he could throw Gerald in front of and be safe.

Brandon chanced a glance over his shoulder and saw Jake looking at him, query written on his face. Brandon couldn't help but wince a little and shrug, trying to convey an apology with a tiny shift of his head toward Rhonda.

"I think ... I think I left the showers running," Jake blurted suddenly as Gerald laughed harder and slapped his thigh. Lena watched him stand up with a slightly outraged look on her face, obviously thinking that he was making a teasing attempt to bypass their annual teams discussion. The head coach waved at them as he gathered up his stuff and glanced up at Brandon again distractedly.

Not sure why he was even trying – other than simply feeling bad for his fellow man – Brandon met Jake's eyes again and subtly turned his head and eyes to the door, indicating he should make his escape while he could. Then he turned back to Rhonda, cleared his throat and spoke a little more loudly. "So, Rhonda, you were going to tell me how the application process for your A.P. class went. What did you tell the school board, exactly?"

"You can't hide from me for long, Campbell!" Lena called as Jake slunk toward the door. He turned around and gave her an irritatingly impish grin and then looked back to the table where Brandon sat, apparently distracting the chemistry teacher. He gave the man a little smile and a nod of thanks as he made a hasty exit.

Watching Jake escape from the corner of his eye, Brandon turned all his attention on Rhonda, who was now waxing rhapsodic over paperwork. He figured he'd done his good deed for the day. Possibly the week.

"HEALTH? You want me to teach freshman health?" Brandon asked for the third time, utterly stunned. He stood in Mr. Berry's office – the same Mr. Berry who had been his geometry teacher – and just shook his head. "I've got honors biology, a sophomore and a junior biology class each and freshman quantitative physical science. I don't have a block for a health class," he pointed out triumphantly.

"But you have a block for the A.P. biology class you applied for," Tom reminded with a small smile as he rocked back in his chair. With a roll of his eyes and a sigh he shook his head. "Look, I know this isn't your cup of tea. But we have no one else even remotely able to teach the course, and we can't get rid of it because it's required. You remember health, Brandon," he went on in his gravelly voice. "You put in a videotape of Rescue 911, and you sit and do your planning while the kids sleep."

"You're cutting the A.P. bio class? Tom," Brandon pleaded. "Can't you hire a sub? A temp to work an hour and a half a day? I do remember health class, that's what scares the hell outta me. CPR dummies and lurid descriptions of diseases and putting condoms on bananas!"

"They got rid of the condoms," Tom retorted with a wry smile. "Parents made a fuss."

"Aw hell," Brandon muttered, sitting down hard in the chair and slumping. "Great. Just great. Freshman health. Jesus, Tom. Fine. I'll do it. It's not like I have much choice, do I." It wasn't even a question.

"Well, I suppose technically you could quit," Tom offered with a shrug. "Unfortunately, health is already scheduled during the last block, so you'll have to shift your planning to second since the A.P. class isn't happening." He pursed his lips in disapproval. It was obvious he wasn't happy about asking Brandon to do this. He just didn't have a choice. "We've lost some staff over the Christmas break, you know that. A few maternity leaves, a few unexpected retirements ... We were also short a baseball coach until someone volunteered," he went on with narrowed eyes. Brandon just grunted noncommittally, already working out the changes he'd have to make in his planning to allow for the change of classes. He wasn't really interested in staff turnover. "Thanks for volunteering, Brandon," Tom went on pointedly, smiling slightly as his eyes danced with affectionate amusement.

Freezing in place, Brandon blinked and looked up slowly at the man who had shepherded his teaching career along for years while becoming a good friend. "What?" he drew out slowly and balefully.

"Don't worry," Tom was quick to go on. "That varsity team is a well-oiled machine, so I hear. They just need an extra set of arms, you won't be doing much. Hell, I don't even know what you'll be doing, but it won't be hard. And since you've got the background to be the team trainer as well, you're the best qualified person on staff. Actually, you're the only qualified person on staff."

Brandon looked at him incredulously. "How in the hell do you figure that? *What* background?" he asked, his voice higher than usual.

"You're male and big enough to keep the boys in check," Tom said before hurrying on. "And you did study anatomy and physiology, did you not? Trainer."

Finally becoming aware that his jaw was hanging open, Brandon snapped it shut. He stared blankly at Tom a bit longer and then rubbed both hands over his face. "Anything else, Tom?" he asked, his voice dangerously quiet.

"Brandon," Tom said softly. "I know this isn't your thing, and I am truly sorry. But I know you understand that the school needs you to be a team player. It's all for the kids."

The science teacher sighed, and his shoulders relaxed. It was the one thing that was unshakable in him and dammit, Tom knew it. Brandon would do anything for the kids. It was why he got up at 4:45 a.m. and drove 40 minutes to come in at six o'clock to tutor, a task almost all other teachers avoided like the plague. "All right, Tom," he agreed wearily.

"Thank you, Brandon," Tom responded sincerely as he stood and extended his hand over the desk. "And unlike the tutoring, you do get paid extra for the coaching," he added optimistically.

Brandon chuckled and stood to shake Tom's hand. "Well, that's something. I'm guessing the health class is already in session with a sub?"

"Jake Campbell has been doing double duty on the health class and senior phys ed until we could find someone permanent. And he's the man you need to talk to about baseball," Tom answered. "Hey, didn't you two graduate close together?"

"Yeah, same year." Brandon said with a small nod. "You still taught geometry then," he added with a smirk.

"I still had all my hair then, too," Tom shot back with a quick grin. "You want me to have someone track Jake down after the class is over?" he offered with a gesture to the public announcement system in the outer office.

Brandon grimaced. "No. I'll wander out to the gym. I think I know where his office is," he said, squinting a little at the school map on the wall.

"If you find him in his office then good on ya," Tom laughed with a dismissive wave. "Kid never could stay in one spot even when he was younger. Thanks again, Brandon. I won't forget it."

Nodding, Brandon headed out and turned toward the athletic complex, walking through the empty halls, his rubber-soled loafers not making much sound. He found the hallway of offices and checked the doors until he found one with a "Coach Campbell" sign tacked up in the window, but the office was closed and dark inside. The science teacher turned around and headed to the gym itself. There were older kids sitting in the bleachers and some shooting baskets, but no teacher in sight. Brandon frowned in consternation before belatedly recalling what Tom had said about health taking his planning period and moving planning to the hoped-for A.P. class slot in second block. Jake was pulling double duty with the health class. Brandon figured this must be the coach's senior P.E. class, left unsupervised as he watched over the freshmen. So the science teacher made his way to the health class and checked his watch. Five minutes until afternoon announcements.

Inside the classroom located just off the gymnasium complex, Jake watched a ball of wadded up paper fly through the air and hit the rim of the wastebasket. It teetered there, seeming to almost cling to the plastic trash bag. Jerome – freshman, wrestler – leaned sideways from the table seven feet away and blew on it frantically as Jake chuckled quietly. The wad of paper wavered some more and then fell with an anti-climactic plop onto the ground just beside the trash can.

"Aw, snap."

"Oh ho!" Jake shouted with glee. "And it's a dollar to teacher for the brick shot." He laughed as he held his hand out and made the universal gesture of 'gimme my money.'

"Man," Jerome whined as he dug into his pocket and pulled out four quarters. He got up and trudged over to slap them into Jake's palm with a sheepish smile. "I got it next time," he said confidently with an inclination of his head before tossing the paper in the can and heading back to his seat. Jake had told the perpetually lazy freshmen that if they shot a trash basket and made it, he'd acknowledge their brilliance in an appropriate manner according to the difficulty of the shot. But if they missed, it was a dollar fine for being too lazy to get up and walk the ten feet to the can.

Brandon stood in the doorway, leaning against the frame, watching the little scene, hard pressed to keep a smile off his face. He wondered what Jake had offered to do if they made the can shot. Then a couple of girls started whispering loudly and looking his way. He blinked, wondering if he had something on his shirt or tie. Glancing down, he remembered he'd taken off his tie and rolled up his sleeves after his last class, and unbuttoned the top two buttons on his shirt in agitation as he'd dropped his glasses on the desk before going to see Tom. He'd even dragged his fingers through his hair enough times while talking to the principal to pull it out of the tie that usually held the shoulder-length dark hair neatly at his nape. Christ. He must look like hell.

When Brandon looked up again, three girls were whispering and pointing and blushing. He raised an eyebrow in surprise and glanced to the teacher at the front of the room. Jake followed the whispering and turned to look at the open doorway with a raised eyebrow. "Mr. Bartlett," he said, covering his surprise and confusion with his usual friendly, somewhat cheeky style of greeting. "What can we do you for?"

The girls squealed quietly, and a few of the boys snickered, while Brandon just shook his head. "I'm the new health teacher," he answered, which caused even more of an uproar amongst the girls. God! Why were they doing that?

Jake frowned at the squeaky little freshmen girls and looked back at Brandon with a slightly confused smile. "My apologies," he offered wryly with a smirk, earning him a few playful boos as he stood up and strolled to the doorway. "Oh boo hoo, go practice your bank shots," Jake drawled to the class. "They're all yours," he said to Brandon softly as he stepped out into the hallway. He stopped and leaned against the wall by the door, peering back inside. "They're a generally good group," he murmured to Brandon softly. "You shouldn't have much trouble." He paused, looking the man over.

Something was different about him, but he couldn't figure out what it was, besides looking a little rumpled. It wasn't the glasses. The missing tie maybe? The slightly annoyed glint in his eyes? Jake gave a mental shrug and pushed off the wall. "Want me to stick around through announcements?"

The P.A. crackled to life, and Brandon smiled a little. "If you don't mind hanging around, Tom said I should talk to you," he said below the front office secretary's voice blaring out of the speakers. When the bell rang, the kids were off like a shot, walking between them, though several of the girls walked more slowly. "Bye, Mr. Bartlett." "See you tomorrow, Mr. Bartlett." "I'm looking forward to health class, Mr. Bartlett." Brandon's face got more and more mystified as the classroom emptied out.

Jake grinned as the last of the class trailed off down the hallway. "You certainly wowed them, Stud," he laughed. "What did you need from me?"

Brandon's brows shot up. Stud? He'd certainly missed that message. "Ah, Tom Berry dropped this class on me like a ton of bricks about half an hour ago – and then he steamrollered me with another small tidbit. I'm supposed to be a coach, too."

"A coach?" Jake asked with a frown. Was his leg being pulled here? "For what team?" he asked suspiciously.

"Your team," Brandon said, a little annoyance creeping into his voice. "He said you were short a baseball coach. And pretty much that I'm the bottom of the barrel." He muttered that last.

Jake blinked. And blinked again as his mouth fell open slightly. They were short a coach? Who? "Do you know anything about baseball?" he asked incredulously.

"I do watch the game. I happen to be a Braves fan, thank you very much."

"Good for you, Sport," Jake responded in slight irritation. "Do you know enough to coach it, though?"

"I would say no. Which is what I tried to tell Tom, only his cheeks and nose were already turning red, and you know what that means." Brandon crossed his arms. "He said something about me being 'male and big enough to keep the boys in check', so I guess that has to count for something," he said, eyes downcast. The comment had stung, actually, intimating that he *couldn't* coach – never mind that he was an excellent teacher. "So. Since it's that bad an idea, you can tell Tom no way, and that'll be it," he proposed shortly.

Jake frowned at the man. "I didn't mean to insult you," he said with a sigh. "It's just that we're looking at state this year, and I didn't even know I was a coach short. I'm sorry," he offered, his tone slightly frustrated and huffy. "God, who did we lose?" he muttered almost to himself.

Brandon looked up at him and saw the truth of his words, and he again shrugged. "Guess I'm the bearer of bad news. Don't kill the messenger?" he asked, a tinge of humor creeping into his voice. "Surely there's something I can do to help. I do happen to be an above average teacher. It can't be that far off to coach, at least small things," he offered seriously. "A shot at State is nothing to sneeze at."

"It's certainly not," Jake responded in a hard voice. "This ain't just a sport here. We've got eight kids who should be scouted this year. We're talking their futures at stake."

"Then don't throw away my offer," Brandon said just as firmly, face set.

Jake met the man's eyes and nodded finally with small sigh. "Just remember to at least act like you know what you're doing. Since you just got this dumped on you, you'll need clothes, won't you?" he asked with a wave of his hand at the man's attire. He was a step away from wearing tweed. Christ, he could almost see the lab safety goggles on the guy.

Brandon blinked at the about face. "Clothes? I've got running shorts, T-shirt and shoes in the car."

"Nah, not workout clothes," Jake huffed. "The coaches dress out every day just like the players do. I'm talking cleats, baseball pants, Under Armour, jersey. You got a number you want?" he asked as an afterthought as he gestured for Brandon to start walking with him.

Baseball pants? "No preference," the science teacher

answered. "You know, the whole 'act like you know what you're doing' thing probably isn't a great idea. The kids, especially yours, being so good, will see right through it. It might be better to say I'm observing or something."

"Nope. Then you'll get plowed over," Jake countered. "They have to respect you or else you're just wasting your time. We'll figure something out. Third base coach, maybe, all you'll need to learn are the signs and know the basics of base running," he mused as they entered the gym to head for his office. A few kids were loitering amidst the bleachers, and Jake narrowed his eyes. His class should have cleared out by now. "Where are you supposed to be!?" he bellowed suddenly, his voice echoing around the gym and causing the kids to jump and scatter.

Brandon pulled back a little at the resounding shout, but he had to smile as he followed Jake back to his office. He remembered that bellow from the football field – Jake had been the star quarterback, of course. "You don't sound much different, you know that?" he said before thinking about it.

"Different?" Jake asked in confusion as he went to the free-standing aluminum locker in the corner of his tiny cinderblock office. "Different than what?"

"You used to yell like that on the football field. I remember. I could even hear you from the far end of the bleachers," Brandon said, hands in his pockets as he watched Jake rifle through the locker.

Jake looked over his shoulder as he pulled out a spare pair of pristine white baseball pants. "Oh," he responded with a slight blush. "I didn't know you ever went to any games," he went on uncomfortably, uncertain of how else to respond.

"A few," Brandon admitted. "Wanted to see what all the hubbub was about when you won regionals," he said. He still didn't know much about football, but it had been an experience.

"Did you?" Jake asked curiously. He remembered the 'hubbub.' The crowd roaring in excitement, the marching band blaring music from the stands, the crunch of pads and the grunts of tackles, the cold, the bright lights and the smells of sweat and grass and perfect fall nights. God, he had loved it. Lived for it.

"Yeah," Brandon said quietly. "It was a world I didn't have any part in. It was exciting to watch." He saw the faraway look in Jake's eyes, so he just stayed quiet until the other man was done reminiscing. He wished he had memories like that. The best he had was the blank calm he'd get when running miles and miles cross country, over flowing fields and through leafy forests. He knew he'd been in the zone then.

Jake looked at the man strangely and nodded. Brandon was an unusual one in that he'd always had the physique to be an athlete, but Jake had never seen him play anything. They'd not even been in freshman gym together because Brandon didn't get to Parkview until their sophomore year. Even back then, Brandon had been one of the larger kids, nearly as tall as Jake himself and filled out through the shoulders, though lanky. He had just never had the desire to use it, losing himself in his intellectual side instead, Jake supposed.

"Well," Jake huffed. "These should fit you," he said as he handed over pants, a shiny blue long-sleeved Under Armour shirt, and a loose-fitting jersey of the same color. "What size shoe are you?" he asked as he lifted his own foot and looked down at his trainers with a distracted frown. "Eh, first day you'll be fine with tennis shoes," he amended. "Hey, thanks for running interference earlier, by the way."

Brandon stuck the clothes under one arm, confused until he remembered Rhonda. "Ah, yeah. No problem. I've seen Rhonda when she's really fixated on something. Granted, it's always been projects or grants or something. But she was getting this scary look in her eyes." He paused. "And size 12."

"You can borrow my spares," Jake nodded. "They're twelve and a half cause I have to wear this lift thing in one of them for my ankle," he rambled as he picked up one of the cleats and poked inside it. It was battered and scuffed, but had a well-loved look to it as he held it in his big hands. "The lift is still in here, actually," he muttered, poking at the thick pad. "They've got stickers on them, I never try to pull them out," he muttered distractedly, "and I sort of walk on the outsides of my feet so the soles wear down funny, but they should do you okay if you don't want to buy a new pair. They run about fifty bucks, I think."

"Thanks, I'll see how they fit," Brandon said. "I'll just change. The locker room's across the hall, right?"

"Yeah, but," Jake cleared his throat and flushed a little. With a little huff and a smile he bit the bullet and asked, "Boxers or briefs, man?"

Brandon held up the pants, looking at them appraisingly before looking back to Jake. "You're not telling me I'm supposed to wear something under these, are you?" His voice reflected his real amusement. There was *no way* he'd be able to get these pants on with underwear.

"You're supposed to wear sliding pants under them, but since we're not playing you'd look a little funny. White briefs are best," Jake answered as seriously as possible. He'd gotten a sudden image of the man standing before him going commando, and he'd rather liked the idea quite a bit.

"Okay, you would know," Brandon said, looking uncertainly at the pants. "I'll be right back." He left the office and crossed the hall, dropping the clothes on the bench in between the rows of lockers and starting to strip down. Maybe it was fate, he thought wryly. He'd worn white spandex shorts instead of briefs today, planning to go running in the park once he got home. At least he wouldn't look like a total nerd with red or black showing through the white pants.

He pulled on the Under Armour shirt, surprised that it was so stretchy and comfortable. Stepping into the pants, he blinked in surprise when they got really close-fitting, really fast. He had to shimmy several times to pull the damn things up, and for a moment he was sure he wouldn't get them over his hips without baby powder or something. Finally they were on, and he looked in the mirror, almost horrified. Second skin had *nothing* on these pants. He tucked in the shirt (as best he could) and slung the jersey over one arm, walking back out to Jake's office barefooted.

"If you're ordering pants for me, I'm thinking these are maybe a size or two small," Brandon said as he re-entered the office.

Jake looked up from his book and blinked at the man. He looked him over appraisingly, noticing for perhaps the first time just exactly how fit Brandon really was. The Under Armour stuck to him like wet paper, outlining muscles Jake had never thought to see on a biology teacher, and the pants were in fact a perfect fit; just loose enough to allow for the usual protective gear but not so loose as to impede movement on the field. *Jesus.* "No," he murmured as he cocked his head and raised an eyebrow. "No, they look perfect to me," he answered distractedly.

Brandon looked down at himself and then shrugged, combing his hair back behind his ears with his fingers. "If you say so. They're going to take some getting used to," he commented, sitting in the other chair and pulling on the blue socks Jake had set out.

Jake watched him with a series of stupid blinks before pulling his eyes back down to the Sudoku puzzles on his desk. Another hobby he hid while at school. Slowly he moved his clipboard over to cover them up and then glanced back up at Brandon from under lowered brows. With his stuffy dress shirt and tie replaced by the tight blue shirt and the clean white pants, he actually looked like an athlete. He looked like someone Jake would try to pick up in a bar. Looking away again, Jake slowly reached for his paperback to put it out of sight as well. When you were a P.E. coach in any high school, no one gave you credit for having actual brains. If you were caught doing something that could be considered intelligent, like reading a book, you were prodded at for trying to 'look smart'. It was more the 'that one doesn't have illustrations, dimwit' kind of thing that he usually got, instead of someone asking if it was a good book. He didn't want to hear any jokes from Brandon.

Jake cleared his throat again and nodded. "Trust me, you'll be glad to have them. We practice from 3:30, when the kids get out there, to anywhere from 5:30 to 7 at night. It'll be cold when the sun goes down. It'll be wet sometimes. Only time we don't practice is when there's lightning, and then we're in the weight room." He picked up a pencil and began to tap it on his desk thoughtfully. "What else..." he murmured to himself as he looked around for guidance. "We do a good bit of traveling, have a few overnight stays, so might want to prepare your girlfriend or wife or whatever," he went on as he dug out a schedule and glanced over it. "We got some Friday and Saturday games," he muttered. "We have a tourney in Florida over spring break, and usually during that first week of May we take the kids to Turner Field for a game or two, that's an overnight thing as well," he went on as he handed the schedule over to Brandon.

"Coaching is a full-time job," Jake murmured softly. That was one of the things most regular teachers never understood. They had the kids from 7:30 in the morning to 2:30 in the afternoon. Most left it at that. Some sponsored clubs or did tutoring, but then they wiped the school smell from their shoes and headed home. The coaches spent nights, weekends, and summers with their kids. They helped them shop colleges. They fielded phone calls from drunken parties and gave advice on love lives. They kept in touch with kids long after they walked and got their diplomas. When Jake had been in college and come to the realization that he might be bisexual, his football coach from high school had been the first person he had called.

"Not married," was Brandon's only quiet comment as he considered the practice time, the weekend games and tournament trips. He'd already committed himself, he knew, so there was nothing to do but give his best. He quickly calculated the amount of sleep he'd be getting and inwardly winced though outwardly he looked calm. Long days. Even longer days. He started each weekday at 4:45 a.m., tutored from 6 to 7 and carried a full class load from 7:30 to 2:30 p.m. Now, instead of working on his doctorate research in the late afternoons, he'd have baseball practice and games, and another skim of the schedule convinced him that his personal classwork would have to shift to after 9 p.m. – after daily planning, grading papers, writing up tests – and with several Saturdays gone, his only free day, Sunday, would be taken up as well. Exercise, he had no idea when he'd fir that in. Maybe after the doctorate planning, late. He could run around the lake at home.

"Where do you want me to start?" he asked the coach.

"You look a little green," Jake observed without answering. "Practice is actually fun after you weed out the whiners," he said, trying to offer some condolences as he leaned back in his chair and propped his feet up on the desk.

Brandon had to chuckle, and he relaxed a little. "Whiners, huh? Whining about what? Taking ground balls in the groin?"

"That's what cups are for," Jake answered instantly, his

standard retort to any complaints about impact pain in that particular area. "And if they get knocked in the nuts it's 'cause they didn't have their glove down and they deserved it. We don't baby these guys," he insisted vehemently. "I know you academics think we treat them with kid gloves, but if they don't pull their weight on a report card they're off the team. If they get hurt, they play through it. If they get sick, they show up anyway. I guarantee you my boys are some of your only students with perfect attendance. And I guarantee you any day of the week you have at least one kid in at least one of your classes with taped fingers, ankle brace, knee brace, or some sort of hellacious bruise they're trying to cover up."

He was bristling protectively now. He knew what student athletes went through. They got labeled with the 'jock' title, put in the easy classes even if they should have been honors students, and when they did do something spectacular academically it got chalked up to luck. Not to mention the injuries, grueling practice schedules, and heartbreaks that could only come with loving a sport. Jake snorted noisily through his nose to calm himself and rocked back in his chair, rolling his sore neck and closing his eyes.

Brows rising as Jake seriously soap-boxed, Brandon knew he'd hit a sore spot, one possibly dating back to their own time in school. And the more Jake talked, the more he made sense. The biology teacher nodded slowly. The coach was right. As much as the nerds had felt put down and razzed for not being athletic or good looking – the jocks had been razzed about grades and attendance. He thought maybe both groups had gotten the short end of the stick. "I'm sorry," he said quietly.

Jake stared at the man for a moment and then broke into a disarming smile. It was another thing he was good at, glazing over bursts of emotion and pushing it back until it was quickly forgotten. He was also good at playing up the dumb brute image when he needed to. The everyday game face. "I get carried away," he offered, his usual wry smirk back in place and his eyes warm brown again. "It usually happens when they don't give me my juice at lunch," he joked with a sheepish grin, reaching behind himself to rub the back of his neck and roll his head, forcing his spine to crack loudly.

The phone on his desk began to ring demandingly, and Jake glared at it. He held up his hand, indicating for Brandon to wait, and removed his feet from the desk to reach for the speaker button. "This is the Literacy Self Test Hotline," he drawled in a deep, businesslike voice. "After the tone, leave your name and number and recite a sentence using today's vocabulary word. Today's word is *supercilious*."

"Is there a student sitting with you?" Troy Peterson's voice asked warily over the phone.

"No," Jake laughed with a wink at Brandon.

"Go fuck yourself then," Troy muttered. "Did you send in this announcement to be read with the morning report tomorrow?"

"What announcement?" Jake asked in an attempt to sound innocent, barely able to keep his voice from wavering in amusement. Brandon tilted his head and smiled at the change in the other man. How bizarre that he could switch so quickly from one mood to the other.

"I quote," the speech teacher and fellow coach responded, obviously reading from something, *"At precisely 11:42 this morning, maintenance will be blowing the dust out of the phone lines. All teachers should cover the earpiece of their classroom phones with a bag to catch the dust."*

Both Brandon's brows rose, and he stifled a snort. Jake was laughing quietly as he listened, shoulders shaking and hand covering his mouth, hissing a little as he tried not to laugh out loud. "Wasn't me," he managed finally.

"I'm running with this," Troy said accusingly. "All blame will be placed squarely on your impressively built shoulders, darling," he warned before hanging up.

Jake practically guffawed. Brandon joined in with a chuckle. "That was funny," he commented, eyes dancing. He was quickly discovering there was a lot more to Jake Campbell than the jock stereotype.

"Hey, I've got to entertain myself somehow." Jake snickered as he grabbed his clipboard and stood. "Now the real fun will come when we see how many people actually do it," he practically giggled as several sheets of Sudoku puzzles fluttered to the floor.

Brandon leaned over to gather up the papers, looking at the filled-out puzzles. "God, I hate these things! I have the worst time figuring them out," he said as he offered them back to Jake. "You must have more patience than I do. I get frustrated with them. Give me a crossword instead."

Jake laughed a little uncomfortably and nodded as he took the papers back. "Crosswords require a bit more knowledge than one through nine," he murmured as the bell rang for last bus – that meant it was 3:10. "Shit, I gotta get dressed," he huffed, putting his clipboard back down and moving around Brandon in the small space to grab his bag.

Frowning slightly at Jake's awkward and self-deprecating reply, Brandon stood up. "I'll wait outside at the main diamond." The school complex had three fields, two baseball and one softball, as well as the football field and track, two soccer fields and six tennis courts.

"Yeah, yeah, we're all meeting there this week. Then the teams get split," Jake answered distractedly as he stripped off his shirt and tossed it into his chair. "Hey," he said quickly. "Thanks," he added softly as he looked up at Brandon and began to undo his shorts.

Brandon stopped, surprised – not to mention blindsided by the ripped chest suddenly bared to his eyes – but he managed to give Jake an honest, open smile. "Sure thing," he said. He closed the door behind him and moved outside, a little bemused on how seeing that chest had surprised him so much ... and why he was still enjoying it now. Oh *man*.

Chapter 2

SEVERAL minutes later Jake was tucking in his shirt as he jogged toward the fields. He made it there before any of the kids, and found the three college guys who were assistants this year standing with Brandon and the freshman team coach, Jonathan. They were waiting for someone with a key to the storage room off the home dugout, and the head coach grumbled as he jogged up and fished the key out of his bag.

"I swear, my office gets further away every year," he growled as he jammed the key in the lock and opened the door. The assistants began to drag the equipment out and set up the field, and Jake turned to Brandon and glanced around the complex with narrowed eyes. "Where the hell is Troy?" he asked with a frown as he pulled a pack of sunflower seeds out of a bulk sell box and shoved it into his back pocket. A stream of blue-clad kids began to filter out of the building in the distance, and Jake growled softly. "He's gonna get a bat up his ass if he's not here before they get here."

Brandon decided right then and there that keeping his mouth shut was probably the best idea, although the thought of Jake going postal on golden boy Troy was funny as hell. Golden boy Troy – the other popular king of the castle – homecoming king when Jake couldn't be, the known 'playboy' of the school, light to Jake's dark. The unholy duo. Brandon shook his head and stood to one side, watching the college guys in case he needed to know how to set up sometime in the future. They were quite friendly, not knowing Brandon from anyone else. None had been Parkview students, they said.

A squeal of little bitty tires and the clink of the electric golf cart shutting off signified Troy's arrival, and Jake growled under his breath as he watched the man hop the chain link on the other side of the dugout and jog out to where Jake stood at home plate. The man was grinning as if he'd somehow dodged a bullet, and Jake smacked him on the side of his head with his glove. "Ow," Troy huffed as he rubbed his ear and sulked. "Is that Bartlett?" he asked suddenly in surprise, looking over Jake's shoulder at the suited-up science teacher.

"That's the new member of our coaching staff," Jake answered in a hard voice, all of his usual good humor gone the second he had stepped onto the grass. "If you want to stay on it I suggest you get your ass in gear," he warned seriously. Troy looked at him, sighed, and nodded, head down as he moved to help set up the equipment. Troy knew how Jake got when he was on the field, whether it was football or baseball. He was like a different person. There was no bullshitting out here. The fun wouldn't start until the teams were set.

Jake stood there and met the boys as they jogged out onto the field. "Take your laps!" he boomed in a voice that carried over all three fields and made the freshmen flinch. The older boys immediately ducked their heads and started into a warm-up trot around the field, leading the new kids by example. There was no first day of practice greeting. There was no explanation of what Jake expected of Parkview's baseball players. There was no lecture about being on time to practice or remembering their gear every day or grades or attendance. The kids already knew all of it. And if they didn't, they'd learn or quit within the next two days. Jake's seniors would make sure of that.

The coach watched them with intent black eyes as he stood like a king at home plate, seeming to tower over the entire complex. He picked out the kids who were lagging at the end of the lap. He remembered them. He picked out the kids who were talking as they ran, and he remembered them. He watched with narrowed eyes as he mentally began weeding out the kids who were already proving themselves to be JV material and no more.

"Who wants to take the running today?" he asked his coaches softly, pointing to his heel in explanation of why he couldn't do it himself.

Brandon looked around at the other coaches. The three assistants were shuffling their feet, a younger coach he didn't know looked unsure, and Troy was oblivious – or at least acting that way. "I'll do it," he volunteered. How difficult could it be?

Jake raised an eyebrow at Brandon and looked him over carefully. He certainly had the look of a runner, but looks could be deceiving. Hell, if Troy could look like he knew what he was doing, then Brandon could look like an athlete, right? "All righty," he said as he waved Brandon closer. "To warm them up we make them run suicides against a coach," he informed the man as the first of the herd of ballplayers began to come down the third base line. "If they beat you, they get bragging rights. If you beat them..." he trailed off and smiled wickedly as he waved his hand at the field.

"Suicides?" Brandon murmured.

"Oh, yeah," Jake answered as he pointed down to the third base line. The assistants were setting up cones marking lines across the field as the older players filed up obediently at the painted white line and instructed the younger boys to follow suit. "Start here at the line, run to the first cone line and back, run to the second line, then back, and so on with all five lines," he told Brandon as he pointed out the cones. "I can make one of the kids do it," he added in a lower voice as he waved his hand at the college kids. "That's what they're here for, after all. $9.50 an hour for me to torture at my whim."

The science teacher chuckled. "No, I don't mind. So is the point speed or endurance?" he asked curiously. "Do I just do it once the fastest, or over and over?"

"Speed," Jake answered immediately. "If you beat them, they know what comes next. So they'll be gunning for you," he warned as he wagged a finger and walked toward the dugout to grab his bullhorn.

"He thinks he needs that thing to be heard," the freshman

coach murmured from Brandon's side. "What a joke, man, he could whisper and these kids would hear him. Hey," he said as he stepped up next to Brandon and offered his hand to shake. "Whatever you do, just don't *let* them win. Don't pull your punches, right? He hates that."

Smiling, Brandon shook his hand, then grabbed one foot at a time, stretching a little by pulling them up behind him. "I'm Brandon. New assistant coach. Of some kind," he said with a half grin.

"Jonathan," the man offered. "Freshman head coach. I go by 'hey you,' mostly," the man offered as Jake's voice boomed over the field. The bullhorn hung unused at his side.

Leaning over at the waist to stretch, Brandon chuckled as he looked over toward Jake. "You were right about the bullhorn," he said, standing and turning his waist each way in a slight warm-up. He saw the kids trotting in their direction. "Do you teach?" he asked as Jonathan walked with him over to the starting line.

"Over at Trickum, the middle school up the road, yeah," Jonathan answered as he watched the boys line up. "Here we go. Good luck, Coach," he offered with a pat to Brandon's hip as he jogged away from the starting line.

Brandon blinked at the familiar touch, but didn't say anything as he moved to stand at the line. At least there was someone here who wouldn't judge him by his past, unlike Jake and Troy. And as the students lined up around him, he realized he would be new to some of them, too. He only had one class of freshmen this year, whereas most upperclassmen he'd taught sometime in the last three years.

Some of the older students and seniors nearly matched him in size, and they were in great shape. Brandon hoped to be able to at least keep up with them. This sort of running was new to him. He glanced over to Jake, squatting slightly to keep his weight balanced. Just like starting any other race, he told himself. Take deep, even breaths.

Jake stood near the plate, his eyes scanning the line to make sure there were no cheaters leaning forward. He placed his whistle in his mouth, met Brandon's eyes briefly, and blew a sharp blast.

Whether it was because he was a teacher or something else, none of the kids crowded him, so Brandon got off to a swift start, reaching out with one foot to touch the first line as he stretched back into the run, trying to use his long legs to his advantage. At the second line, he was keeping up. By the third, most of the younger kids had fallen behind. As Brandon ran for the fourth, he hit his stride, his breathing settling in, and he was hard put not to laugh as he swiftly ran back toward home plate, matching a handful of seniors.

Jake was momentarily shocked at the quick burst of speed from Brandon, and he watched the man in astonishment as he displayed that – in this case – looks were not deceiving at all. The man could run. He pulled his attention away enough to observe the boys, which ones ran well, which ones looked like Bambi on ice, and which ones were lagging too far behind. When the lead group came close to the finish, he dragged his eyes away from Brandon one last time in order to watch the finish. A couple of the boys, his speedsters, beat Brandon to the painted line by a fraction of a second, and Jake blinked again.

"Damn, that was close," he muttered to the man at his elbow, who happened to be Troy, standing there to watch the finish.

"Dude can run," Troy muttered in return. "Shit, who'd a thunk it, huh?" he joked softly, and Jake shook his head and smiled as the stragglers passed the line.

Brandon was grinning when they finished, only slightly winded, even more pleased when several of the older students who knew him came over to compliment him. "Wow, Mr. Bartlett, I didn't know you could run." "Mr. Bartlett, you the man!" "Good job, Teach." "How can you run when you spend all that time in the lab?" Brandon just laughed, pulling his feet up behind him again to stretch a little more.

"You all have Marshall and Tyler to thank for your sorry asses not having to run any more!" Jake boomed as he walked over and gave Brandon's hip an absent-minded pat, just like Jonathan had. He began to separate the boys by grade, sending an assistant or coach to go with each of them. When they had all dispersed, Jake turned to Brandon and grinned widely. "Nice run," he said to the man with a smack to the arm, the compliment a rare and sincere one. "Stick with me today, you'll get a feel for it," he went on.

The pat, the compliment and the smack all gave Brandon's ego a boost, and he nodded, flushed with warmth, pleased to have done well on the first day. At least there was something he could do – there wasn't much of a way to mess up running. He was sure there'd be plenty of yelling in his direction going forward, but running he could do. Brandon started watching Jake as he put the kids through practice, coming to appreciate that the man was not just a good teacher. He was a *great* teacher. It was an eye-opener.

As the sun began to set on their first practice, Jake sent one of the kids over to the control box to switch on the lights. They flickered on in the growing darkness, bathing the field with light once more. "If you're thinking about what momma has on the table for dinner," Jake bellowed as he walked over the grid of kids now doing push-ups like they were in a boot camp, "then you can get your ass off my field and go home! *I* am your momma now! And *I* say when you eat! *I* am your daddy now! *I* say when you sleep! The only time I am *not* your momma or your daddy is when you want money for new shoes!" he shouted, his voice booming over up and out into the darkness. He walked the rows of panting, sweating, whimpering kids. They were the best, and this was how they got that way.

Brandon stood off to one side, next to Jonathan, just watching. The kids were tough, he had to give them that. But, he supposed, you didn't get to be a team that went to State if you weren't tough. He hadn't become a cross country runner over night. It had taken months and months of grueling, exhausting, mind-numbing running to condition himself properly, and even then it didn't stop. So yeah, he felt for the kids, but more in the way of having been there. He wondered how many would quit. Jonathan had told him earlier in the afternoon that these were supposed to be tryouts.

"The juniors have everything to lose," Jonathan murmured. "They can't be on JV, too old. The seniors have the leg up just 'cause they were all on varsity last year. The juniors are the ones digging in this week."

Jake let them go for another full minute before calling a stop to it. "Now!" he boomed. "Get your lazy hind ends up and into the showers! Go home!" he ordered amidst an array of thankful groans and moans. "And if there is one stitch of equipment left on this field, tomorrow you will all wish you hadn't been born!" he threatened, and kids scurried to put up the stuff they'd been using.

The science teacher watched them react to Jake and had to smile just a bit. It was obvious the coach didn't have discipline problems. Jake handled it in a totally different way than he would have, but it was extremely successful.

Hands on his hips and watching the kids like a hawk, Jake kept his presence big and hulking and threatening until the kids were all gone. Then he seemed to deflate a little, becoming less large, becoming more approachable. He looked over at his coaches and smiled slightly. "What do we think?" he asked no one in particular.

Brandon glanced among the other guys. He knew it certainly wasn't his place to say anything right now. He had a few opinions about some of the kids, but they were only based on what he'd seen tonight, so it wasn't a reliable sample. He needed more data to generate viable conclusions.

"Yeah, me too," Jake agreed with the silence. "Go home, guys. See you tomorrow," he told the men staring at him, heading for the gate a little stiffly.

Raising a brow, Brandon nodded a goodbye to Jonathan and made to follow Jake back to the gym. He had to get his clothes and head back to his classroom. He had two blocks of papers to grade and more planning. He was trying to decide if he wanted to stay here at the school to do the work or pack up and head home when his stomach growled.

Jake turned to see Brandon pacing him, and he stopped for a beat to let him catch up and walk beside him. "That you growling at me?" he teased lightly. "What, the grapes at lunch weren't enough to go to six o'clock?"

"The grapes were dessert, actually," Brandon said with a chuckle. "I'd eaten a sandwich in my office before that." He wouldn't mention what type of sandwich, it would probably get him laughed at. Peanut butter and jelly was still his favorite. "But yeah, growling. 11 a.m. was a ways back."

"Tell me about it," Jake grumbled. "Might want to start stealing snacks from the cafeteria for just before practice. Stay away from the gray stuff," he warned absently. "How long's your ride home?" he asked suddenly.

The sound of "gray stuff" made Brandon cringe. "About 40 minutes, depending," he answered. "I live out in Mountain Park."

"Damn," Jake exclaimed in his usual 'act first, think after' method of communicating. "That's one hell of a commute. Hey man, I hate to ask you this, but would you maybe mind giving me a ride home?" he asked with little to no shame. "I live on a side road just up the way and on nice days I walk in. But my damn ankle is giving me fits tonight," he explained with a slow blush that crept up under his high blue collar and into his cheeks. The truth was, no one would ever know just how much Jake hurt all the time. To let them know would be to admit that all his years of playing the sports he had loved, balls to the wall the entire time, had done him more harm than good.

If Jake was man enough to admit his ankle was bothering him and ask, then Brandon was adult enough to help him out. "Don't mind at all. I need to change and stop at my classroom, but then I'm good to go," Brandon said as they walked back into the gym. "The commute's not bad, actually. It's only about 25 miles. It's just on curvy country roads," he added as he pulled open the locker room door. "Want me to meet you here?"

"I'll meet you up at your room," Jake offered automatically as he bypassed the locker room door and kept on going. "Err ... actually, I don't know where your room is," he corrected as he stopped and turned back around to face Brandon. "I'll just be wandering around looking lost near the parking lot," he told the man with a careless wave of his hand that was typical of Jake's easy attitude. "Can't miss me," he laughed, turning back toward his office door.

"That's fine. For future reference, I'm in old man Rayburn's room," Brandon said before disappearing to change clothes.

Heading on to his office and stepping inside, Jake tugged off his Under Armour cage jacket and tossed it onto his desk. For a first day of practice, things hadn't gone so badly. The real shocker today had been Brandon Bartlett, and Jake's thoughts couldn't help but linger on the man as he dropped his baseball pants and slid back into his khaki shorts. Jake knew the terrifying feeling of being dropped into something you knew little about. He knew the freefall effect it had on your stomach and your nerves. Brandon had handled the day in a way Jake respected: silent, observing without interfering, but willing to step into it without even knowing what to do. A sudden overpowering guilt swept him as Jake thought about the man as someone he could respect, maybe even like. No matter how much he thought he'd learned since high school, he was still discovering things about himself that he didn't really like all that much.

After changing clothes, Brandon gathered up the uniform, figuring he could wear it again tomorrow before washing it. Christ; he was a coach now. Shaking his head, he walked out of the locker room and headed back into the school proper, navigating the darkened halls to his office. He shoved several stacks of papers and his planner and calendar into his backpack – he refused to carry a briefcase even now – and laid the uniform in on top. He grabbed the cleats, figuring they'd do well to air out, and was on his way.

Jake stood at the large circle in back of the school where parents dropped off and picked up their kids, his heavy equipment bag over his shoulder and his face turned up to the cold night sky. His entire body hurt. It wasn't the pleasant ache of muscles being used hard after a long break. It was pain, pure and simple. He stood stock still, waiting for his ride.

Brandon pushed out of the side door, and he saw Jake at the circle, so he went ahead and got the car rather than making the guy walk. He slung his backpack and the cleats into the back seat of the Jetta and climbed in. Because of his long legs, both seats were pushed all the way back, and he found the car roomy enough for him, so Jake shouldn't be too uncomfortable, he thought. A few seconds later he pulled up in front of the coach and rolled down his window with a spur of the moment smile. "Need a lift?"

Jake huffed, not sure how to respond as he stepped forward and opened the back door. If it had been someone he knew well he likely would shown some leg and faked thumbing a ride. But he just didn't know Brandon well enough to know where the joke line was drawn. He laid his bag carefully in the back and then climbed into the front seat. "I never hurt this much when I played," he complained with a groan as he stretched his long body out.

The science teacher shrugged a little. "Sucks getting older," he muttered. Sometimes he felt it in his knees when he ran, but his college sporting career hadn't really lasted long enough to do serious damage, and now he ran for simple exercise and enjoyment instead of seriously training. "Where to?" he asked politely.

"Ah, take a right at the exit," Jake answered with a frown. "I'm not old. *You* might be old, but I'm not," he said with a small smile and a sideways glance at the man driving.

Turning as directed, Brandon glanced over at his passenger. Now obviously worn out, Jake did look a little older. But it wouldn't be polite to mention it. "I didn't say we're old. Just that we're *getting* old," he said. "We're only 32 or so. We got at least 30 years to start approaching old."

"Pfft," Jake offered as he watched the school pass by. "I was getting old when I was seventeen," he muttered as his ankle and knees screamed at him.

Hearing the edge in Jake's voice, Brandon looked at him again. "You okay?" he asked quietly, not wanting to pry, but the other man looked like he was hurting. Pretty bad.

"Nothing some ice won't fix," Jake answered with an attempt at a smile.

Brandon nodded and let it drop, pleased that the other man had at least replied civilly. "Any ideas about what I might be doing with the team?" he asked after Jake directed him through another turn.

Jake gave a short, sharp laugh. "My God, he wants me to think!" he exclaimed sarcastically, glancing over at Brandon and smiling to let him know he was joking. "If I had to say right now, I'd tell you you're going to be working with me on varsity. Third base coach, probably, since you mentioned at least being a fan, right?" He paused. “You were taught to run, weren’t you?” he asked suddenly. He recognized training when he saw it.

Blinking at the sharp segue, Brandon stopped the car at a light and looked at Jake, one brow raised. “Yeah. In college. How did you know that?”

Jake shrugged and looked out the window. They were at the intersection he’d been crossing this morning when his heel had suddenly decided to have a shit fit. “You have the look,” he answered vaguely. It was difficult to describe how one athlete was able to spot another. “Sorta like gaydar for athletes,” he offered, laughing a little.

Brandon’s mouth pulled into a smile. If only Jake knew how true that was. “Nobody’s ever told me I had ‘the look’,” he commented, starting to drive again at the green light. “I wanted something to do at school to counteract the classes and workload, and my adviser introduced me to some guys on the track team. Figured running was good for focus. Turned out I was better at the endurance races, so I switched to cross country.”

“You still run?” Jake asked, glancing over at the man. To be honest, he had never had much respect for track and field. In high school and college the joke had been that they had no “balls.”

“Yeah, I try to get in at least an hour a day. Seven, eight miles maybe. Helps me clear my head,” Brandon said distractedly as he made a turn into a nice neighborhood. “Usually in the park at home or around the lake if it’s nice. It’s a chunk of time I really need for other things sometimes, but I try hard to resist skipping it. I feel like shit if I do.” He had no idea why he was chattering so much. Maybe it was because it had been so long since anyone asked about him directly. He didn’t have friends outside a few teachers at the school because he worked too much to socialize. It didn’t look like that would be changing anytime soon.

“I never got much out of running,” Jake admitted. “I always wound up talking to myself,” he said with a slight blush.

“Yeah, I had that problem at first. Too much going on in my head. To really get into it you have to get past that, sort of zone out. For distance running, I mean,” Brandon said as he pulled the car into a driveway. They were about a mile from the school, half a mile as the crow flies, in an older, upper-class subdivision with large, wooded lots. It reminded him of Mountain Park a little. He leaned forward to look at the house with green trim. "Nice house," he complimented.

"Thanks," Jake responded, reaching for the door handle. "You want a drink or something?" he offered as he popped the door open.

Brandon's stomach chose that moment to growl loudly. His lips twitched. "I'm thinking I better go look for some dinner. Thanks, though." He tilted his head, a thought occurring. Surely Jake was just as hungry as he was. "You going to eat?"

"Sometimes I do, yeah," Jake laughed softly. Truth was, if he didn't eat dinner then whatever he took for his aches would hit him quicker. But he didn't say that. "I've got sandwich stuff," he offered with a shrug.

"Well, I was going to suggest Mimi's after you got some ice, but sandwiches would be fine," Brandon said. "I'm not much of a cook myself. Cold cuts, microwave. Roll-out cookies from a can," he said self-deprecatingly.

"Hey, I'm a great cook. All I need to fix a meal is a phone and someone to answer the door," Jake responded as he got out of the car and closed the door. He opened up the back and retrieved his bag. "I need beer," he added before closing the back door.

"Unless Mimi's got a liquor license, you'll have to provide that," Brandon said, climbing out of the car. "But if you want to get your ice, I can make the sandwiches."

"Sounds like a plan," Jake agreed as he straightened his back and popped it slowly. "I'm not helping you do teachery things," he warned with a wave of his finger as he dug out his keys and turned to head for the door.

Brandon paused at the hood of the car. "Teachery things?" he asked, wondering if that was a hint that he could bring his grading in to work on while they ate.

"Yeah, you know, with pens and papers," Jake said with a wave of his hand over his shoulder as he mounted the stairs. "I don't do those," he said with a shake of his head.

Figuring that was as close to a sign as he was going to get,

Brandon ducked into the rear seat to grab his back pack and jogged to catch up. "How can you not do pens and papers? I remember taking tests in P.E.," he said, curious. How could he get away with giving grades without giving tests?

"Tests?" Jake asked incredulously. "No, no, they moved that to health and somewhere else," he answered as he pushed the door open and stepped into his house. It smelled cool, with an undercurrent of something that might have been a melon of some sort. He snapped on the lights and headed for the kitchen, trusting that Brandon would follow. "The only tests we do in P.E. are the President's Fitness tests, and those are usually 8th grade, I think," he added. "P.E.'s just pass-fail."

Brandon looked around as he followed. It was a really, really nice house. Not at all what he would have expected for a.... Brandon winced at the track his thoughts were taking. He figuratively kicked himself and entered the kitchen behind Jake. Once another set of lights flipped on, he slung his backpack onto the bench of the breakfast nook. He needed to work on changing his preconceptions. They'd already been tilted several times today.

"I grew up here. My parents moved to Florida about five years ago," Jake told the man, knowing he had to be wondering how he afforded this house on a teacher's salary. "I took the house in exchange for hauling all their shit down there for them," he smiled as he went to the refrigerator and opened it. "Want a beer?"

"Sure," Brandon said, looking around a little more and out at a rolling, wooded back yard. The neighbors looked to be a good fifty yards or more away. "Got my house pretty much the same way. Well, inherited it, I mean," he said, pausing for a moment as he remembered his parents, some years gone now. He turned back to Jake abruptly. "Okay – ice? Blender? What do you need?" he asked efficiently.

"Heh," Jake laughed as he tossed Brandon a beer. "Rookie," he scoffed as he opened up the freezer and pulled out a frozen gel pack. He plopped it onto the counter and reached in for another, and with it pulled out a wrap that was specially made to have one of the gel packs inserted into it and then fit over his ankle.

Brandon nodded – he'd seen braces like that before. "Modern technology is a wonderful thing," he commented, setting the beer on the table. "Sandwich fixings?" Brandon was trying very hard to distract himself from looking at Jake's close-cropped dark hair, the curve of his neck. Oh, not a good thing. Nope. Move on, Bartlett. Nothing here to see. He walked over to the bread box, lifting the door experimentally and pulling out the loaf he found there.

"Everything else is in the fridge there," Jake said with a nod at the stainless steel appliance as he lifted his foot onto a stool and gave his sore ankle a brief rub before sliding into the compression pack. He gave all the Velcro pieces some tugs and made sure the ice was on his heel, then slid around Brandon and reached into the freezer again for a wrap that went around his knee.

Brandon had mayo and mustard in the crook of his arm, and he was picking up packages of deli meat when he felt the other man's body close, so he shifted his hips over so Jake could open the freezer door. He rifled through the cold-storage drawers, finding a couple kinds of sliced cheese, some shredded lettuce, even a few tomatoes. He pulled it all out in a huge armful and spread it out on the table, nabbing the bread. "Plates? Knife? Cutting board?" he asked as he watched the coach adjust the wrap. By the looks of his movements, he was very well-versed in putting the things on. He suddenly wondered if Jake had continued to pitch in college, or if he'd played outfield or first base instead.

Jake tapped a drawer to signify the knives were in there and reached behind him as he stood on one leg, his hand holding the knee piece together while he plucked out a cutting board and set it on the counter. "I'll get the plates in a sec," he muttered as he pulled the compression brace tight and felt the cold of the ice pack within press around the inside of his knee. He smoothed out the Velcro and then sighed heavily as he straightened back up.

Watching the production, Brandon began to understand a little bit of what Jake was going through all without saying anything. He would never have thought the coach hurt that much until less than an hour ago, but now it was getting obvious. He'd learned this afternoon, though, that with Jake silence was more valued than chatter, so he kept quiet about it, taking the cutting board and a knife he'd pulled out to the nook table where he started slicing the tomatoes.

Jake glanced up at the man as he reached into one of the glass-fronted cabinets and retrieved the plates. "I blew out my knee freshman year," he told the man in answer to the unasked questions. "It still aches on me sometimes, when it's cold like it is now."

Brandon looked up at Jake, face even. He didn't pity the man. He was sure Jake was doing something suitably athletic at the time, but he wouldn't wish that sort of pain on anyone. "Saw that happen to runners a few times. Painful," he commented quietly, going back to slicing. "Ligaments, anyway."

Jake raised an eyebrow but said nothing. He doubted many runners got tackled from the side by wild bears in thick pads as they trotted down the trail or something, but he left it alone. He also hadn't explained the bone spurs in his ankle or the utter destruction of his shoulder that his dumbfuck high school baseball coach had wrought by pitching him too often and too much. He just let it go at the knee and twisted open his beer. It didn't occur to him that most people used bottle openers to do that.

"I'm guessing since this stuff is in your fridge, you'll eat it all," Brandon said as he built two large sandwiches, heavy on the meat and cheese. He stole glances at Jake, seeing the play of emotions across his face. He was curious, but it wasn't right to push. For all that he'd gone to school with and now worked with him, Brandon barely knew him. It felt awkward standing in his kitchen making him a sandwich.

"I'll eat anything," Jake responded automatically. "I'll eat bark if you put beer on it," he assured the man as he popped a few pills and took a long gulp of his beer to wash them down.

"Bark?" Brandon asked with a snort. "That would certainly take care of your fiber for the day," he joked, setting the plate with the bigger of the two sandwiches in front of Jake on the bar that faced the nook. He sat at the table and rifled through his back pack to pull out a folder of papers. Then with a glance up – though he wasn't sure why he was embarrassed, he wore them all day when teaching –

he pulled his glasses out and slid them on. "Good with the sandwich?" he asked.

"Mm hmm," Jake answered as he straddled the nearest bar stool. He watched Brandon silently as he ate, glad that he didn't have to deal with grading papers.

Nodding and taking a bite of his own, the science teacher started reading and marking, scribbling a grade at the top of each paper and circling it before setting it aside. He kept eating as well for several minutes, pretty much caught up in what he was doing until he glanced up to reach for his beer and saw Jake watching him. He froze in place. How had he not felt the weight of those black eyes on him?

"What?" he asked suspiciously.

"Nothing," Jake answered with a small smile. "Just another one of those times where I'm glad I'm me," he laughed softly with a gesture of his beer at the stack of grade papers.

Brandon cracked a grin. "You already said you wouldn't help with the teachery things, too. Bastard," he muttered under his breath.

"That's the rumor," Jake answered with a shit-eating grin as he pushed his empty plate away and finished his beer. He plunked it down on the counter and leaned back on his stool, trying to reach the refrigerator without having to get up.

"I'll get it," the science teacher said, pushing his glasses up with one finger and crossing to the fridge. He took out a beer and pressed it into Jake's hand, then went and sat back down, going right back to eating and grading.

Jake frowned a little. "Thanks," he muttered, looking at the man closely. He wondered how much of a doormat the guy really was, or if he was just too nice. There was such a thing as being too nice.

Back at his marking, Brandon made a noncommittal noise. "Just don't get used to it," he said, not even looking up from his papers. He wondered how long Jake would let him stick around before kicking him out. He was getting a decent start on his grading now.

"Hmph," Jake offered as he twisted off the top and kicked back a large portion of the beer. This was his nightly ritual. Get home, get ice, take drugs, and chase them with alcohol. He knew he likely should have been embarrassed to be doing it in front of Brandon, but frankly, after ten years he had lost the capacity to care. In fact, he had rarely cared what people thought of him; it was one of the qualities he supposed had made him so popular everywhere he went.

"That reminds me, every Wednesday the coaches all gather somewhere under the guise of team meetings," he said as he watched the pen move. "Usually we drink and make fun of the Dugout Club, but it's always a good time. If you're interested."

Brandon glanced up – Jake was inviting him to hang out? How wild was that? His glasses had slid down enough that he could look at Jake over the frames. "The Dugout Club?" he asked, smiling a little.

"Yeah, you know, the parents who can't keep their noses out of the game long enough to let us breathe?" Jake answered with a raised eyebrow. "Don't get me started on the Diamond Girls," he warned.

Smile getting bigger, Brandon chuckled. "You know I'm gonna ask," he pointed out. "Better I know now than look like an idiot if I have to ask later," he pointed out reasonably.

"Cheerleaders for the baseball team," Jake grunted. "Baseball shouldn't have cheerleaders," he protested grumpily.

The science teacher's eyes got really big. "We have baseball cheerleaders?" he asked in utter disbelief. "Oh *God.* Don't tell me it was one of Misty's ideas. I knew she wanted to figure out a way to be around the field in the spring, but this?" He threw down his pen and leaned back with a groan.

"Don't say that name to me," Jake warned good-naturedly. "I tried to fight it, but the girls started shouting discrimination." He grunted in distaste.

"Oh, good Lord. Does the softball team have cheerleaders?" Brandon asked, tossing his glasses to the table.

"Not that I know of," Jake answered wryly. "As long as they stay away from the dugouts we deal with it," he added. "That's another thing. When you're in the dugout with the guys, make sure they know you're willing to smack them around if they get out of line," he advised as the warmth of the beer began to flood through him.

"You know why you have a cheerleading team, right?" Brandon asked. It was an open secret, really. Misty ran her mouth about it even in the ladies' room – or so Rhonda had told Brandon. The cheerleading coach was gunning for a handsome husband; specifically the Prom King to her Prom Queen.

Jake leaned back warily and narrowed his eyes. "Why?" he asked with a slight touch of dread.

Brandon looked uneasy. He'd never been one to pal around with the guys, comparing cock length and notches in bedposts. He wasn't really comfortable with that kind of talk. "You remember how Rhonda was looking at you like an appetizer?" he asked.

Jake blinked at the man and then shifted uncomfortably. "Oh, that," he muttered. "Misty's tenacious," he huffed uncomfortably.

"She looks at you like you're a side of high-grade beef, man," Brandon said with more than a tinge of sympathy.

"She always has," Jake shrugged. "Senior year I thought she was going to kill me if I didn't take her to the prom. I skipped last period one day, drove over to Berkmar, grabbed the first girl I saw and asked her to go with me. Just to save myself the trouble."

Brandon's jaw dropped. "Wow. No *wonder* she was so pissed. I remember that hissy fit very clearly, and I was all the way across the cafeteria. Sure as hell went a long way to making me swear off...." He snapped his mouth shut and shook his head. "You were smart," he finally added.

Jake cocked his head questioningly at the truncated sentence, but left it alone. He smiled fondly at the memory. "I almost married that girl later," he told the man with a small smile. "She couldn't take the 'brutality' of the sports, though. And I couldn't take ... well, the thought of being married."

The smile reappeared. "Almost married, huh?" Brandon tilted his head, looking over Jake. "You've got closer than I have," he added with a shrug, finishing off his sandwich.

"Too busy with the learning, huh?" Jake ventured.

Brandon played with his glasses, tapping them on the papers. This discussion wasn't where he wanted to be – it edged too close to dangerous territory. "Yeah, I guess. College, grad school while teaching, moving back here. That and no real interest in dating," he said. "I wasn't exactly coveted by girls in high school, as I'm sure you know."

"Nothing bad about that. You don't have Misty on your tail fifteen years later, hmm?" he pointed out.

Shaking his head, Brandon made a face. "How someone that pretty can be so ugly, I don't know," he said, his voice filled with obvious distaste.

"Looks can be deceiving," Jake crooned with another gulp of beer. "I mean, for some reason I've been thinking about high school a lot lately," he admitted. "Thinking about what shits all kids are and how many friends I could have had but didn't 'cause I wore a letter jacket. You still see it today."

Among the teachers as well as the students, Brandon added silently. "Well, I can honestly say I never thought I'd be sitting at your kitchen table grading papers and drinking a beer," he said, thinking back to how defined the cliques had been when he was in school. Except for very few, those lines just didn't get crossed, and the groups didn't mix. "In high school, you just don't know how to break those walls down," he added quietly. He knew from experience, and now he sensed Jake knew, too. "But I'm sure I was just as much a shit as you were," he poked, trying to lighten the tone of their discussion.

Jake bristled mightily and then sighed, the beer and pills loosing his tongue more than he would appreciate when tomorrow came. "I wasn't such a bad guy," he mumbled defensively.

Brandon looked at him closely when Jake dropped his eyes. No. No, he hadn't been, not really, not compared to many. A sudden tenseness filled Brandon, and he knew he needed to leave. He wasn't sure he liked this sudden interest his body seemed to be taking in Jake's body. *Gah*. "It's late, I need to get home and get more work done. I've got baseball practice after school tomorrow. Imagine that," he said, standing and shoving all the papers in his back pack, that whole shell-shocked look returning.

Jake looked back up and watched Brandon with his dark eyes. "Something I said?" he asked curiously.

"Something you...? No," Brandon said, sinking back into the booth, sliding on his glasses to hide behind them just like he did at work. "I'm just not really good with people," he said. "This whole baseball thing will be a real challenge for me. And not just learning the rules." He'd been an introvert for so long, it was really hard for him to break the habit. Teaching was different.

"With people?" Jake echoed, brow furrowing in deeper confusion. "Oh," he murmured as if trying to understand but not really getting it. "Yeah, no. No, I'm sorry," he went on as he stood up slowly. The gel pack on his ankle made a loud squishing sound in protest but he ignored it. "I'll walk you out," he offered.

Standing up again, Brandon grabbed his back pack and headed to the door, feeling awkward once again. This was why he didn't do social things. He stopped outside, turning to look at the tired man in the doorway. "Thanks for the sandwich. I hope you feel better tomorrow."

"Heh," Jake responded as he leaned against the door frame. "I'm sure I'll be right as rain come morning," he asserted with confidence. "Hey, don't forget to bag your phone tomorrow," he told the man with a cheeky grin.

Brandon just stared at him, totally at a loss for what to say. Bag? His phone? He blinked in confusion. *Oh!* It clicked, and he chuckled, rolling his eyes. "Sure. I'll have to remember not to laugh when Troy announces it. It would be *supercilious* of me not to follow instructions," he teased, shuffling a little.

"Like I know what that means," Jake scoffed with a grin. "See ya tomorrow, man. Don't forget your clothes."

Starting down the stairs, Brandon raised a hand and nodded. He got settled in the car and drove off, all the while feeling very self-conscious because Jake stood there in the doorway, watching him the whole time. Jake waited until the headlights were gone, then turned back into his house and shut the door slowly. It was a habit learned from his father, to watch a visitor leave until they were out of sight. He didn't even know that he did it. With a sigh, he trudged toward the stairs and the shower on the upper level. Something about Brandon was ringing in his ears, but he couldn't place it. It left him unsettled and cranky, and Jake didn't like being either.

The drive home seemed to whip by because Brandon's head was full of new images and ideas – baseball, tight white pants, health class, Jake Campbell. He stopped the car in the driveway and climbed out automatically, looking at the rustic white bungalow surrounded by wild flowers. So different from Jake's house. But tonight, Brandon thought they might have discovered they had at least a tiny something in common. He headed inside, deciding to finish grading the essays and the other block's work before taking a run around the lake. It was going to be a long night. The first of many.

Chapter 3

THE science teacher leaned on the third baseline fence next to Jonathan as the younger man mused over the reasoning behind some of the drills Jake was running to evaluate the kids at tryouts. About four had dropped out from yesterday to today, fewer than expected, according to the freshman coach.

On the field, Jake was a force. Even Troy the pretty boy was eclipsed by the sheer power of Jake's personality, and Brandon could readily see that popular homecoming king in the head coach. But now the allure was transformed into a man comfortable with his confidence and not afraid to put it to use. Again Brandon tamped down the flicker of interest beyond professional involvement. He was determined to quash it, to not let the idea even see the light of day.

Although Jonathan had offered, Brandon had run the suicides again today. He remembered Jake's pain from the night before and was unwilling to let the head coach do the running. Three guys instead of two outran Brandon this time, but he'd not even been a half step behind. Maybe he'd do some speed drills in the park to practice.

Jonathan pointed out how the kids were practicing sidestepping, and while Brandon recognized the effort, he could tell the balance involved wasn't a strong skill for most of the players. It didn't help when Jake's voice lashed out.

"You don't even have a glove in your hands!" Jake bellowed. "How the hell are you gonna field a ball if you can't stay on your feet?" he questioned as he walked through the lines of boys doing the complicated drill. The first and foremost reason for it was to teach them the most effective way to turn and run by ingraining it in their muscle memory. But it also doubled as a good base running drill, and as a way to weed out the waverers who had stuck through after yesterday.

"Pick your feet up!" Troy shouted from the other side of the grid of players, the two of them double-teaming as they circled the kids like vultures. Jake glanced over at the fence where the other coaches were calling out encouragement to the kids, thinking how the staff formed a pretty decent good cop/bad cop crew. He caught sight of Brandon, standing there beside Jonathan and murmuring to each other, and he looked away quickly before he could let himself be distracted. He remembered some of the things he had told the man last night, things he shouldn't have said to anyone probably, and he flushed a little with the memory. He made it a point of keeping his private life private for a reason. And really, this sudden interest in the man, it wasn't a good thing.

"Well, I'm not sure I'd do so well with that my first time, either. But I've got pretty good balance," Brandon said. He glanced up to see Jake look over them and then go back to the kids. "Should we be doing something?"

"Nah, wait 'til the drill's over or we'll just be in the way," Jonathan answered with a wave of his hand. "And watch the kids. Pick out the weakest ones from the herd, that sort of thing."

Brandon nodded slowly, adding what he was seeing to the information he'd gathered last night. On a whim, he'd jotted some thoughts last night in a small pocket-sized notebook that was now in his back pocket. "Did you play ball in school?" he asked.

"Yep, right here at Parkview. I was a freshman when Jake was a senior," Jonathan answered with a nod as he squinted into the sun. "Every once in a while our coach would have us stop practice and watch the varsity just to learn," he laughed. "God, what a crop of talent they were. What some of those guys could have done if they'd been given the chance," he mused, watching Jake stalk up to a kid who had fallen and yank him bodily off the ground by his belt.

Suppressing a laugh at the look of horror on the kid's face,

Brandon shifted sideways to face the other man. "I didn't know you went to school here. I wonder how many people come back over time." He started trying to count. There'd been several who drifted through, especially his first few years here, many doing student teaching and then heading off to bigger, more moneyed schools in Atlanta or even out of state.

"I'd say anyone who washed out in college comes back," Jonathan ventured with a nod at Jake.

"Next person to fall down will owe everyone a lap!" Jake shouted as he tossed the kid back into line and continued his prowling. The drill went on for another minute or so, and Jake called a halt to it just before he knew kids would start falling over and not getting back up. "Go get water!" he ordered, stalking back to the fence. Behind him, some kids literally crawled to the dugout.

Brandon was momentarily shocked by Jonathan's comment, but then realized he was talking about sports. Jake would have had to complete his degree to teach, but not playing sports wouldn't have stopped him. The blown-out knee was starting to make more sense. And why Jake was here and not playing professional ball somewhere. He remembered there'd been talk. He watched Jake approach, straightening a little and pulling out his pad to make a few notes, checking the numbers on a few of the players.

Jake frowned at the little pad of paper and raised an eyebrow in question as he came up to the fence and leaned against it. "That little dude is gonna be your leadoff hitter, I guarantee it," he said to Jonathan with a nod at a freshman kid who was little more than five feet tall. "Shortstop."

Jonathan nodded. That was one of the kids he didn't know, who had filtered in from another middle school. But he could see what Jake saw clearly enough.

"Any observations?" Jake invited of Brandon as Troy came trotting up to them noisily.

Brandon glanced over his shorthand. "Jack will be a good runner, so will Evan," he said of two juniors. "Jimmy's not very fast or suited to running, but solid. First base, maybe. And Junior in the outfield, he's got the endurance to do the distance. Not sure about the eye, though." He looked up to see all three men staring at him. It was starting to get a little unnerving. "What?" he asked for about the millionth time.

Jake stifled laugh and shook his head. "All right, then," he responded without answering. "Let's break 'em up," he ordered as he stepped away from the fence and bellowed the order.

"Do I want to know what that was about?" the science teacher muttered as they followed the varsity coach back out onto the field.

"You never know," Jonathan laughed with a shake of his head. The kids trudged out obediently and began to work the same drills from yesterday. Jake worked them until the sun started to go down, then called a halt to the activities and had the kids start putting up the equipment.

"You put up your own equipment until the day someone offers to pay you to play ball!" Jake was shouting as he watched. "If I see you letting someone else do the work, I'll *make* work for you!"

Brandon stood near third base, watching the tired kids scurry. Hell, he was tired just looking at them. Soon the field was clear, and he walked to join the others at home base.

"Tomorrow we'll start making lists," Jake told the coaches as they gathered around him. Light was fading quickly now, and he glanced around the field to make certain it was clear. "By Friday we'll have the teams set. Sound about right?" The others nodded obediently, and Jake refrained from rolling his eyes. "See you guys tomorrow," he told them, giving one of the college kids a slap on the back that had him staggering forward as Jake turned and headed for the gate.

Jonathan waved goodbye to Brandon, who nodded an answer before starting to walk back to the gym himself. Troy whizzed off in that golf cart – where on *Earth* did he get that thing and why did Jake tolerate it? – and the biology teacher found himself walking through the parking lot in the dusk. It was quiet and cool, and he shivered a little.

Jake flopped down on the steps near the entrance, dragged off his cleats, slid into his trainers and stood again slowly, shouldering his heavy equipment bag as he watched the other guys head off. He watched Brandon for a moment, not even sure what he was thinking at that point. It annoyed him that he couldn't make up his mind about the guy. He stood and stretched, his long body arching gracefully, then he turned to head for the road and the walk home.

Spur of the moment, Brandon piped up. "You good to get home, Coach?" he asked neutrally as he came to a clacking stop on the concrete with the cleats.

Jake turned around and looked back at the man. "Yeah," he called in answer. "I plan to hijack Troy on the road and steal his golf cart," he said seriously. "I figure even if he hits me with it, it can't do much damage," he snickered.

Brandon's nose wrinkled in a smile. "Why the hell do you let him drive that insane thing?" he asked.

Jake veered off the grass and strolled back into the parking lot. "He drives it to work," he answered with a smirk. "He lives about a mile that way," he pointed in the opposite direction of his own house. "He's cheap and lazy. A fearful combination when you add shameless and resourceful."

Unable to stop the snicker, Brandon just shook his head. "That's just incredible," he commented, eyes dancing.

Jake gave a slight smile and nodded, looking out into the darkness of the road he would be walking. It was an interesting mix of feelings, the need to get home combined with a curious desire to keep talking with a man he had never had much to do with before. Well, there was an easy way to solve that predicament. "You know, if you don't mind, I might take you up on the offer of a ride," he said with another glance at Brandon. "Gets dark too early."

"No problem," Brandon replied easily, stopping at the door. "I just need to grab my pack and change my shoes. Be right back." He ducked inside, shoes clacking on the hard floor.

Jake groaned quietly and flopped his big body to sit on the steps to wait. He was going to have to start actually driving to work. Just because he felt like a walk in the morning didn't mean he would twelve hours later.

It only took Brandon a couple of minutes, and then he was back outside. "I parked back here this morning," he pointed to the car about halfway back in the lot. "Figured it would make the evenings easier." He offered Jake a hand up.

Jake reached up for the hand without a second thought, letting the man pull him to his feet with a slight groan. "My ass is too old for this," he complained good-naturedly as he walked beside Brandon toward the car.

Brandon laughed. "Yesterday you said we weren't old!" he pointed out.

"It's just certain parts of me, that's all," Jake answered defensively, grinning as he hitched his equipment bag higher.

"The whole young at heart thing is clichéd, but I think it still applies," Brandon said, digging into his pack for his car keys as they approached the Jetta. "To you, anyway."

"Oh yeah?" Jake asked in slight amusement. "Why's that?"

"That it applies to you?" Brandon opened the locks with the fob and tossed his pack in the back seat. "You still love it. The game. You still have passion. Even though it's a pain in the ass sometimes, and you hurt at night, you still love it."

Jake felt himself flushing in the darkness, and he cleared his throat as he opened the back door. "Yeah, well, yeah," he muttered in response as he tossed his bag in and closed the door again.

Brandon smiled a bit, recognizing the other man was a little embarrassed. So he just let it drop and climbed into the car. Soon they were off, headed to Jake's house, classic rock playing quietly on the radio from where he'd left it on that morning.

Jake wasn't quite sure what to say on the quiet drive. He felt like he needed to say something, but he was finding that he just didn't know enough about the other man to converse comfortably. They didn't even really have work in common. They were both teachers, technically, but not the same kind.

He wracked his brain, trying to think up something. "So, uh, did you know Jonathan before yesterday?" he finally asked, remembering the two men being chummy on the field.

"No, I didn't know him. I don't think he knows I went to Parkview, either," Brandon answered, stopping the car at the same light as the night before. "He said he knew your name, looked up to you," he ribbed a little.

Jake blushed harder and bit his lip. "Yeah," he agreed as he looked out the window. A lot of people had looked up to him, thinking he of all people would be going on to bigger and better things. Football and baseball scholarships, scouted by Major League and NFL teams.

But here he was instead.

Smiling, Brandon let it go, not wanting to prod Jake into annoyance rather than slight amusement. He drove across the intersection and within a minute he pulled into the driveway and shifted the car into park. "I meant to ask before practice," Brandon said quietly, "if you were feeling better today."

"Eh," Jake responded automatically. "All I had to do was put one of those lifts in my shoe again and it solved the ankle thing. Thanks for asking," he added sincerely.

"Good," Brandon answered with a nod, and then he was out of things to say. He sat there wracking his brain, trying to come up with something, anything to say, though he had no idea why. Actually, no, he knew *exactly* why. He just didn't want to admit it.

"I would offer you food and beer, but..." Jake turned to the man and smiled slightly. "I'm not good company after 3 p.m."

Brandon compressed his lips to hold back a snicker. When it was safe, he said, "You were fine last night," rather evenly. He understood, though. Last night was an aberration. Brandon could be on his way now. It wasn't like he didn't have plenty to do. "Have a good night," he murmured, caught looking at the other man's shadowed face.

Jake smiled slightly and said, "I'm always fine *last night*," barely able to stop the snicker as he elbowed the man. "See you tomorrow, man. Thanks for the ride."

Shaking his head at Jake's banter, Brandon raised a hand to wave. "Bye," he said quietly, reminding himself to stow these odd twitching feelings and get back to the real world. He moved to shift the car into reverse.

Jake gave a wave and stepped away from the car, then gave a little hop and banged on the roof, leaning over to open the door and stick his head back in. “Coach’s night tomorrow,” he said to the man. “We’re coming here after practice. Pizza, beer, more beer...”

Brandon startled when Jake hit the car, but had his breath back by the time he was done talking. He had to smile, just a little. “I guess since I’m a coach, I’m invited. Should I bring anything?”

“Only if you have a certain type of beer you like or chips or something. Seriously, it’s just an excuse to drink. If you bring any Zima or shit like that, you’ll get beat up,” Jake teased with a wink.

The look on Brandon’s face was one of mute horror. “Don’t tell me Jonathan did that.”

“No. Troy did it,” Jake laughed, grinning widely at the man as he leaned over and looked through the door.

“Jesus Christ. Where did he go to school? If you were caught drinking something like that at Tech you’d have been dumped off an overpass onto I-75,” Brandon said, still cringing.

“He swears it was a joke,” Jake snickered. “I just think he’s a closet queer,” he giggled with a shake of his head as he stood back up and gave the car another slap with his hand. “See you tomorrow, man,” he said with a smile in his voice, turning to head into the house.

Stuck in place, Brandon just watched Jake walk up the stairs, intensely glad the other coach wasn’t looking at him at that moment, because he was sure all sorts of things he didn’t want seen were written all over his face. Closet queer. *Fuck*. Brandon ran a hand through his hair and pulled out of the driveway. He really hoped Jake had meant what he said in a somewhat affectionate, teasing manner, rather than a dirtier, more ignorant meaning.

Brandon had heard enough of that to last a lifetime.

“MORNING, Mr. Bartlett,” one of the bouncy little

cheerleaders greeted the next morning. "Morning, Coach," the boy walking with her said, nodding at Brandon respectfully and smiling as they headed for their seats.

"Katie," Brandon said distractedly, ticking her name off the list, but Jimmy's greeting caught him off guard, and he looked up. Pushing his glasses up, he had to rally. "Ah, good morning, Jimmy."

"Morning, Coach," came another greeting almost immediately, followed by a smattering of other good mornings as the kids filed in. The first class of the day usually saw tired kids trudging in and flopping down with grunts. But every boy who had been at tryouts the last two days greeted Brandon that morning in a semi-cheerful manner.

Blinking, he remembered what Jake had said about the players always being in class, and looking at his grade book, he had to admit the coach was right. They all had perfect attendance. Pleasantly surprised, Brandon moved to his desk off to the side of the room to grab his teaching list for the block. "All right, break into groups of four, please, and pull some desks together for each group. We're doing interactive exercises today." It was one of the activities Brandon consistently received positive feedback on: Students working together on something besides book work. He personally felt they learned much more by *doing* rather than seeing or hearing. Musing, he got them started on a variation of Biology Pictionary and let them go, listening in on each group.

As the first class of the day got started, the speaker near the door crackled to life for the morning reports. The voice droned on with the usual announcements, the person speaking obviously aware that no one ever listened to these things. At the end, the voice read, "And Coach Campbell would like to remind the student body that the next person caught throwing wet wads of toilet paper at the ceiling of the locker rooms will be ... wait, can I say that over the speaker? I'm not sure I can say that." There was a clearing of a throat and a mutter that couldn't be understood, and then the kid said, "Just don't do it again, trust me."

A few of the boys in the class snickered quietly, trying not to make a lot of noise but obviously familiar with whatever threat their coach had used. Brandon's brow shot up. He could just imagine what Jake had said he would do. Shaking his head, he chuckled, tapping Cynthia on the head and pointing to the trash can for her gum without having to say a word. Too bad Troy couldn't find other upperclassmen to keep reading announcements along those lines. It would be amusing enough to keep him going all morning.

As he walked around, Brandon noticed that one of the baseball kids was having trouble drawing, using his left hand instead of his right. He was about to say something when he saw the kid's right hand. His fingers were taped. The teacher stopped before commenting and just watched, not wanting to interrupt. It was awkward for the boy, he could tell, but the kid got it done, and the other students guessed correctly. Brandon smiled and patted the kid's shoulder. "Good job," he murmured before moving on to the next group.

"Thanks, Coach," the kid muttered automatically.

The rest of Brandon's day went much the same. Third block, a cheerleader had to sit with her leg extended because she was wearing a knee brace. Fourth block, it was a softball player with a wrist brace. Fifth block, a lacrosse player with a black eye. The teacher couldn't figure out how he'd missed all this before. It was all right there in front of him. It wasn't that he'd thought badly of the kids or didn't pay attention to them, it was just that he hadn't noticed the injuries or the way the kids dealt with them. That embarrassed him a hell of a lot. In the nine minutes before sixth block, Brandon crammed papers and files into his pack, snagged the duffle from under his desk and headed out to the gym and the 'beloved' health class. He had plans for the anatomy lesson he figured the students would get a hoot out of, and since he was still trying to build rapport with them, he figured some fun would go a long way toward helping that. He got to the classroom in the gym complex just a couple of minutes before the bell.

Somewhere in the maze of hallways that connected the gymnasium to the locker rooms, offices, and classrooms, an angry bellow echoed off the tile and out through the open doors. It sounded again, clearer this time, accompanied by running footsteps.

"Snakes in the grass," an amused voice said to Brandon as he stood in the hallway. The science teacher turned to see the School Resource Officer leaning against the wall in the dark end of the corridor, his handcuffs and gun seriously out of place in the school hallway. Another shout echoed and a door slammed somewhere. "He's been after those little shits for weeks," the cop said with a laugh.

"What's going on?" Brandon asked, stopping outside the classroom as students filed in past him.

"Kids loitering in the locker rooms, that sort of thing," the SRO answered. "Hell, they're more scared of Campbell than they are of me." He laughed softly as he put a Pepsi can to his lips and spit tobacco into it discreetly.

Brandon had to grin. "Hell, I know I am," he said. His smile grew when a couple of kids smashed through the double doors just past them and raced toward the breezeway leading back to the main building.

The SRO laughed hard as the kids flew by him, and a moment later the doors were pushed open and Jake came stalking out. "Little bastards," he growled, completely unaware of the presence of anyone else until he turned around. "Next time just shoot 'em, man, I won't tell nobody," he huffed to the cop. Brandon and the SRO looked at each other before dissolving into laughter. "Shut up!" Jake called grumpily as he pushed through the other pair of doors and into the large gymnasium. *"Get the hell off that rim*!" he bellowed suddenly as the doors creaked closed behind him.

The two men left behind just kept laughing until the bell rang. "Welcome to the nuthouse," the SRO said before sauntering off. Brandon went into class still grinning and grabbed up his grade book. What a hoot. Sitting on the edge of the front of the desk, he took role, still trying to match names to faces.

"Ladies and gentlemen. And *Rodney,*" Brandon had to call to one kid staring out the window. The student jerked his head around while the others tittered. "Today we're going to learn about anatomy."

There were giggles and whistles in response to this news. The only kids in the rowdy class being quiet were the several girls who were batting their eyelashes at Brandon and the two kids who had been at baseball tryouts and knew Brandon as a coach.

"All right. Did anyone read the assigned pages? There were only five," he reminded them. "Raise your hands if you did."

A few hands raised, a few throats were cleared. "I looked at the pictures!" one kid offered cheekily.

Brandon waved Cheeky up to the front. "What's your name? Larry Wallace? Okay." He looked back at the few hands and chose one of the quiet girls. "Come on up, Melissa. The purpose of this exercise is to identify parts of the body by their proper name."

Melissa blushed mightily as she was called to the front of the class, but she shuffled up obediently and stood there as Larry grinned at the rest of the class, drinking up being the center of attention. Brandon noted the reactions of his two 'volunteers'. "The rule of the exercise is to touch the piece of anatomy with one finger."

There was a ripple of giggles and Melissa blushed harder. "Are you sure, Mr. Bartlett?" she asked in a slightly squeaky voice.

Brandon squeezed her shoulder supportively. "If you break the rule, *Larry*," the teacher emphasized to get the kid's attention, "meaning, if you cop a feel, you get to choose between two results."

"Get slapped or keep going. Like that's anything new," Larry responded with a snicker.

"You either get to explain your actions to Melissa's father or Coach Campbell," the teacher answered.

Larry's smile fell, and his shoulders slumped as the rest of the class snickered. Brandon continued. "Of course the same applies to Melissa. I can just see her explaining why she grabbed Mrs. Wallace's baby boy's butt, right? Right. So. Are you two comfortable demonstrating the exercise or shall I ask for different volunteers?"

Both kids nodded dubiously and glared at each other in mutual silent warning. Brandon barely restrained his chuckle. "Oh. And did I mention we're keeping score?" he asked innocently.

Both kids squeaked again and another ripple of snickers went through the room.

An hour later, loud cheers echoed down the hallway, despite the closed classroom door. They would stop, then erupt. Stop, then erupt again. Then there'd be booing. Then cheers again. And then chanting: "Ry-an, Ry-an, Ry-an, Ry-an" and "Go Nelly, Go Nelly, Go Nelly, Go Nelly!"

The door jerked open suddenly, and Jake stuck his head into the room, glancing around with narrowed eyes at the kids and Brandon. The desks had all been pushed to the sides of the room, making space in the middle for the guy and girl who faced off. The other students, divided by gender, grouped on opposite sides, cheering on their 'champions' while Rodney kept score on the whiteboard. Brandon sat on the edge of the desk, one foot on the floor, the other swinging as he pitched out words, anatomy book in hand, glasses mostly slid down his nose.

"Okay. Girls 4, Boys 2. Ryan: Deltoid," Brandon challenged. Nobody had heard the door open over the cheering. Ryan considered carefully, looking over the girl's body, then reached out with one finger and prodded the front of her shoulder. The girls groaned and the guys cheered as Brandon said, "Correct," and Rodney added a tick mark next to Ryan's name.

Jake raised an eyebrow and cleared his throat. "Is there *fun* being had in here?" he asked pointedly.

Brandon looked up with a smile while some of the students called out greetings to the other coach. "Girls 4, Boys 3. Nelly: Humerus," the science teacher said. The girl wilted, but the others cheered her on. After a moment she shrugged, stuck out one finger and touched Ryan right on the tip of the nose.

Jake raised the other eyebrow and met Brandon's eyes briefly, seeing that he obviously had this under control. He'd have to apologize for interrupting later. "Carry on then," he laughed softly as he pulled back out of the doorway.

Right before the announcements came on, there was much happy female shrieking and male groaning. When the bell rang, the students left, most bouncing and saying "bye" to Mr. Bartlett as they went, commenting on the "instructional" exercise. Once they were gone, he chuckled and started pushing the desks back into line.

Through the open door more shouting could be heard and laughter echoed off the tiles. "If God wanted you to hang from the rafters he'd have given you tails, you damn monkeys!" Jake shouted. The smile in his voice was obvious as more laughter met his words. P.E. teachers were likely the only ones in the school system who could cuss at a kid and not get in trouble. A moment later, Jake was standing in the open doorway and leaning against the frame with a small smile.

Having heard the now more familiar Campbell-bellow, Brandon glanced up as he shifted the desks back into place. "Hey," he greeted.

"Hey," Jake returned with a small smile. "Sorry about barging in earlier," he offered. "Usually in these parts when there's yelling it means the teacher's been hung from the ceiling by his toes."

"Not by his tail?" Brandon joked. "They're good kids. I'm glad they enjoyed the game. Helps make them more at ease with me, at least." He straightened up and stretched before shoving his glasses back up his nose. "How was your day?" he asked politely, looking at Jake curiously.

"There's a reason we're not allowed to torture kids anymore," Jake groused seriously. "I gotta run, got bus duty today," he practically growled. "See you in a bit."

Left behind, Brandon reflected on how much he'd laughed the last three days. He just couldn't help it, especially with Jake's insane sense of humor. With a sigh he sat at the desk and pulled out his folders, settling in to do some – hopefully most of – his grading. He had an hour before he had to be on the field.

So fifty minutes later he was in the visitors' locker room, stripped down and just into the white baseball pants when he started stretching. He wanted to be ready to run the suicides, and it was easier to do it here than out at the field. Jake had said they'd be narrowing the team down today. He distracted himself from the slow stretches by mentally reviewing his notes on the players.

Jake was doing his last survey of the locker rooms before classes were let out to clear them of anyone that shouldn't be in them, and he pushed through the door with catlike silence and crept into the rooms. He peered around the first rows of lockers and into the showers and found no one, then stepped through into the other bank of lockers to find Brandon there, half dressed and stretching out his long legs slowly. *Jesus.*

The coach stopped short and blinked, a rush of lust assaulting him before he could stamp it down. He swallowed heavily and watched for a moment longer before retreating quietly, licking his lips nervously as he pressed against the cinderblock wall near the sinks. *Wow.* He knew he should creep back out of the rooms before Brandon sensed someone around, but he couldn't seem to force himself to move. He couldn't remember ever being hit that hard by the desire to pounce on someone before. Just like that, right out of the blue. Was that what that niggling feeling had been the last few days? Unrealized lust? Christ.

Sighing quietly, Brandon slowly bent over at the waist, grasping the backs of his thighs, eyes closed. After holding the position he straightened and stretched both arms up into the air, groaning when his neck popped. He yawned involuntarily and grunted, shaking his head to try to ward off the doze as he held the stretch.

Jake shook his head and told himself to move. Walking in on the man innocently was one thing, but standing there and listening while he considered the shape of his ass was bordering on territory that would have him feeling dirty. Yeah, he definitely felt dirty. He crept out into the other side of the room, flushing hotly even though he was the only person who would ever know what he was thinking. He pushed at the locker room door. "Bed check!" he shouted, his usual bellow somewhat ineffective as it came out slightly croaked.

Brandon's eyes flew open, and he turned in place, then moved to stick his head around the corner of the lockers. "Bed check?" he echoed. "Are we in the Army now, Sergeant?" He tilted his head, noticing that Jake looked out of sorts.

"Any kids in here?" Jake asked the man without responding to the tease, already knowing the answer. His voice was tight and clipped. The last thing he needed was an attraction to another teacher. Another teacher who knew him from before he'd grown up.

Not to mention that he really didn't want to be outed at any point because he was ogling the man, thank you very much. So he overcompensated, his black eyes hard and his body tense.

Feeling an unexplained wave of coldness, Brandon shook his head and dropped the attitude. "No," he said shortly before leaving Jake's view to finish getting dressed. He just didn't know how to deal with Jake. He yelled at the kids, but took care of them. He could be friendly, and he could be cold. He could explain or he could browbeat. He could do a hell of a lot, Brandon admitted silently. "Just not predictably," he muttered under his breath as he pulled the Under Armour over his head.

"What?" Jake called as he turned and headed for the door. He felt almost physically ill, and he was desperately trying to think of some sort of joke to break the tense mood he'd created. But he could think of nothing. *Goddammit*!

"I'll see you out on the field," Brandon called out, feeling really off-balance. He had to figure out a way to relate to Jake or he just might lose his mind. Or worse. He dropped his head into his hands, trying to shake the odd warm flush that filled him every time he saw the man. He just couldn't afford this kind of reaction right now.

"Yeah," Jake agreed woodenly, making his escape as quickly as possible. He needed some ice water or something. He needed to deal with this and fast.

Chapter 4

"DOES anyone else wanna bitch about being tired?" Jake practically screamed as the unfortunate kid in question started on the first of his five laps around the field. His tone was different today than it had been before. Jake always shouted. But shouting and angry were two different things, and Jake was rarely angry. Today he was, though, and the kids could tell. Dark was soon approaching, but no one dared hope it meant the end of practice was coming. Even Troy was frowning at the man and watching the kids closely. He seemed to want to step in, but apparently even Troy knew enough to be afraid of Jake when he was in a mood. He also knew that no matter how angry he was, Jake would never let the kids come to harm.

Brandon stood nearby, nearly wincing, though more at Jake's language than the tone. But the angry note was a little distressing. Brandon knew Jake wouldn't have the reputation of an excellent coach if he truly abused the kids. Still, in Brandon's own quiet opinion, the kids needed to be running more. They needed to build up their endurance. Some of them wouldn't last a mile before dropping.

Finally Jake dismissed the kids in disgust, waving them off the field without even a word as he turned away from them. There had been misplayed grounders, dropped balls, swings that were a mile off target, not to mention the complainers who always got on his nerves. It was days like this when he questioned whether he was in the right place. The other coaches just waited quietly, knowing not to poke the growling tiger. Even Troy kept his mouth shut, which surprised

Brandon.

Jake grunted at the other men and shook his head. "Beer," he snarled at them as he passed them by. Shrugging, Brandon led the way, following Jake. They were supposed to go to the head coach's house tonight, and he figured that was still on despite Jake's wretched mood. "You guys want a ride? I can drop you back here after," he offered to Troy and Jonathan.

"I'll take you up on that," Jonathan grinned as Troy shook his head.

"Thanks, but I'm good," Troy answered as he watched Jake stalk ahead of them. "Jake drove today, so...." He trailed off and cleared his throat as Jake stalked up to an old Chevy truck and chucked his equipment bag into the back, an action he usually undertook with great care. "Actually, yeah. Shotgun," Troy said to them, and Jonathan scowled at him as they continued on to Brandon's car.

Brandon snorted and unlocked the car doors so they could climb in. "Don't sit on the limes," he warned Troy, who was about to flop into the passenger's seat. There was also a six-pack of bottled Corona in the floorboard.

"Is that legal?" Troy asked as he slid into the seat and plucked the beers off the floorboard. "Damn! Jake told me I couldn't bring alcohol onto the campus," he sulked, pulling the door closed.

In the back seat Jonathan laughed and reached up to pat Troy's head. "That's 'cause you were trying to bring it for lunch, man."

"Fuck you," Troy sneered, hugging the beers to him. "Fuck you all," he declared as Jake's truck pulled up beside them.

"I'll meet you boys there," Jake said to them as he stuck his head out the window of the truck. "I've got to run by the store and pick up a few cases, y'all go on ahead."

"You might pick me up another pack of Corona, Troy seems to have gotten attached to mine," Brandon said drolly, glancing to the blond man now crooning to the clear bottles.

Jake peered past Brandon to look at Troy and then rolled his eyes. "Corona?" he asked, just to make certain.

Brandon nodded. "Yeah." He tried reaching over to get the six-pack from Troy, but got his hand slapped. "Bastard!" he barked at Troy, though he smiled while Jonathan just cackled in the back seat.

Jake watched with a smile as Brandon asserted himself and slowly realized that the feeling from the locker room was returning. "Don't let him into the limes, you'll be scarred for life," he warned, his voice slightly strained as he tried to fight back the sudden attraction. He gassed the truck before he could stare any more and drove quickly out of the parking lot.

Muttering and mock-glaring at Troy, Brandon turned on the car. "My luck. I bring beer, and you filch it," he said under his breath.

Jonathan hung over the seat, still laughing. "Wait 'til you see what Troy can do with a lime."

"That's, yeah, that is pretty impressive," Troy chuckled evilly. "Hey, what crawled up Jake's ass and died, huh?"

"Shit, I thought maybe he needed some fiber or something," Jonathan said.

Brandon choked back a laugh. "I don't know. He was fine after last block," he said. "I noticed tonight he sounded a little more..."

"Mad."

"Yeah."

"I haven't seen him that mad since –" Troy stopped suddenly and simply stared out the window, shaking his head as if muttering to himself. "Must have had a bad day," he finished finally without moving.

Jonathan prodded Troy's shoulder. "Since what? Is this something we should expect to see more of?"

"I don't know," Troy answered reluctantly. "I mean, I dunno what set him off, is all. Last time I saw an extended pissy fit like today was when he found out that his shoulder couldn't be operated on."

Brandon's hands tightened on the steering wheel as Jonathan launched into a rant on how ten years ago players got pushed too hard and how many careers had been ruined because of it. Jake's shoulder? Along with his ankle and a blown out knee? What the hell had he gone through to compete? Brandon realized he just had no concept of how much Jake must love to play. He drove, deep in thought, while the other two men ranted.

When he pulled into Jake's driveway, Troy was still clutching the Corona. "I'm not getting those back, am I?" Brandon said flatly.

"Nope," Troy answered with a big grin as he got out of the car.

"You're not getting all the limes," Brandon retorted.

"You won't want 'em when I'm done with them anyway," Troy twittered as he strutted up the walk to the front door like he lived in the place. He fished out the spare key from a hidden spot over the door and unlocked the door, inviting them in with a cheeky grin.

Jonathan laughed and bounded up the steps. "C'mon, Brandon. If you want one of those limes you need to get it as soon as possible," he said, making Brandon grab his pack and run up the stairs and into the house.

Jake pulled into the drive not long after and sat there glaring at his front door. "Get a hold of yourself, you fuck," he muttered as he sat with his wrists resting on the steering wheel. He had dealt with this before, an attraction to someone he shouldn't be attracted to. He could do it again. With a grumpy snort he got out of the truck, slamming the door loudly so Troy would know to get out of his stuff, and grabbed the several cases of beers he had bought and lugged them up to the front door.

Having heard the car door slam, Brandon loped to the front door and opened the screen for Jake. "Watch out for Troy, he's on a tear," Brandon warned just as the blond came sliding into the hardwood hallway in his sock feet, singing into his stolen Corona bottle like it was a microphone.

"Oh Jesus," Jake groaned as Troy turned, shook his ass at them, and strutted off. "You let him into the limes, didn't you?" he muttered at Brandon, smiling slightly and heading into the kitchen with his load. "Sit down!" he shouted at Troy in his loudest, most authoritative voice. Troy plopped down on the couch obediently and sulked at him. "Before we get too trashed, we do need to divvy up the teams," Jake reminded him.

Troy huffed, and Jonathan chuckled as he flopped down next to the man with a bag of Doritos. Brandon just shook his head and watched in fascination. Jake growled softly and went to the sunroom to retrieve the rolling whiteboard he kept out there. He pushed it back into the living room, settling it in front of the television, and then he stalked to the kitchen to dig out the markers. On his way he grabbed a cold beer and opened the cabinet where he kept his many little bottles of pills.

Brandon had come around the other door into the kitchen, planning to get a second Corona and lime, and he paused in the doorway when he nearly ran into Jake standing at the cabinet. "Sorry," he murmured, moving past the other man to the fridge.

"No problem," Jake muttered as he poured out a handful of pills and then picked out two of them. "Small kitchens make for close families," he said without thinking, the words his mother had loved to say, even though the house was sizable and the kitchen wasn't that small.

Straightening, Brandon looked curiously at Jake as he moved to the cutting board for a slice of lime. It was an interesting aphorism. He could see that applying at the house where he'd grown up, the house he still lived in. It sounded loving. He twisted the top off the bottle and shoved the lime down the neck, watching Jake chase the pills with beer. Were it anyone else, Brandon knew he would have said something.

Jake glanced over his shoulder at the man as he realized what he'd said, and that Brandon was silently watching him. "Hmm?" he asked in what he hoped was an innocent tone as he flushed slowly.

The attraction Brandon had been trying really hard to bury reared its gorgeous head again, and all he could do was blink and look at Jake – at what must be the real man. Not puffed up, not coaching, not yelling, not joking. Just him with a tired sag to his shoulders, bobbing Adam's apple, mussed hair, and warmed skin. The science teacher had to close his eyes fully to break the tableau. "Ready?" he asked, voice rough, tipping his bottle toward the other room where he could hear Troy and Jonathan squabbling good-naturedly over *American Idol*.

Jake took the opportunity to think seriously about slamming his fingers in a drawer. That would distract him easily enough, right? Right. "Yep," he muttered as he grabbed the three markers and his beer and headed back out into the other room.

Brandon followed him, trying really hard not to look at Jake's ass in the white baseball pants. Really hard. *Oh, man*. Not the thought to have. He sat on the couch, pushing Troy over and away from the Doritos as Jake went to stand at the whiteboard.

"C'mon, Bartlett, be a pal," Troy whined, practically climbing on top of Brandon trying to reach the bag of chips while Jonathan convulsed with laughter, rolling off the couch onto the floor.

"Troy!" Jake shouted, fed up and tired and hot and dirty after a long day. "Get back on the fucking Ritalin or something!" he barked in annoyance as he uncapped a marker.

Troy flipped him the bird but moved back to his end of the couch. Brandon grabbed the bag of chips and tossed it against the other teacher's chest. "Now behave," he said quietly as Troy stifled a cackle and sat back, a look of childish glee on his face.

"God," Jake groaned, the tip of the marker just touching the whiteboard before he withdrew his hand again. "You get your cheese rush, I'm going to change," he muttered dejectedly as he put the marker down and headed up the stairs, stripping off his shirt as he went and using it to wipe at his chest.

Annoyed on Jake's behalf, Brandon reached and bapped Troy on the back of the head. "I thought you were his friend. Can't you tell how tired he is? Button it up, Troy."

"Fuck. If I button it up whenever he's tired I'd be perpetually buttoned," Troy muttered, glaring at the biology teacher.

"Cut him some slack, man," Jonathan said from his spot on the floor. "Or never mind the kids, he'll be making *our* lives hell, too."

Troy and Jonathan continued to murmur, and Brandon just watched the stairs, remembering the bared chest and back he'd seen, muscles shifting. He pressed his lips together and took another long drink, despite the fact this was supposed to be his last beer for the night.

Jake didn't shower, but just putting on fresh clothes made him feel better as he thumped back down the stairs. He was wearing loose sweats and a worn fraternity T-shirt that fit him like a soft, thin, second skin. Comfort clothes. He brought a T-shirt for each of the others and tossed them in the general direction of the couch as he grabbed up his beer again.

"Okay," he huffed, picking up the marker. "Have we settled down?" he asked them in a tired voice as Troy stripped off his Under Armour and slid comfortably into Jake's T-shirt. Jonathan took the shirt, but merely folded it back up and laid it aside. Apparently the slighter man was either comfortable in his Under Armour or he knew he'd look like a five year old in his dad's clothes if he wore Jake's shirt.

Brandon held up the shirt Jake had thrown at him. 'Co-ed Naked Wrestling: The Mat Is Where It's At'. *Quaint.* He half-smiled and pulled off the jersey as Troy murmured an apology to Jake. Next went the Under Armour, and Brandon was surprised at the cool air that hit his skin. He hadn't realized he'd been so warm in the uniform. Just cooling off, he sat there holding the T-shirt, listening with half an ear as Troy promised to sit back and try to act at least half his age.

Jake turned around to say something and stopped short, his eyes catching Brandon's bare chest. He blinked and looked away quickly, staring at the whiteboard for a minute as he tried not to flush. God, this was just getting worse and worse. Without a word he began to write the last names of boys who had tried out for baseball. All sixty of them, from memory. In alphabetical order. By grade.

The science teacher took a moment to yawn and stretch the kinks out of his back before he pulled on the T-shirt, surprised to find it actually fit well over his frame. It had that well-worn feel of a favorite. He smoothed his hand over the lurid words and stifled a chuckle.

"We've got twenty-two freshmen," Jonathan said to Jake as he settled on the floor with his back against the couch. "At least five need to go."

"Fifteen seniors," Jake replied with a nod. "God, the juniors are going to be murdered," he murmured with a wince as he began the next line of names. He stood for a moment, tallying the count.

They could take twenty on varsity, no more. And that was really pushing the limit. "Somebody get the book, we're going to have to look at their birth dates and not their grade levels. And the stats from last year. Christ," he murmured to himself as he rubbed his neck.

"This is going to slaughter my team. And yours next year," Troy said, his voice finally sobering. "Juniors will be ticked if they're left out this year, and some might bail. Maybe even transfer to Berkmar to get playing time to prep for college."

Brandon shifted and nabbed Jake's bag, dragging it over to his feet and fishing out the book the other coach asked for. He opened it up to the bio pages and glanced up to the head coach. "Want me to just read them off?"

"Hold on, hold on," Jake murmured as he shook his head. He rubbed the back of his neck and frowned at the names on the board. "God, this is gonna be okay. We do it purely by skill first run. Narrow it down to twenty each. Then we go from there, okay? I don't care what grade they are, they deserve varsity if they get it first run. Then we tinker," he said, turning to look at the other three for confirmation.

The science teacher shrugged, glancing to Troy and Jonathan as they both nodded. Brandon sat back, putting his feet up on the coffee table and crossing them at the ankles. It was going to be a long night.

Jake nodded and turned back to the whiteboard, going down the list of names and checking the kids who were definite varsity material. He crossed out the definite freshman cuts, a few kids who just weren't meant to be playing for one reason or another, and then he stepped back.

He had fourteen varsity marked, five of whom were juniors. He sighed and glanced back for guidance. Troy shrugged and nodded. "Cutting seniors?" he asked dubiously.

"Some of them got outplayed," Jake murmured with a slight frown. "And that little Garner bastard needs to be stuck in a tree until he ripens somewhere," he added as he crossed out the kid's name with a vengeance.

"You might consider cutting Garrett," Brandon suggested quietly, naming a senior who'd been on varsity last year. Not a stellar player, not a star, but usually solid.

"Cutting?" Jake asked seriously, not even blinking at the fact that he was asking advice from the science teacher.

"Yes. He's at practice everyday, and he plays, but his heart's not in it. He daydreams when you're looking the other way. I also heard..." Brandon stopped talking, not sure if they'd want to know information that didn't have to do with baseball.

"Go on," Jake invited with a nod.

"I heard he asked Rachel Richards to marry him over Christmas break. Rumor is she's pregnant and he's over the moon about it."

Jake stared at the man for a moment and then groaned, rolling his eyes as he cracked his neck and went back to the whiteboard. "Good luck with that one, kiddo," he murmured, crossing off the name.

Brandon shrugged. "Clark might be a problem, too. Not with a girl. With grades. Marty told me in the lounge today he's looking to drop out and join the Army."

"He does like to kill things," Troy muttered with a little snicker.

"Yeah, we had to warn him last year not to hold his bat like a gun in batting practice," Jake muttered as he crossed the name off the list.

Jonathan had been quiet to this point, and he piped up with a question totally off-topic. "Who gets locker room duty this year? Are we splitting it up?"

"Just like last year," Jake answered with a nod. "Troy, who do you want?" he asked suddenly as he examined the lists. Troy shuffled over to the board, and for about five minutes the two men stood side by side, shoulders touching comfortably as they played a morbid sort of tic-tac-toe with the names.

Jonathan craned his neck and grinned at Brandon. "Want another beer?" he offered quietly.

Brandon shook his head. "Two's my limit when driving. And really, I should eat something since I skipped dinner," he added. "Anything to eat besides Troy's Doritos?"

"Hey Coach, how about some pizza?" Jonathan asked with a pat to Brandon's knee.

Jake turned around to look at them and blinked stupidly at the two of them as he stared. He nodded as he forced himself to get over the fact that he was actually *jealous* of Jonathan. God! Jonathan was as straight as they came, he knew that for a fact, and so was Brandon as far as he knew. What the hell was wrong with him? "Money's in the drawer," he muttered distractedly with a wave of his hand.

Jonathan clambered to his feet and took a moment to lean over Brandon and whisper, "He lets you stay the night if you drink too much. It's gonna be a long one," he murmured in the other teacher's ear before standing up and adding, "Any toppings requests?"

"*Meat*!" was the demand from Troy, who then went right back to the whiteboard. Brandon shook his head. He'd eat about anything and pick off what he didn't want. When Jonathan lurched, about to lose his balance, Brandon reached out and shoved his ass up. "If you're calling Morelli's, just tell them to get it here fast if they want to see Parkview go to State," he said. "The owner's an alum."

"Yeah yeah yeah," Jonathan huffed with wave of his hand as he went to the kitchen for the phone. "No free grabs," he added with a smirk. Brandon waved him off with a roll of his eyes.

Jake growled a little and leaned back to watch Jonathan with a frown. "Put green peppers on that," he added, trying to tell himself that Brandon grabbing Jonathan's ass had nothing to do with him. "And mushrooms!" he added as Troy tried not to laugh beside him. "Ooh! And onions!" he added as Troy began to shake uncontrollably. "Shut up."

"What put that look on your face?" Troy asked between insane giggles, chancing a swipe from the head coach.

"What look?" Jake asked defensively.

"That somebody-kicked-my-puppy-and-I'm-pissed-off-about-it look," Troy tried to describe. "Christ. I don't think I've seen that on you before. C'mon, what's the problem?"

Brandon listened from the couch, looking from man to man before settling on Jake, trying to see what Troy was describing. Jake looked fine to him.

"Shut up," Jake grumbled as he crossed another name off the list. Troy just fell over onto the couch, laughing.

"How many Coronas have you had, man?" Brandon asked, nearly agog.

"Just the one," Troy snickered as he pointed at Jake. "But I know that look. I remember that look now," he crooned as Jake turned around to glare at him. "You've found a girl," Troy accused in a sing-song voice. "Oh oh! Did she turn you down? Is that why you've been spitting nails all day?" he asked with glee.

Brandon's brows shot up. Christ. It was like they were back in high school, and once again, he was relegated to the silent watcher. Jake's face darkened like a thundercloud, and Brandon started to wonder if he might ought to go join Jonathan in the kitchen, so there'd be no witnesses.

"Your mom always turns me down," Jake finally answered with a flicker of amusement in his eyes as he turned back to the whiteboard. He easily caught the empty beer bottle that was tossed at him and snickered when Jonathan came back into the room with his arms spread wide, asking what the hell he'd missed. As Troy collapsed back on the couch, Brandon wondered what Jake hadn't said. There'd been a little too long of a pause before his snappy comeback, not that Troy noticed. Apparently the blond was quite the lightweight; a few beers and he was gone. Brandon scooted to make room for Jonathan on the couch between himself and Troy, not even noticing when Jonathan put a hand on his shoulder to balance himself as he threaded between the couch and coffee table.

After seeing Jonathan touch Brandon again, Jake's shoulders tensed further, and he began to wonder if he wasn't just imagining it all. "All right," he practically growled, sighing and rolling his neck to ease the tension. "We have thirteen cuts to make," he announced as he counted. "Who has the book?" he asked, flopping down on the coffee table. Brandon lifted the binder and waved it in the air. "Look through there and see if any of those kids were born after September," Jake ordered, pointing at the names he had circled.

Brandon started looking through the pages. "Ellis. Walker." Several more pages. "That Stithton kid. That's it."

"JV, all three of 'em," Jake declared immediately, leaning back to snag his beer. "The rest... shit, this is the part that just sucks," he groaned as he curled back into a sitting position and pinched the bridge of his nose.

Troy sighed, once again muted by the tough choices they had to make. Ten more kids had to go. "I nominate Miller and Rodriguez to go," he said quietly.

"Reasons?" Jake requested hopefully. Reasons meant easy decisions.

"They're single position players, with only one strong point. All the others have multiple skills," Troy answered. "Increases varsity flexibility."

Jake mused over that point for a moment before nodding regretfully. "We'll have to make sure they know to come back next year and try again," he noted as he got up slowly and headed back to the whiteboard to cross them off. "Any problems with grades on any of these kids?" he asked.

Brandon checked the names still up there. Eight more had to go. "Gregory was just referred to tutoring because he's dropped below a C average in Chemistry," he offered.

"Actually, cut Manero and Slodamesh. If I catch those sons of bitches smoking in the bathroom again I'm gonna whip their asses," Troy said. "They know well enough it's against team rules."

"Ooh," Jake responded excitedly. "Fulk and Gilliam were busted for drinking over the winter," he told them, knowing he'd meant to write that down. He crossed off the five names they'd mentioned and then cocked his head at the last two. "What do you think, Troy, can you take a crew of nineteen?" he asked.

"What the hell. If they get tired of riding the bench, they can be the JV cheerleaders," the blond-haired coach drawled, earning a chorus of groans.

"Oh Jesus," Jake murmured as he remembered the other cheerleaders they'd have to deal with. Sometimes he thought his life would be so much simpler if he'd just married that woman and made her miserable. "Okay," he said after a moment of staring. "We have our teams," he announced in a slightly surprised voice. It had happened so quickly. As if in celebration, the doorbell rang.

"Ooh, I got it," Jonathan cried excitedly, practically climbing over Brandon to get off the couch.

Brandon grunted and gasped as he was for all intents and purposes kneed. "Goddamn, Jonathan, be careful!" he hissed, smacking the back of the younger man's thigh as Jonathan trotted to the hall that led to the front door. He rolled his eyes and shifted, glaring at Troy, who was snickering. "Watch it, limey boy," Brandon growled.

"What?" Troy asked in confusion, and the look on his face was enough to have Jake smirking as he walked out of the room back toward the kitchen for plates.

Sighing, Brandon leaned his head back onto the edge of the couch, pretty much sprawling out. He was tired enough to not care much for propriety at this point. And since it was *certain* that Troy wouldn't even know propriety if it walked up and bit him on the ass, why should Brandon care? If it pissed Jake off, he wouldn't hesitate to say something. "Blech," he finally muttered, looking at the ceiling, thinking about the next day.

"We'll post the teams on the main boards," Jake responded to Brandon's expression of distaste, taking it as a declaration of his thoughts on the cuts. "They'll announce that they're up in the morning report and we don't have to watch the kids be crushed. Coward's way out," he admitted as Jonathan came back in with two large pizzas. Jake laid out a stack of plates and handed everyone a fresh beer.

Brandon eyed the beer, really tempted. But if he stayed here tonight – not that it was really that much longer, it was pushing 9 p.m. now – he'd have to get up that much earlier to drive home, change clothes, and drive back into town for tutoring before school. He sighed and set the bottle on the coffee table and pulled a few pieces of pizza onto his plate, sitting back and munching, listening to Troy and Jonathan chatter about plans for their teams.

Jake flopped onto the ground in front of the coffee table, grabbing a piece of pizza out of the box and eating without bothering with the plates. "You done drinking, man?" he asked Brandon with a glance at the untouched beer. "I've got four bedrooms and couches to spare," he joked, half serious. Sometimes Troy slept on the floor just to feel like he was roughing it.

"I really need to drive home tonight," Brandon said through a mouthful of sausage and pepperoni. "I'd have to get up a hell of a lot earlier if I stayed here, had to go home, and then turn around and come back into town."

"Man, there's no early that's early enough to keep me from crashing here instead of home," Troy declared with a sort of childish glee. "How long's your drive?" he asked with a frown.

"It's a little under 40 minutes to Mountain Park. Longer if it's after dark, lots of deer," Brandon answered, leaning forward to snag a piece of supreme. "If I stayed, I'd have to leave here about 3 a.m. to make school on time."

"What?" Jonathan asked in horror.

"What time do you get to school every morning?" Jake asked, telling himself even as he questioned it that he didn't want to know, it was none of his business, and stop staring at Brandon's throat!

"Little before six," the science teacher murmured. His eyes sliding from side to side, he saw the other three men looking at him with varying degrees of horror. He was *not* going to say it, he wasn't... "What?" he blurted.

"Why?" Troy demanded in a slightly higher voice than usual. He sounded outraged for humanity.

Brandon swallowed his pizza. "I tutor," he said shortly, shifting to pull a leg up under himself.

"On purpose?" Troy asked in the same disbelieving tone.

"Yes, on purpose," Brandon said defensively, withdrawing a little at what he perceived to be an attack.

Jonathan was frowning. "Didn't I read in the district memo that they hired somebody to do that full time?" Brandon shrugged awkwardly. He wasn't about to tell them it was an unpaid position.

Jake watched the man closely and saw him begin to pull back into his shell a little. There was no reason for him to, and Jake wondered what he must think of all of them to be embarrassed over the fact that he helped kids study in the mornings. For some reason it irked him a little, but it worried him more that Brandon was uncomfortable. "Not much different than the weekends we were taking with the team last fall," he pointed out to Troy softly.

"Well, yeah, but 6 a.m.?" Troy said. "That's torture! At least we worked after high noon."

Jonathan looked between Brandon and Troy, seeing the discomfort there. "Shut up, Troy. Brandon, are you still going to do this tutoring now that you're coaching? That's going to make for twelve, fourteen hour days, just on practice days. For games – away games, fuck – we don't get home until 1 a.m. sometimes."

Brandon looked up again to see them waiting for his answer. "The kids need me. For the tutoring, for the coaching, doesn't matter. I'll be there," he said quietly. But his voice was firm.

Jake watched the man for a moment longer. He was still wavering between trying to decide whether he liked the guy. He liked him when they were alone, but the awkward way he clammed up when someone else was around – or hell, he'd even done it to Jake – Jake didn't know how to take that. He was used to people being at ease with him when he wanted them to be. "If you start burning out, let us know. You can skip the away games," Jake offered quietly as he opened a third beer and gave it a long pull. The pills and beer were hitting him now, just not quickly enough.

Although the thought of shirking his commitment like that really bothered him, Brandon was already concerned enough about it that he wasn't going to argue. At least not right now. "I'll keep it in mind," he said. "Thanks."

Troy and Jonathan looked at each other significantly. Then the freshman coach piped up. "I can help grade papers," he offered. Brandon glanced to him, a brow raised. Troy grumbled a little under his breath and wrinkled his nose. "I'll help, too," he muttered. Then he brightened. "I can show you the best way to sleep on a school bus seat."

Brandon was so surprised that he didn't know what to say. He hardly knew these guys, but here they were, extending offers of assistance. It was damn humbling, is what it was. Was this what that camaraderie among team members was like? How the team always said they would stick together? Brandon had never experienced it before.

"And the boys would probably do some work if you gave them a little extra credit or something," Jake added as he reached for another piece of pizza, oblivious to Brandon's shell-shock.

"Uh." Brandon was at a loss for something to say. "I appreciate it," he settled on.

Jonathan leaned over and butted shoulders with him. "You're part of the team now, Brandon. We look out for each other."

"Or we hang your underwear from the flag pole," Troy added with a grin.

Jake rolled his eyes, remembering the day years ago when his own boxers had been strung up in celebration of a win over their rival. "We don't do that anymore," he assured the man. "Any sort of hazing these days gets you kicked off the team," he added pointedly as Troy beamed at him.

"Does committing evil and unnatural acts upon my limes count as hazing?" Brandon asked mock-seriously, glaring at Troy. Jonathan snickered.

"Just toss 'em out," Jake said quickly, shaking his head as if to ward off the images. "You know, man, doing that often enough will get you a pretty seedy reputation," he added to Troy.

"I'm secure in my manhood, Curly," Troy chuckled in return, gulping down the last of his Corona with a grin.

Brandon had to laugh. "Curly?" He looked at Jake's close-cropped hair.

Jake blushed mightily and lowered his eyes, practically

waffling as he sat there. "If my hair gets any longer it starts curling," he explained. "You remember school. Curly was the best of the names," he shrugged with a glance up at Brandon as Troy and Jonathan laughed.

The science teacher tilted his head, a mischievous glint lighting his eyes, and he warbled lightly, "Thunder, thunder, thunder, Thundercat!"

Jake's eyes shot up to stare at the man incredulously, surprised at the complete about-face in his demeanor, and Troy barked a laugh and pointed at him, giggling like a little boy. Brandon started laughing hard, almost falling over on the couch. "What?" he asked between snorts. "You don't remember that one?"

"I thought I threatened anyone who remembered that one into amnesia," Jake blurted as Troy held his side and wallowed on the couch, snorting and laughing uncontrollably.

Brandon tried to shrug, but he just laughed harder. "I guess you missed me, then. Lord. It was *all* over the school. Even on the walls in the bathrooms." Jonathan and Troy started up with fresh peals of laughter.

Jake shifted uncomfortably. "Why?" he practically whined. That had been the one call at the football games that he had never understood. The cheerleaders had even taken it up for a few games.

Eyes widening in shock, Brandon just stared at him. "You don't know why? Hell, I even know why. Remember the cartoon? 'Thundercats'? The leader was this young guy who bellowed and led the rest of the team in the fights for victory. It was a compliment, man, when you were on the football field. Even if it *is* funny as hell, now."

"Cartoon?" Jake echoed dubiously. He huffed and blushed even harder as he finished his beer.

"Geez. I'll get it from Netflix for you," Brandon said, shaking his head. "Just believe me, it was a compliment." He smirked again before nudging Jake's knee with one foot, stage whispering "Speedball."

"Okay, enough reminiscing!" Jake cried as he waved his hands through the air and closed his eyes. "God," he groaned. "It was embarrassing enough back then; the years just add to it."

Jonathan and Troy were reduced to nearly crying snickers, and Brandon pressed his lips together, trying to put on a straight face and failing miserably. "Those are a hell of a lot better than anything I was ever called," the science teacher pointed out reasonably.

"You can only compete if you had a bleacher load of people shouting it," Jake challenged, reddening further at the memories of some of the games. It hadn't been all that bad until the other team started laughing. Of course, usually they had only laughed until they were being beaten. "Man, even opposing players called me that."

Troy snorted. "It just made you madder and then we beat the hell out of them." Brandon remembered that Troy'd been Jake's wide receiver. Jonathan, who'd been laughing the whole time, stood up, climbed over Brandon yet again, and sang 'Thundercats' on his way to the kitchen for more beer.

Jake growled dangerously and hunched his shoulders, still blushing heavily and glaring at them all. Brandon couldn't help but titter again, then he took pity on Jake. "Sorry, man," he murmured. But he was still smiling widely.

"Bastards," Jake responded sulkily. God, it was embarrassing, having those memories dredged up. And he wasn't quite sure why. He wondered if perhaps the fact that he'd been lusting over Brandon all fucking afternoon, that all the man remembered of him was these stupidass nicknames, and that he yelled had anything to do with it.

Jonathan came back with another three bottles and a Coke for Brandon, handing them around. "Now," the freshman coach said. "Any other juicy gossip we need to know about?" he asked.

"Gossip? I've got some on Parkview, but do you know the staff?" Troy asked the middle school teacher. Jonathan just beamed. "Fine," Troy said. He glanced around at the other guys. "I heard Renata caught Jason Beals and Tammy Parker in the art studio closet."

"Hell, I've run them out of the locker rooms before," Jake laughed with a shake of his head. "Ugh," he added as he realized what he'd said. "I think I need to go duct tape my mouth closed now," he groaned, standing up and grabbed his three empty beer bottles. "Pills have kicked in, boys."

"I need to get going," Brandon said regretfully. "You guys crashing here?" he asked Troy and Jonathan.

"I'll take a ride back to the school, if you're offering," Troy nodded as he stood with an uncharacteristically worried frown, watching Jake walk into the kitchen.

"Me too," Jonathan answered, beginning to gather up the pizza.

Brandon followed Troy's eyes. He figured those two were pretty good friends, despite the blond's constant ribbing. And if he looked worried.... Brandon shook his head and shoved the book back into Jake's duffle, gathering up empty bottles to take to the kitchen. Troy and Jonathan followed him, each carrying a pizza box and a few bottles. Jake was seated on his kitchen counter, legs swinging free and beer in his hand, and Troy chuckled as he placed the pizza on the counter.

"Man, how many nights did we do this after games?" the blond mused, suddenly serious again. He turned to Jonathan and Brandon and smiled. "After every Friday night game we'd come here. Nearly half the team. Everyone in school thought we all went out drinking and partying and shit. But we'd come to Campbell's house, his mom would make us fried chicken, and we'd hang out in the back yard all night with a bonfire. I don't even remember there being beer, man," he said to Jake fondly.

"Hell no," Jake huffed. "My dad would have skinned us all." He laughed with a shake of his head. "Doritos and Gatorade, man. Food of the gods."

Troy snorted and pointed at Jake, grinning widely. "You remember that night we were driving home from that tournament in Atlanta?" he asked with a laugh. Jake smiled and shook his head at the memory, glancing at Brandon and Jonathan apologetically for the reminiscing that was leaving them out. "We had driven there for this Saturday tournament," Troy went on, telling them the story, "and on the way back it was us and two other guys in Jake's car. We stopped at a gas station somewhere and got some snacks to hold us over, and when we got back in the car Jake just drank his drink from the bag as he drove."

"We had Doritos and Dr. Pepper," Jake interjected.

"So this cop sees him driving and drinking from this brown paper bag, right? And he pulls us over," Troy went on, laughing as he spoke. "And he must have had something against sports, man, 'cause he was all over us. We were all still in uniform and everything, and he makes Jake get out of the car to walk a line, right? Like he's drunk! And he gets all up in Jake's face and says, 'Let me smell your breath, boy.' So by this time the rest of us are just dying in the car, because Jake was like a foot taller than this cop anyway, and the guy's all puffed up, and Jake's been eating Doritos for like the entire day. And Jake goes, 'I really don't think you want me to do that.'" Troy was laughing so hard now he could barely keep up the story, pointing at Jake, who was grinning in amusement. "And the cop gets even more puffy," Troy went on, snickering, "and Jake just shrugs and gives him a big ol' whiff of Dorito breath," Troy cackled. "God, it was funny," he chuckled fondly.

Brandon's eyes were wide. "So is that where the rumor that you got arrested came from?" he asked Jake.

"Maybe," Jake drawled with a small smile. "No matter what I said, no one believed it had never happened."

Brandon just shook his head, looked at the clock, and winced. 9:15. "I gotta go. C'mon, guys. Bus is leaving." He headed back to the living room for his pack.

Jake was silent, pondering the sinking feeling in his chest. He could not be doing this. He could not be lusting after this guy, not Brandon Bartlett, not right now, not ever. He kept admiring the man, then reminding himself who Brandon was, and then either beating himself up for doing it or beating himself up for admiring Brandon in the first place. It was frustrating, to say the least.

Troy clapped Jake on the shoulder before following Brandon as Jonathan called out a pit stop on the way. Brandon leaned over to dig in his pack for his keys and slung his jersey over his arm. "Hey, Jake, you want me to wash this T-shirt and bring it back?" he called out as he stuffed the Under Armour in the back pack.

"Nah, just whatever works," Jake murmured with a slight shiver.

Brandon nodded slowly, looking over to the man standing in the door. "See you tomorrow," he said.

"Have a good night," Jake offered, watching Brandon oddly. He started violently when Troy cleared his throat, ducked his head, and flushed slightly. "I'm going to bed," he added in an embarrassed tone.

Troy looked at him sideways and nodded. "Night," he said, following the other two men out to the car, leaving the head coach standing in the doorway to see them off.

"How many of those pills is he taking now?" Jonathan asked in a murmur as he walked with Troy.

"They're just Tylenol Arthritis," Troy answered with a shrug. "Whatever's making him weird, it ain't chemical."

"Tylenol Arthritis out of a prescription bottle?" Brandon asked quietly as they climbed into the car.

Troy was silent for a moment, pondering. "I don't ask about those bottles," he finally answered.

They all fell silent until the stoplight, when Brandon remembered something odd Jonathan had asked about. "What was that about locker room duty, Jonathan?"

"Ah," Jonathan murmured in response, obviously glad to change the subject. "Well, we usually make the rounds before games, sort of to keep things in line when the boys are all worked up."

"Meaning?" Brandon prodded, wanting to know what to expect.

"Meaning the guys get a little riled up, both before a game and after a win, understandably. Just got to make sure they don't get out of hand with the jokes, pranks, slap and tickle," Troy said.

"Slap and tickle?" Brandon asked, astounded. *In the high school locker room?*

Troy simply shrugged and neither he nor Jonathan seemed to

find it at all unusual. “Usually all you have to do is be in the locker room,” Jonathan added. “Just your presence keeps them calmer.”

Brandon swallowed the questions that popped to mind as he pulled the Jetta into the parking lot and stopped at Jonathan’s car. “I’ll see you tomorrow, guys,” he murmured.

“Thanks for the lift,” Jonathan returned as he slid out of he back seat.

Troy sat there in the front for a moment, his hand on the door handle and his eyes watching Jonathan stroll to his car. “The prescriptions,” he finally said slowly, “are better than what he could be doing.”

He looked more serious than Brandon had ever seen him. “You know him pretty well, right?” the science teacher asked.

“Yes,” Troy answered as he jerked his head a little and his jaw tightened.

Brandon nodded slowly. “Okay,” he said softly. He wouldn’t pursue it. Not as long as Troy knew what was going on.

Troy waited for a moment, seeming to want to say more, but finally he tugged the handle on the door and pushed it open slowly. “Thanks for the ride,” he said softly before exiting the car and walking to the golf cart parked in the grass.

Brandon thought about that look on Troy’s face a lot on the way home.

Chapter 5

IT was the second day of March and a Friday night, which meant the home team's supporters were out in full force. Jake liked to have the first game of the season be an away game. It took some of the pressure off, for the most part, but there were drawbacks. Like the loss of the home field advantage and the hourlong bus drive to Powder Springs.

The McEachern Indians weren't in Parkview's region, but they were fighting like they were. Jake supposed the embarrassing loss they'd suffered at Parkview's hands last year lit a fire under the other team, and as the 7th inning came around the Indians were ahead 4-3. The dark sky above rumbled threateningly, and Jake watched it from the dugout, wondering if they'd be able to get in the rest of the game.

He swiped his hand across the letters of his uniform, touched his nose, and then tugged at his ear. Swing away, the sign said. The kid nodded, giving his bat a few more practice swings before dropping the blue donut weight to the ground and heading up to the plate. Jake spit out a few sunflower seeds and clapped, calling out a stream of what would have been meaningless phrases that ended in the kid's name as he shouted encouragement – baseball language that everyone in the dugout clearly understood.

Brandon stood next to third base. It had been a nerve-wracking first game for him with lots of hits and running, scaring him to death in the meantime. But so far he'd done fine, apparently. Jake hadn't yelled at him anyway. Unlike the first base assistant, who'd gotten a chewing for waving a kid to second for an out. The science teacher listened to the words from the dugout, recalling what at least some of them meant and focused his attention on the batter.

It was a new pitcher on the mound, and he was throwing hard but slightly wild in the drizzling rain. Four pitches later, the cleanup hitter racked up three balls and a strike on his count. Jake called to him and touched his nose, then tugged his ear, then swiped his hand across his letters and touched his chin. Don't swing, the sign said to the kid.

One more pitch and the kid earned himself a walk. They were on their way to a rally. And then it rained. And rained. And continued to rain until the umpires called the game. Unfortunately, since they were past the 6th inning, the game was considered complete, and the Parkview Panthers were handed a frustrating loss in their first game of the season.

Brandon packed up equipment in the rain along with the college guys, knowing he was getting soaked, but better him than the kids who were gathering their heavy bags and running to the bus. They got the stuff together and stowed in the compartments and then got on board. Brandon pushed past Jake and one of the seniors, who were talking quietly, seeking the seat he'd claimed about halfway back. He flopped, wincing a little at the squish. *Note to self: Pack towels and a change of clothes, even when rain isn't in the forecast.*

After a brief discussion, Jake sent the kid to his seat and slid into the driver's seat. Being given an okay that everyone was on board and seated, Jake closed the door and shook most of the water off as he started the bus. He didn't say anything to the kids about the loss. They knew they'd been coming back, and they knew they'd played well. That was all that needed to be said, really. Thirty minutes later Jake pulled the cumbersome bus into a Wendy's parking lot and stood to turn around and peer at the tired, damp kids. "Seniors first," was all he said in a loud voice before nodding at Brandon to come on up.

Brandon picked up his pack and followed the head coach off the bus, walking into the restaurant where they quietly ordered and took a table toward the back of the room. They kept an eye on the kids filing in, and the two college assistants brought up the rear.

Jake hunched over his tray of fast food and poked a fry into a puddle of ketchup disconsolately. “You did well,” he murmured to Brandon finally. “Were you nervous?”

Tearing open the package of almonds to top his salad, Brandon muttered, “Nervous, he asks. Yeah. Scared to fucking death,” he said under his breath without even looking up from his meal.

Jake smiled and looked down at his food, fighting back the warmth and familiarity that had been building ever since the first day of practice. “Me too,” he admitted simply.

Brandon glanced up, surprise in his eyes that turned to gratitude for Jake putting him at ease. He went back to his salad, topping it with half the dressing before starting to mix it all up, still thinking about how they seemed to get along pretty well after about a month of almost-daily contact. Jake still caught him off guard a lot, though. “Guys did okay, huh?” he said between bites.

“They did really well,” Jake agreed as he looked the kids over. They were still mostly in uniform, still damp and dirty and tired, but they crowded around the tables that were lined together and sat in a big group, talking, joking, laughing. Jake smiled at them fondly and went back to his food.

Sitting back with his salad, Brandon watched the team with interest, seeing them interact and get along, reminiscing about good plays and ranting about missed opportunities. He shivered from being more than damp and set down the mostly empty bowl. Looking down at his pack, he remembered something. “Be back,” he murmured, heading for the bathroom with the bag.

Jake watched the man go with a look of open longing for a brief moment before lowering his head again and poking at his fries. He’d have to do something about this little infatuation he’d developed. Take a trip into the city, maybe, get it out of his system.

Once in the single bathroom, Brandon dropped the bag and pulled off his jersey, then the wet and clammy Under Armour. He turned up the spout on the hot air blower and stood over it with a groan, leaning against the wall for a long moment. When it shut off, he dug into the back pack and pulled out that T-shirt – 'Co-Ed Naked Wrestling'. He snorted, looking at it again. If it weren't for Jake, Brandon would never have worn this thing. He pulled it over his head, happy to be dry. Shrugging back into the damp jersey, he left it unbuttoned and headed back out to the table.

Jake glanced up when Brandon returned, taking a second look as he caught sight of his own T-shirt. A dry one at that. "Ah, you cheater," Jake grumbled with a small smile. "Just don't let the kids see you dry, we'll never get out of here."

Brandon cracked a grin. "Why do you think I put the jersey back on?" he asked, sitting back down and looking over the guys eating. "How long, you think?"

"Are you kidding?" Jake laughed softly. "They're not eating. They're inhaling. Five minutes," he wagered. "Eh, ten for the Frosties."

Brandon decided he'd pass on grading papers. He couldn't believe he was already so wiped out and figured on catching a nap on the bus. That way he'd be good for the drive home and a couple hours of work after. "Mmmm. Frosty," he murmured, considering.

"If you're gonna do it, do it now," Jake warned as he gathered his trash up. "No second trips through the line!"

Sighing, Brandon passed. He'd have to skip his run tonight, no point in taking in the empty calories. He packed his trash and headed out to the bus, not far behind Jake.

The head coach slid back into the driver's seat, telling himself he should at least look busy as he sat there waiting for his team to stagger back out. Whenever Brandon was near him, he found himself feeling guilty for not having work to do. That was definitely a new feeling for him. He watched Brandon mount the steps to the bus out of the corner of his eye and followed his progress discreetly in the large rearview mirror.

Rubbing his eyes, Brandon sat back down, dropping his pack in the seat next to him. He managed to keep his eyes open until Jake had the bus back on the road, but the relative quiet and regular motion soon had him drowsing, head leaning against the cool window. Jake found himself glancing into the rearview more often than he should have in the dark and rain, and finally he forced himself to keep his eyes forward and off Brandon. A half hour later he was pulling the lumbering bus into the school parking lot and honking the horn at the group of parents waiting there.

The boys filed off the bus, saying goodnight to Jake as he stood to the side and gave them each a pat on the head. They had a game the next afternoon, which was a Saturday, and he knew each one of them would be ready for it. Not many teenage boys would have given up their Saturdays. Only the dedicated ones. Once the guys were moving, Brandon sat up, bleary and blinking hard, trying to get his bearings. When the kids were off he stood up, making it a couple steps before turning around and snagging his bag. He rubbed at his eyes as he got to the front of the bus. "Equipment?" he asked quietly.

"I got it," Jake answered with a shake of his head. "They're all tired, need to get home," he declared as he watched the kids scatter to their various rides. He turned to look at Brandon and frowned. "You look wrecked," he told the man bluntly. "You sure you're okay to drive all that way home?"

"Yeah," Brandon answered automatically, though he stopped in place at the bottom of the steps, so out of it he could barely stay on his feet. "Maybe not," he corrected.

Jake smiled a little and then flushed with cold as he realized what he was going to do. He knew he shouldn't, but it was rather like watching a 300-pound man hurtling toward you and knowing that if you ditch the ball, he won't hit you. Jake had never been able to let go of that ball, even though he knew it was going to hurt. "Gimme your keys, you can crash at my place," the coach ordered with a demanding waggle of his fingers.

Brandon turned exhausted eyes to look at Jake and knew he was in serious trouble when he couldn't even string together a semi-serious disagreement. Instead of digging out the keys, he just held out the pack. Jake took it and began to go through the smaller pockets carefully until he found the keys. He used the remote to unlock Brandon's car, which wasn't far away, and pointed the man to it. "Go get comfy, I'll just be a minute," he ordered in his coach's voice, giving Brandon's shoulder a little push.

The science teacher didn't even think about objecting. He had no idea how far gone he was. He just wished he'd stayed asleep on the bus. He collapsed into the passenger's seat and closed the door, immediately leaning against it. It was almost as if his body knew he'd gotten to Friday night and was crashing regardless of what he wanted.

Jake watched Brandon get into the car and then turned back to the pile of equipment the kids had left by the side of the bus. He took his time lugging everything to the dugout, not wanting to irritate any of the various aches and pains he knew would show up when he got home. He locked the door when he was done, moved the bus into its parking space, and walked slowly to Brandon's car. His stomach flipped nervously, but he told himself to stay calm. He was being childish and idiotic, and this had to stop soon. He couldn't keep crushing on the man like he was without something giving. Probably his sanity.

He got into the car quietly. Brandon appeared to be asleep already, breathing silently, face looking hollow under dim lights that exaggerated the dark shadows under his eyes. He didn't move when the car door shut. Jake sat looking at him for a moment, taking in his features. He wished he had some way to relate to the man, but he could never think of anything that would do more than embarrass him. With a soft sigh Jake started the car and drove out of the parking lot, heading for his house and leaving his own truck behind.

When the car stopped and the engine shut off, the sudden lack of soothing movement made Brandon stir, who dragged his eyes open to look out the rain-glazed window. "Wha'?" he mumbled, trying to sit up.

"We're home," Jake told him as he dragged himself out of the car and reached back in to snag Brandon's bag for him. "You need any of this stuff?"

Brandon climbed out of the car into the light rain and looked up at Jake's house, just now wondering if this was such a great idea. "No," he answered, shutting the door and thinking about sagging against it.

"Inside then," Jake ordered as he came around the back of the car and gently took Brandon's elbow. "Shower, dry clothes, and bed," he coaxed with a small smile.

Unwilling to move for a minute, Brandon watched the moment freeze in a snapshot... Jake standing next to him in the broken moonlight, the rain falling around them both, a soft expression on Jake's face, an even softer look in his eyes. Then the moment broke, time started moving again, and Brandon let Jake guide him into the house.

"Go up the stairs, down the hall and to the door at the end, that's my room. You can use the shower in there; there's shampoo, towels," Jake instructed, setting the bag down by the door, wishing for his own sake that the other bathroom was ready for guests. "And, uh, I'll get you some clothes while you're in there."

Brandon was already moving when he realized he hadn't said anything. He turned, opening his mouth to speak, and was surprised by Jake right behind him. Jake stumbled against him, grabbing him by the arms to keep his balance. "Oh, sorry. I mean, thank you. Yeah. You know, for..." Brandon waved his hand a little.

"Don't mention it," Jake murmured in reply to the stuttered ramble. His fingers dug into Brandon's arms slowly as his body tensed at the unexpected contact.

Brandon lifted his eyes to look at Jake, trying to tell himself he didn't feel a tingle where they touched. They just stood there for several heartbeats when Brandon realized Jake must be waiting for him to move. He dropped his eyes quickly. "Ah. I'll hit the shower." He started to shuffle forward again.

Jake let him go as if he had been burnt, standing there holding his hands out with his fingers splayed as Brandon moved away from him. "I'll get your clothes."

Brandon nodded and followed the directions to the bathroom, where he pushed the door shut and sat down hard on the commode, bone weary. Five hours of sleep a night at best was not going to cut it, he could tell already. He dragged his hands over his face, then leaned and turned on the shower before stripping down, hanging the damp clothes on the empty towel bar, and leaving his shoes on the rug. He pushed aside the shower curtain and climbed in, groaning as the hot water hit cool, clammy skin.

In the hall, Jake stood unmoving. What in God's name was he doing? What was he expecting to come of this potential disaster? He could already see that he was going to have to either start distancing himself from Brandon, which was nearly impossible until the season was over, or just – no. He couldn't act on it. That was unthinkable. Wasn't it? He shook his head and forced himself to move. First he went into the guest bedroom, his old room, and made certain there were fresh sheets on the bed. Then he went into his own room and began to go through his closet slowly, looking for something suitable for the other man to wear. Jake listened to the water running as he laid out a pair of sweats and a T-shirt. Giving the man boxers was ...was it inappropriate? He would have given Troy or Jonathan some to sleep in. He sighed and fished out a pair of boxers and threw them onto the bed with the other clothes, then sat on the bench at the end of the bed and began to untie his shoes, moving sluggishly as the day caught up to him.

Staying in the shower a little longer than his usual one-minute wash down, Brandon leaned on one arm to brace himself before he realized he was in danger of falling asleep standing up, still thinking about Jake in the rain. Brandon bit his lip. Dear God, this had to stop or he was going to be horribly obsessed. He shut off the water and grabbed a towel, rubbing it harshly over his skin until he felt as dry as he could get, besides his hair being damp. Luckily, it was an extra-large bath towel – all the easier to wrap around Jake's extra-large frame, that evil little voice crowed – and Brandon banged his forehead a couple times against the wall before folding the towel around his hips and opening the door halfway, looking out into the bedroom.

Jake stood at the end of his bed, stripping off his soaked Under Armour with a little difficulty as his shoulder began to act up because of the cold and wet. He tossed the shirt to the ground in disgust when he finally got it over his head, and ran his hands through his short hair before realizing that the door had opened. "Hey," he said in surprise, as if he hadn't quite expected Brandon to come back out. "I, uh, didn't know what you liked to sleep in, so...." Jake blushed a little, gathered up the entire bundle from the bed and walked it over to Brandon, averting his eyes as he handed him the clothing.

Brandon took the clothes, murmuring a thanks under his breath. He saw how Jake was holding his arm and shoulder as still as possible. "I'll pull these on and grab the wet stuff and get out of your way," Brandon said, hoping a hot shower would help the other man before he was in more pain.

"No hurry," Jake told the man softly as he turned away. He hesitated there, unsure of what to do for a moment. Finally he headed out of the bedroom, still in his soaking wet gray away-game pants, and he dragged down the hall, thumped down the stairs, and trudged into the kitchen in search of his pills.

Brandon watched Jake walk away, and he was far too tired to make himself look away from the other man's ass in those tight pants. Instead he closed his eyes and turned around. Back in the bathroom, he dropped the towel and pulled on the boxers and T-shirt, considering the jogging pants. Now pretty warm, he left them folded on the sink. He gathered all the wet stuff and his shoes and headed down the hall toward the stairs, figuring he could get a bag or something to put it all in.

Jake stood at the counter with his eyes closed, pill bottle in one hand, edge of the granite counter top gripped in the other. He could deal with sharp pains and injuries. It was this throbbing and aching shit that wore him down. He heard the soft pad of feet behind him and opened his eyes, placing the bottle back in the cabinet where it belonged and closing the door carefully. "Find everything you need?" Jake asked in what he hoped was a normal voice.

"Yeah," Brandon answered softly, seeing the strain in Jake's body and hearing it echoed in his voice. "I was going to grab a bag for these. Should I pick any room to crash in? Don't want to be in your way. I'm sure you're at least as wiped as I am."

"Yeah, I made up the bed in my old room for you," Jake answered as he turned around slowly and grabbed the half-empty Gatorade bottle on the counter. One of the boys had left it on the bus, but Jake had never been picky. He popped the pills and washed them down with a gulp of the sharp lemon-flavored drink and then shivered all over. "I've got some grocery bags," he offered as he shivered again and his jaw tried to lock.

"Okay," Brandon said, wincing in sympathy. "Jake, is there anything I can do to help?" he asked, hurting just looking at him.

"Help?" Jake asked in confusion, momentarily distracted by the very thin material of Brandon's borrowed clothing. Jake wondered if he himself looked as good in his clothing as Brandon did.

Knowing exactly where the muscles ran, Brandon lifted his hand to slide his thumb along the knotted shoulder. "You're hurting and protecting your shoulder, but it's still seizing up," he said evenly.

Jake tensed involuntarily and quivered at the touch. "Yeah, it, uh, it aches sometimes," he mumbled, trying to decide where to let his eyes settle. "I have to remind myself not to favor it," he added as he desperately tried to think of something to say.

"You've got some liniment, right? Go get in the shower, and I'll rub it in so you can get some rest," Brandon offered before he could think better of it. He knew, intellectually, what had to have happened to Jake's shoulder for it to act like that, how the muscles and ligaments could be stretched and abused, torn and pinched. He knew how all the layers of muscle overlapped, what would hurt where the most, what would cause the worst of the knotting. It was simple anatomy.

Jake frowned worriedly at him but nodded obediently in the end. The truth was that he would do anything if it offered relief for the parts of him that hurt like they did. Brandon nodded and dropped his hand. "Go on, then," the science teacher urged. He could find the bag himself or drape the clothes over the bar in the meantime.

Jake licked his lips and set the Gatorade down, stepping to the side and around Brandon as he headed for the bedroom and the shower. "Bags are in the pantry," he called over his shoulder as he undid his belt. "Actually, just leave 'em on the counter, we'll throw them in the wash," he added. "Game tomorrow."

Nodding, Brandon laid the pile next to the sink, taking a long minute to peer out the window at the rain. He let his mind wander as he heard the water come on upstairs. Game tomorrow. Late afternoon home game, which meant he wouldn't have to be in too much of a hurry the next morning. He needed a good rest, and he was going to *have* to take one.

Jake stepped into the still steamy shower and groaned softly as the scalding water hit his skin. Just one night with Brandon down the hall. He could do that without spazzing out, right?

Right.

He showered quickly, letting the hot water warm his cold body and loosen tight muscles. When he'd gotten all the benefit the shower could offer, he turned off the water and hesitated briefly before getting out and patting himself down with a soft towel. He pressed his lips tightly together and then hissed a curse as he realized that he'd forgotten to grab any extra clothing before getting into the shower. Wrapping the oversize towel around his hips, he stepped out of the steamy room hesitantly.

Brandon was still mentally wandering when the water shut off. He took a few steps toward the stairs, but stopped and went back to the fridge to dig through it for something decent for Jake to drink. Beer. Beer. Coke. Beer. *Ah ha!* Gatorade. He snagged a couple of bottles and started down the hall.

Jake rummaged through one of his drawers for some more boxers and another T-shirt as he clutched at his towel. He felt his shoulders tensing back up as soon as he heard Brandon approaching. Fuck, he was going to have to shake this. It was getting ridiculous.

Stopping on the threshold, Brandon shook the bottles. "I brought Gatorade. It'll help with the muscle spasms," he said, though he knew full well how inane it sounded. But he was too busy trying to keep his eyes off the large amount of lightly furred, muscled skin that filled his vision.

"Urgh," Jake responded, accepting a bottle. "The horse liniment is in the drawer there," he murmured as he twisted off the top and pointed to the bedside table closest to them.

Brandon sat on the edge of the bed and pulled out the

drawer. As soon as he looked, he knew he was on thin ice. A small rounded bottle of lubricant rolled on top of a stack of magazines that just happened to be face down, so Brandon couldn't read the titles without deliberately looking. There was an accordion of unopened condoms, a large tube of Thermaflex, a television remote of some kind, a dog-eared James Patterson mystery. Nothing all that shocking. Brandon pulled out the Thermaflex, revealing a couple of photographs, one half over the other, and he chanced a glance. The first was Jake and another man with their arms around each other, looking like they were yelling at the camera. The surroundings looked like they were smack in the middle of a Mardi Gras parade. The other photo was black and white, artistic – and provocative. Brandon pushed the drawer shut after a few-seconds delay.

Jake stiffened as he remembered the various items he kept in that drawer, too late to stop Brandon from going into it. He watched the man's reaction carefully. There wasn't really anything in there that would scream 'Coach Likes Dick,' but you just never knew with the smart ones. They thought differently than most of Jake's acquaintances. They thought in terms of the bigger picture. He stood watching Brandon expectantly.

Shaking the bottle, the science teacher looked up and gestured for Jake to sit down in front of him. While he could read whatever he wanted into those photos, there was really nothing at all damning about them. Not even close. He could hope, but that would only lead to things that just really shouldn't happen. Like getting even more obsessed. He squeezed some liniment onto his fingers. "Right shoulder, correct?" he asked evenly.

"Yes," Jake answered softly as he sat down on the edge of the bed and looked up at Brandon expectantly. He was actually glad for the towel. Somehow it felt more like something to hide behind than clothing.

Brandon spread the liniment lightly along the line of Jake's shoulder. "Is the damage in the scalene, the trapezius or the deltoid?" he asked before starting to rub in the gel.

"It wasn't muscle so much as tendons and ligaments," the coach said. "I had bone spurs from overuse. By the time anyone realized I wasn't just complaining when I said I hurt, it was too late to do much more than clean it out and send me on my way," he rambled as Brandon's hands moved over his skin. "But mostly it hurts right along here," he added in answer to the question as he traced the line of the pain along the front of his shoulder with his finger.

Brandon rubbed lightly at first, slowly strengthening the grip of his fingers until the liniment was starting to soak in. He traced his finger along the same line. "This is the coracoacromial ligament. It holds together the coracoid process, the acromion –" He slid his finger along Jake's collarbone, "and the head of the humerus," he completed, rubbing in the rest of the liniment on the ball of Jake's shoulder. "I'm sure it was very painful."

"It was," Jake murmured as the names just flowed through his ears. He concentrated instead on the warm hands on him, the familiar scent of his own shampoo and soap on a man he was entirely unfamiliar with. He turned his head to the side and closed his eyes as the liniment began to make them water. His skin grew warm under Brandon's hands as he continued to press against the shoulder muscles, rubbing, then smoothing, rubbing, then smoothing, working to push the lactic acid out of the area so the muscles could calm and rest.

The motion was repetitive, and Brandon was caught by the heat radiating off the man next to him. Jake had closed his eyes so Brandon took the opportunity to study his features closely. The muscles of his jaw were jumping as he ground his teeth, but his face was otherwise calm and almost tranquil.

Jake had obviously done this many times over the years, let himself be doctored. He shivered violently as the cool air licked at the liniment on his skin. Brandon lifted one hand under the man's jaw, sliding his fingers along the back of his jawbone to rub at the juncture. "Relax," he urged, trying to stop the uncomfortable-looking grinding. "You relax one place, tense up another," he muttered, trying not to let the concern be too evident in his voice. "How do you get any sleep?"

Jake smiled crookedly and opened his eyes. "The pills and alcohol help," he answered in a rumbling murmur.

The odd moment of tension lightening, Brandon shook his head. "You ought to get yourself a masseuse and a hot tub," he suggested, rubbing at the last of the liniment and wishing it hadn't been absorbed so quickly.

"Hell, do you work weekends?" Jake asked with a small smile as he cut his gaze to meet Brandon's eyes. They were an odd mix of green and blue – almost a sea green – that Jake wasn't sure he'd ever noticed, and he forgot what else he was going to say as he looked at the man.

The corners of Brandon's eyes crinkled in amusement as he thought about what he would want to do with Jake's body spread out in front of him. *Fuck*. Figuratively, hell. Literally. *Down, boy*. He's never going to be interested. "I'm sure something can be arranged," Brandon answered without censoring his thoughts. He swallowed and scrambled. "After all, not too many guys with a degree in anatomy and physiology running around, are there?"

Jake raised an eyebrow and smirked. "What do you expect in return?" he teased. "I barbecue pretty well," he offered.

Brandon grinned, a bright light snapping in his eyes. "Barbecue. Sounds great," he answered. "Sleep space works, too," he said, thinking of tonight and the guest room Jake had mentioned, not anything else.

Jake's eyes widened slightly, and he cocked his head, wishing the man meant what it sounded like he'd meant. "Are you suggesting I'd whore myself out for some pain relief?" he asked jokingly. "You'd be right." He laughed softly.

Although Brandon felt a strike of panic, it faded as he realized Jake was kidding. He smiled, lips twitching as he sifted through any number of responses to such a loaded comment. "I don't know if anything I have can match that offer," he finally replied, letting his hands drop to his thighs, the liniment and his excuse to touch gone.

Jake looked up at him with unreadable dark eyes, smiling tightly. "Thanks," he whispered, unable to make his voice work.

The tension in his gut and chest was suddenly unavoidable and unbearable and Brandon had to move or he was going to do something really, really ill-advised. So he nodded and stood up. "Good night," he murmured, putting the liniment tube back into the drawer before turning to the door.

"Night," Jake practically croaked as he sat with his head down, refusing to watch Brandon walk away for fear of tackling him.

Brandon padded down the hall, finding the room with the bed turned down, and he disappeared inside, the light from Jake's room giving him enough illumination to see. He sat carefully on the edge of the bed, his racing heart holding off exhaustion for now. *Oh God*. It was too late. He was hooked and it could only end badly if Jake ever got even a hint. The teasing, it had been driven by something in Jake's voice, something visceral that Brandon could almost see, could almost identify, but not quite. A deepening friendship, maybe? Trust building between two co-workers? Two men figuring out how to get along instead of butting heads? Or, as his body wanted him to think as he lay back and squirmed, two men feeling each other out for something more? Brandon rolled over and pulled a pillow over his head.

Jake sat there in his towel for another moment and finally released a long, steady stream of breath. He got up and walked over to turn off the light, then let his towel drop to the floor and crawled into bed, nude and smelling of liniment.

Chapter 6

BRANDON'S eyes blinked open to sunshine and he immediately turned his face into the pillow to block the light. He was confused at first; he didn't have a window on the left side of his room, and the pillows didn't smell right. He sat up, looked around and remembered. Jake's house. In Jake's old room, there were trophies on neat shelves on the walls, with tons of ribbons and certificates all nicely framed, obviously the work of a devoted mom. Brandon shifted on the bed. The sheets tangled around his legs and it took him a moment to extricate himself. He sat on the edge of the bed and wondered what time it was. Late, for him. He was usually up and moving before sunrise. Feeling the heat of the sun, he would bet it was late morning. He'd slept hard, and he felt a little disconnected.

A loud clatter came from downstairs, followed by a muttered curse and another series of clatters. Frowning a little, Brandon stood up and walked to the door, sticking his head out into the hall. There was some more noise of pans shifting, and he chanced a trip down the hall and the stairs to stop at the door to the kitchen.

Jake looked up from where he knelt on the floor, gathering up the spilled pot lids and baking pans. He winced at the other man and smiled a little. "Sorry," he said. "I was trying to be quiet, and I opened the Cupboard of Doom by mistake."

Brandon couldn't help but smile a little. "I've got one of those, too." His mother had loved to cook and bake, and the cabinets were full of pots and pans and cookie sheets that he never used. "Morning," he added.

"Morning," Jake returned with another sheepish smile. "Did you sleep well?" he asked politely, unable to think of anything else to say as he averted his eyes.

"Out like a light," Brandon said, leaning against the door frame. "I was really wiped. Longer week than usual for me." He couldn't look away from Jake. Now, in the light of day, he seemed more approachable, but no less attractive. *Attractive. Right*. Brandon mentally whimpered. Jake's hair, even short, was rumpled, and he didn't have any tough guy image going on. Making him alluring, too. Brandon resisted the urge to sigh.

"I'll bet," Jake agreed as he finally got all the pieces stacked and stood up, bending back over to lift them up and place them on the counter. He rubbed his eyes and then stretched his hands over his head, glancing at the clock on the wall. It was just after 9 a.m. "You eat breakfast?" he asked Brandon as he looked over at the man. Something about this interaction felt so right somehow, and Jake found himself panicking a little as he thought about it. Why was he torturing himself like this?

"Usually something in the car. Granola bar, Hot Pocket, piece of fruit," Brandon answered. "Me and cooking don't get along, not that I have the time anyway." Seeing Jake's look to the clock, his eyes followed. It wasn't as late as he thought. Still, he'd slept nearly seven hours. A new four-week record.

"Well ... that's disgusting," Jake responded with a small laugh. "How about bacon and eggs?" he offered.

Brandon laughed at the expression on Jake's face. "Bacon and eggs is good," he agreed. "I'm going to clean up a little," he said. "Unless you need some help?

"Nah," Jake responded with a wave of his hand as he turned to the fridge and fished out the breakfast foods. "Go ahead, this should be ready in a few minutes."

Brandon nodded, though Jake wouldn't see, and backed away, watching the other man until he was a bit down the hall and had to turn to avoid falling over. He chastised himself for his behavior and got to the bathroom. Done after a few minutes, he pulled the T-shirt back on and remembered he needed to wash his uniform. Once back in the kitchen he stopped where the pile of clothes sat on the counter. "Mind if I throw these in the washer?" he asked.

"Yeah, it's just around the corner there," Jake answered as he poked at the eggs scrambling in the frying pan and nodded at a door just off the kitchen. "Would you ... would you mind grabbing mine, too? I sorta left it all in a pile at the end of my bed," he said with a jerk of his head.

"No problem," Brandon answered. He retrieved the clothes and started the laundry, using the supplies on the shelf above the washer. Then he stood there, thinking about how odd all this was. And how odd that it didn't *feel* odd. He closed his eyes. When did he get so comfortable around Jake? It seemed sudden. He thought about how much time they'd been spending together, usually talking after last block in the health classroom, baseball practice, team meetings, games, coaches' nights out. Brandon realized Jake had dangerously and silently become a part of his life. He opened his eyes and rolled them at the thoughts, knowing they would come to nothing. He'd had no indication whatsoever that Jake might be attracted to men. Just two little photographs upon which to pin his hopes.

Jake shook his head as he cooked, muttering to himself. He wouldn't do this again. He'd let Brandon go home on his own. Or hell, drive him home. Something. Anything else. He growled softly as he stood there and jabbed at the eggs. And they had roughly two more hours left to deal with each other.

Finally sighing, Brandon peered out the window. It looked really nice outside. Maybe he'd borrow some shorts, go for a run after breakfast. As soon as he thought of the idea, he discarded it. He was sure Jake wouldn't be running, not with that knee, certainly not the distance Brandon usually ran. And it would be rude to literally run out of the house. He stepped back into the kitchen, quietly moving to pull plates out of the cabinet.

Jake glanced over at him as Brandon came back into the kitchen. "Thanks for ... uh, last night," he said haltingly as he waved his hand through the air nervously. "It helped."

"I was happy to help," Brandon answered. "I'm surprised it didn't heal better if they scoped it."

"Yeah, well, it might have if I hadn't kept playing after," Jake admitted as he scooped the eggs into a large bowl.

Brandon hitched himself onto a stool at the end of the center island. "What happened? If you don't mind my asking?"

Jake shrugged as he dished out two helpings of scrambled eggs and a load of bacon that he had cooked in the microwave – it made it floppy, just like he liked it. "I had a scholarship," he answered. "Full ride, football, wrestling, and baseball. When I started having trouble with my shoulder I bailed out of wrestling. Then it got worse, and the docs told me I had to pick one sport or the other. I would lose half the scholarship," he explained in clipped tones. "I couldn't afford to do that. My grades alone wouldn't have kept me at Clemson. So they did the surgery and I kept playing. Finally my arm got too bad to pitch and my knee got too bad to keep playing football. And that was it," he finished with a shrug. "I was just lucky to get through the four years."

The rigidity had returned to Jake's shoulders and neck, and he jerked his limbs. He was still in pain over it, after all these years. *He destroyed his knee and shoulder to keep his scholarship.* It was enough to make Brandon feel ill. "Nasty business," he murmured, thinking of the scholastic measures he'd had to meet to keep his scholarships and fellowships. It was nothing compared to what Jake had gone through. It put Brandon's struggles at Tech into sharp perspective.

"Well," Jake responded as he jabbed at the eggs on his plate. "We can't all be Major Leaguers or NFL quarterbacks," he joked lightly.

"You're a great coach, you know," Brandon said seriously, offsetting the injected humor.

Jake looked up at the man, dark eyes serious for once and slightly melancholy. He smiled a bit and looked away. "Those who can't do, teach," he recited with a little nod.

The rest of Brandon's good mood melted away. "Yeah, I guess," he murmured, thinking back to eleven years ago. Unaware of the change in his expression, he hunched his shoulders and frowned.

"You look like you have a story, too," Jake prodded as he could practically see the dark cloud forming over the other man's head.

Brandon glanced up, jaw set. "My undergrad degree is in biology. My first Master's was biology and human systems. The second's anatomy and physiology. I was getting ready to go to med school," he said. His voice was as flat as Jake's had been, a big change from his normal buoyant self.

"What happened?" Jake asked with a frown as Brandon morphed into someone Jake had never seen before.

Sighing, Brandon shifted. "My parents died," he said quietly.

Jake was silent for a moment, watching Brandon closely. He wanted to ask why Brandon had ended his schooling because of that, but he knew better. "I'm sorry," he offered finally.

Brandon nodded. "I had to come home to handle things, and I ran into Tom Berry. He came to the visitation. He talked me into trying a year teaching, just to get my head on straight. I never went back to school."

"But you enjoy it, right?" Jake asked softly.

"Oh yeah," Brandon answered, brightening a little and meeting Jake's eyes. "I found out that my rapport with patients translated really well into teaching students. I really do like it." He tilted his head, wistful. "Just a missed opportunity, you know?"

"Just a different road," Jake offered, something he had told himself many times before.

Brandon's smile grew. "You say that like a man who knows."

"Pfft," Jake responded with a small smile. "I enjoy what I do. I just hurt while doing it," he joked.

Chuckling, Brandon thought about the equipment he'd packed away in his closet. "I really can help with that, you know. If you're not already seeing someone for regular ultrasound and therapy."

"Therapy," Jake huffed with a small smile. "I haven't been seeing anyone, no," he laughed softly with a shake of his head. "They frown on alcohol therapy."

"Yeah, well, I understand where they're coming from,"

Brandon poked a little. Then he hesitantly added, "If you're not doing anything tomorrow, I could bring some stuff over. See if it makes a difference." The urge to help was undeniable.

Jake hesitated a moment as he looked up. "Stuff?" he echoed dubiously.

Brandon snorted at the uncertain look on Jake's face as he pushed away his empty plate. "Ultrasound machine, Biofreeze, heat wraps," he said, brows raised like Jake should know what he was talking about.

"Ah," Jake responded with distaste. "Ultrasound machine. With the clear gunk that freezes your balls off when they put it on you," he clarified with a nod. "Great," he laughed wryly.

Brandon's answer was a sharp bark of laughter. "Funny guy. You want to try a pain-free Sunday afternoon or not?"

"Why, you bringing weed with your ultrasound machine?" Jake asked teasingly. He had little to no faith in the abilities of therapy to ease pain. He never had. That was probably why it had never worked for him.

The tone of Jake's voice made Brandon think. "You don't think it'll work. It didn't work in the past, did it?"

"Nope," Jake answered with a smirk. "I'm what they call a 'difficult' patient."

Brandon rolled his eyes obviously. "That's *not* a news flash. Will you let me try?"

"If that'll make you happy, darlin'," Jake drawled without thinking.

"My heart's set on it, babe," Brandon retorted right back, inwardly amazed at how easy it was to talk to Jake. Brandon hadn't spoken about his parents in years, but when Jake asked, it had just come out.

Jake chuckled and glanced up at Brandon with a smirk before going back to finishing his breakfast. A comfortable silence was beginning to settle but Jake didn't want silence. He searched for something else to say, but came up empty.

Brandon fidgeted a little on the stool. He thought of several things he could be doing – grading papers, reading the doctoral guidelines – hmmm, hadn't mentioned that to Jake – planning for next week, but none of those things would involve his host. Again, rude. "Do you have plans? I could take you back to your truck at the school and get out of your hair," he offered hesitantly. He didn't want to leave, even though he knew he should.

Jake took the last bite of his eggs and placed his fork down, his chest twisting a little at the proposal. It became more and more apparent as they spent more time together that Brandon didn't enjoy it quite as much as Jake did. He shrugged as he chewed. "I mean, all I have to do is go over the stats from last night, decide on today's starting lineup," he answered finally. "I just have to be at the field about noon to get it ready, so I was going to do that as the boys warmed up. Actually I was just gonna sit and stare at the wall for a few hours this morning," he admitted with a flush.

Screwing up his courage, Brandon asked, "So you don't mind if I stick around? I thought if you had something going on I would go do some grading in my classroom, but frankly, I'm sick to death of seeing those four walls," he muttered. "Not to mention, you're a hell of a lot better company than James."

"James?" Jake asked curiously, keeping his mind as blank as possible so as not to have to deal with the novel emotions assaulting him this morning.

Brandon smiled, amusement shining in his eyes. "The anatomy skeleton. The kids named him James after Boney James, the jazz musician."

Jake stared at the man for a moment and then laughed softly. "I don't even know who Boney James is, but okay," he snickered as he leaned on his elbows and grinned. For some reason the fact that Brandon wanted to stick around, or didn't mind doing so, anyway, put Jake in an incredibly good mood.

The science teacher just shook his head. "Did my backpack make it inside?" he asked, standing from the stool and gathering his dishes.

"Yeah, I dumped it at the door," Jake answered sheepishly.

"You said you've got grading to do?"

"When don't I have grading to do?" Brandon asked drolly. "Not too bad, though. Only two blocks, no essays," he said, rinsing off the plate in the sink. "If I get it out of the way I won't have to deal with it tomorrow," he added.

"Right," Jake nodded seriously, privately wondering how godawful boring a biology essay had to be. "Because you have plans tomorrow," he reminded with a smirk.

Brandon laughed. "Right. I have hot plans tomorrow that are not to be missed," he teased. Inwardly, he knew he was in for trouble. Oh God, yes. The awkwardness between them seemed to have disappeared, leaving a comfortable camaraderie tinged with humor and warmth. And it was oh so seductive to think it could last.

Hot plans. God, did Jake wish. He was really going to have to plan a trip into the city soon, just to relieve some of the tension building inside him. Once again he found himself watching Brandon with nothing to say. And so he simply watched, uncaring of the silence now.

Seeing the teasing fall flat, Brandon's smile faded. He left Jake sitting there, regretting the words now. Obviously Jake didn't feel as at ease around him as he felt around Jake. He wondered if the allowance to stay was out of pity. Pity for the brainy teacher who had nothing better to do than grade papers on a Saturday morning. He jerked up the bag, intending to turn around and tell Jake he'd changed his mind, that he needed something back at the school.

Jake watched the light fade in Brandon's eyes before he turned, and he frowned, chewing on his lower lip as he pondered the situation. His knee bounced nervously, and he stared at the floor, worrying, wondering too many things and imagining too many things to even categorize. He wouldn't allow himself to hope that he was sensing what he thought he was sensing. No way was he going down that road.

Brandon walked back up the hall with a purpose, stopping in the doorway to look at Jake, and he froze. The look of indecision on the coach's face arrested him, the obvious worry there surprised him. What on Earth? "Jake? You okay?" Brandon asked, completely forgetting about what he'd planned to say.

Jake jerked his head up in response and blinked at the man. The desire to just come out and ask was almost overwhelming. But Jake knew on a basic level that he didn't have the balls to do it. "Yeah," he answered belatedly. "Sorry, just floating," he said with a smile and a slow flush.

The urge to go over and do something about that smile was painful. Brandon cleared his throat. "I'm going to sit in the living room, be comfortable." And he fled, afraid of what he might do to get himself in trouble. Big trouble. He flopped on the couch and stared at the fireplace, but all he saw was brown eyes. "God. I'm so, so fucked," he muttered.

Jake rolled his eyes to the ceiling and pressed his lips tightly together as he was left alone in the kitchen. "Get it together, sport," he murmured to himself. He thought he heard Brandon speaking in the living room, but it wasn't loud enough for him to be certain. He sat there for another moment and then stood abruptly. He might as well get the lineups together now. Then maybe he wouldn't feel quite so stupid as Brandon sat in the other room being a real teacher.

Snapping out of it when he heard Jake scoot his stool around, Brandon huffed and pulled his pack open, yanking out portfolios of papers and digging in the zipper pocket for his glasses. He found a pen at the bottom of the bag and sat back against the arm of the couch as he slid the metal-rimmed glasses on. Work. Work work work. Work is good for distraction, he told himself. Work, he repeated, every time he heard Jake moving.

After looking through the third place Jake thought he might find his scorebook, he stepped into the living room and glared around at the surroundings, trying to think back to last night. "Well, fuck a duck," he finally spat. "Is the scorebook in your bag, by any chance?"

Brandon's chin snapped up as a strangled laugh escaped him. "Fuck a duck?" he asked as he bent to dig in his pack, successfully finding the book and holding it up.

"Don't tell me you've never heard that one," Jake growled as he thumped over and snatched the scorebook. He flopped down onto the couch beside Brandon and flipped through the book grouchily.

Brandon sniggered, relaxing unconsciously as the easy banter seemed to be back. "You've got an awfully inventive vocabulary," he said. It was sort of a backhanded compliment.

"Shut up," Jake grumbled good-naturedly as he sank further into the couch and propped his feet on the coffee table. "My momma taught me how to cuss," he drawled with a grin.

Brandon hooted, slumping against the arm of the sofa. "That's one momma I'd like to meet," he said with a snort. "Sure she didn't do that just so she'd have a chance to go at that mouth with a bar of soap?"

"I learned to talk early," Jake blurted defensively, smirking as he tried not to laugh.

"And often," Brandon shot right back.

"Ooh," Jake cried as he pressed a hand to his heart. "Truth hurts," he laughed, eyes dancing.

Brandon licked the tip of his finger and hooked it in the air in front of him, making a fizzing sound. "Score one for the nerd."

"Even a blind squirrel finds a nut every now and then." Jake snickered.

The other teacher's jaw dropped, but he came back with a quick jab. "It's easy when the ground's littered with them."

"Shake that tree enough, and you get hit in the head," Jake practically giggled.

"So *that's* what happened to you!" Brandon exclaimed with exaggerated, huge eyes.

"Hey!" Jake barked. "Momma fumbled a lot," he huffed, barely keeping a straight face.

Brandon opened his mouth, but stopped and pressed his lips together. He rolled his eyes and sighed, shaking his head. "Goddammit," he muttered, unable to think of a good comeback. Jake chortled with gleeful relish as he settled back into his scorebook. On the coffee table, his toes twitched and bounced to a tune only he could hear.

Picking up his pen, Brandon again shook his head as he started back on the grading. The banter shocked the hell out of him. It came so easily with Jake. *Like they'd known each other for years*. But now he was relaxed, he could focus on his paperwork, and he could deny how happy he felt because Jake was sitting right next to him.

It was a full thirty minutes later before Jake got his stats tallied and the lineup solidified for that day's game. He tapped his pencil against the list of batting averages and fielding percentages that he'd figured up in his head, groaning loudly as he realized that it was almost time to start getting ready to head to the school. He tossed the scorebook to the coffee table and flopped sideways on the couch, jostling Brandon with his feet.

Shaken out of his concentration, Brandon pulled back as feet attached to long legs pushed onto his lap, nudging the papers. He lifted a brow and tipped his chin to look at Jake, glasses sliding down his nose. "Is this your way of telling me you want my attention?" he asked. Yep. Still feeling happy. *Shit*.

"No, but feel free to keep my feet warm," Jake ordered haughtily as he waggled his fingers at Brandon and then tucked his hands under his head, long body stretched out comfortably.

Brandon now had ankles on his multiple-choice tests, and he looked at them, bemused. Without thinking, he dropped his pen and pressed a finger to a whitened scar and slid it along the tendon.

Jake's leg jumped, and he shivered violently, but he didn't pull his feet away. "Careful there," he warned seriously. "It's tender. Prod too deep and I kick."

"Dare I even ask how many scars like this you have?" Brandon asked sadly. "Tender, still, after how much time?"

"Years. And it's just the two long ones like that," Jake answered with a tap to his shoulder. "My knee was arthroscopic."

Brandon turned serious eyes on him. "Like that makes it better. 'Yeah, I went under the knife, but they did it by camera instead of looking with their own eyes.' " He shuddered, obviously not liking the concept despite where he'd been headed in med school. "I'm sorry you still feel it after all this time," he said, unconsciously caressing the scar with one hand.

Skin prickled all over Jake's body as he watched Brandon's hand move with dark eyes. That was a decidedly tender gesture. Christ, could he be right about Brandon? Was it really more than just in his head and wishful thinking? He swallowed heavily and watched the man wordlessly.

Seeming to realize what he was doing, Brandon sat back and pulled his hand away with reluctance, fingers brushing along the skin before leaving it entirely. He glanced to the other man and murmured a weak apology. His touch had been beyond that of a doctor or therapist and well into something more intimate.

Jake pushed up onto his elbows and licked his lips as he watched Brandon intently. His stomach was churning after that gentle caress, and he could see that Brandon was embarrassed by the touch. Perhaps thinking he'd overstepped his boundaries? What if Jake was right? What if Brandon *was* attracted to him? The likelihood was slim, but Jake had reached the point where he just couldn't tolerate not finding out somehow.

"Can I ask you a question?" Jake blurted before his better senses could stop him.

Brandon glanced at him. "Of course," he answered, pulling off his glasses and setting them on the pile of papers he'd just slid to the couch's arm.

Now that Jake had embarked on this road, he didn't quite know how to proceed, and he certainly didn't know how to turn back. He sat up and tucked his feet under him, peering at Brandon intently as the man turned on the couch to face him. Jake wasn't a wordy person, and though he was quick with the insults, having a serious conversation about what he wanted to ask just wasn't in his makeup. Actions spoke louder than words to Jake. So instead of asking the question he'd intended to, he reached out quickly, tugged Brandon closer to him – and kissed him.

It was the last thing Brandon expected.

He froze for the first few seconds as his heart tried to tear out of his chest. Then the heat swamped him and he practically melted against Jake's strong chest and firm lips, a soft moan in his throat.

The best way to tell if the answer to Jake's unasked question was a resounding 'no' would have been a swing of some sort. He half-expected Brandon to push him away and hit him. What he didn't expect was the responsive sound. It sent a fire through him he hadn't quite foreseen, and he nipped at Brandon's lower lip experimentally as he crawled closer. Brandon shivered and opened his lips slightly, softening and molding to Jake's as his head spun. God, was this really happening?

Jake leaned closer and kissed him harder, finding himself enjoying it even more than he'd thought he would. He kept his hands carefully off Brandon's body, that last mental barrier still yet to be broken down. Finally he pulled back and pushed himself off the couch, standing quickly and breathing hard. "Ha!" he shouted as he pointed down at Brandon. "I knew it," he announced with relish.

Brandon's eyes were wide and surprised, and he flinched when Jake practically yelled. "Knew what?" he asked, raising a hand to touch his lips.

"You're gay, right?" Jake asked in a slightly amused voice. "Or bi, anyway. I knew it," he repeated as he took a step forward and bent over Brandon again, bracing his hands on the back of the couch and trapping the man below him. "Aren't you," he said softly as a smile pulled at his lips.

As Jake leaned close, Brandon first considered panic. Second, denial. Third, he thought flying off the fucking handle might fit well here. Instead he just nodded, studying the other man's face for warning signs. *Jake* had kissed *him.* Surely it wasn't a damn joke.

A happy flush spread through Jake's body as Brandon nodded slowly. "Can I kiss you again?" he asked impulsively as he hovered. If possible, Brandon's eyes got bigger. Unable to form words, he nodded again. Jake brushed his lips over Brandon's as soon as the tentative permission was given. He growled softly and finally let his hands move until they were resting on Brandon's shoulders, holding him down.

Clearing his throat, Brandon tilted his head up. "Why?" he asked softly before his mouth was taken again.

"Why what?" Jake asked a little breathlessly against Brandon's lips, telling himself that if he didn't get calm very fast the cup he never wore to games would have to make an appearance this afternoon just to preserve the innocence of the children.

The moan escaped before Brandon could stop it. "Why this? How did you know?" Brandon's voice was deepening to a rasp and his hands clenched on the couch cushions.

"Hope," Jake answered immediately. "Sheer hope," he murmured as he kissed Brandon again gently.

Jesus. Brandon leaned slightly into the kiss and raised his hands to touch Jake's chest and shoulder lightly. "Christ," he whispered. If he thought his head was spinning before... he had no concept. "Jake," he breathed. The other man hummed in response and slid one hand behind Brandon, pulling at him gently. He wallowed in the contact, kissing him languidly over and over. Already aching, Brandon leaned into Jake when he was pulled toward him. He didn't mind at all letting the other man take the lead. There was certainly no denying the attraction any more, and the slow, warm kisses soaked through him until he whimpered from the pleasure of it.

Only when Jake's thigh muscles began to complain about the odd position he had put himself in did he pull back reluctantly. He licked his lips as he met Brandon's eyes, which had turned stormy dark green. The coach's heart was pounding; his breath was coming in little panting gusts. It occurred to him that he needed to say something. Anything. "God," he whispered finally.

Brandon blinked and bit his bottom lip against a nervous laugh. "Not last time I checked," he tried, gripping his own thigh when he noticed his hand was shaking.

Jake reached down and grabbed the clutching hand, threading his fingers through Brandon's and bending again to brush his lips against Brandon's. "Wow, I wish I'd had the nerve to do this last night," he laughed softly, not pulling back yet for fear of looking into Brandon's eyes again. Remaining this close to him offered a bit of anonymity or something.

The soft words made Brandon's insides clench, and the sentiment spurred him to clasp Jake's face between both hands and kiss him with a hint of desperation, a tinge of hopefulness, and more than a little agreement. When he pulled back, he murmured, "Would have been more than kisses."

For the first time since walking in on Brandon stretching in the locker room weeks ago, lust hit Jake like a physical force. He practically whimpered against Brandon's mouth, his big hands sliding along Brandon's body and taking liberties he wouldn't have dreamed of an hour ago. "Christ, if you knew how little self-control I have you wouldn't say things like that," he growled.

Brandon arched up into Jake's touch, the wanton actions moving him without conscious thought. "Hell, Jake, you blew my self-control all to hell with the first kiss," he admitted hoarsely. "I never expected..." He touched Jake's lips in wonder. "Tell me this isn't just a momentary lapse of judgment."

"It is an extremely big lapse in judgment," Jake murmured regretfully. "I'm afraid as soon as we move it'll go away," he added with a nudge of his nose against Brandon's cheek and another gentle kiss.

Exhaling with a shuddering sigh, Brandon's fingers tightened around Jake's, his other hand clutching at one bicep. "No. Please, don't, not yet," he whispered against Jake's lips. It had been so long since he'd been touched at all, and the fact that it was Jake was almost too much to believe.

"I'm not going anywhere," Jake growled as his fingers dug into Brandon's hips and gave him a little yank sideways. He scooted and tugged and pulled until he had Brandon under him, lying flat on the couch. Logically he knew that they only had a little less than an hour and that wasn't nearly enough time to do what he wanted to do to Brandon. He could see already that they were both going to head to school for the game frustrated and probably very cranky.

Wiggling and scooting to help, Brandon moaned happily when Jake's weight settled on him, and he curled his arms around his neck, pressing his lips to the strong chin and sliding to his ear. "You're driving me crazy," he whispered. He pulled one knee up to slide Jake's body more firmly between his thighs.

"Short drive," Jake managed to groan as Brandon moved under him. "Stop moving," he growled, panting against the other man's neck while his body throbbed.

Brandon actually whined. "You've got to be joking!" he said as he dragged his hands down Jake's back, tracing the shifting muscles.

"I'm not that funny," Jake growled, nipping at Brandon's neck and sliding his hands under the man's shoulders.

Tilting his head back, Brandon choked off a soft groan as he felt Jake's teeth. "Fuuuuhhck…" he hissed, lifting the propped up leg and curling it around Jake's upper thighs. He just couldn't resist. Too many nights of heated dreams, too many mornings of cold showers.

Yet again Jake found himself surprised by Brandon's actions. He wasn't nearly as inhibited as Jake had imagined he would be, and for a moment it threw him off almost to the point that he forgot what he was doing. He scraped his teeth along Brandon's collarbone and then pushed up onto his elbows and looked down at the man. "I, fuck, we should get moving," he breathed.

"You just told me not to move," Brandon said in exasperation, opening his eyes to see melted dark chocolate ones staring down at him with heated intensity.

"I meant stop wiggling," Jake growled, his voice low and rumbling and intimate. "We don't have time for you to wiggle," he added with a predatory grin.

Brandon's eyes flashed and slowly a wicked smile took his face, and he deliberately wiggled. Jake pressed him down hard into the couch cushions and groaned as his body responded to the provocative movements. "You have no idea what you're getting into," he warned seriously.

That heated smile faded into a visage of longing. "Probably not," Brandon agreed. "Doesn't mean I don't want it."

"Tonight then," Jake purred as he brought one hand up to run it tentatively through Brandon's hair, brushing strands away from his face. "We can pick up right here. We just need to get through three hours of ballgame first." He practically whined before giving in and pressing his lips to Brandon's once more.

"Tonight," Brandon sighed into the kiss, aching and hoping it wouldn't all disappear like a popped soap bubble.

Jake pushed up and off him suddenly and stood, knowing if he lingered he would drive them both crazy. He pressed the back of his hand to his mouth and looked down at Brandon for a moment of indecision before nodding and turning abruptly to clomp down the hall. Sucking in a deep breath, Brandon covered his face with both hands, groaning and squirming. He was almost afraid to look down – although if he'd busted out of the boxers he was sure Jake would have had something to say (or do) about it. By force of will he kept his hands off himself and climbed off the couch, heading to the kitchen to get their uniforms out of the wash.

Chapter 7

BRANDON grinned as the kids pumped their fists in the air and cheered at closing out the final inning on a win. He jogged over to join the line as the two teams passed each other, slapping hands and congratulating each other. He had a few words with the other team's assistant coach and then headed back to the dugout to start packing up equipment. It had been a great game, in his opinion, with most all of the players staying invested and focused.

"They can do that," Jake told him after Brandon had started on the equipment. He was smiling slightly, patting kids on the back as they passed by him, telling them first what they had done right and then what they could do better next time.

Sitting down on the bench, Brandon watched the kids pass by, complimenting them on particular plays he remembered, taking high fives. It pleased him how much the team accepted him. With that thought, his eyes strayed to Jake. During the game, he'd been able to stay focused. But now there was nothing to keep him from thinking highly inappropriate thoughts about the head coach in a high school setting.

Jake glanced down at Brandon and met his eyes, looking at him for a much longer time than he probably should have. The curl of nervous anticipation he hadn't felt for a very long time had started as soon as the last inning began, and he had been damn lucky that his boys were well-trained and could play without a heavy hand from the dugout. He was nervous enough that he thought he might be ill, but the excitement overpowered that feeling. It was one that came when you were about to get something you never thought you could possibly get. Jake didn't get that feeling often, and he intended to enjoy it. Every time he looked at Brandon, it got stronger.

Catching the look in Jake's eyes, Brandon swallowed hard and got up to help with the equipment again. He couldn't sit still under that scrutiny, not if he was to have any hope of walking even somewhat normally. He chatted idly with a couple of the sophomores who were toting bats, and when they were done, he stood at the fence, leaning and looking out over the field as he listened to the cars depart.

Jake made one last survey of the dugout, making certain there was no trash or sunflower seeds or God knew what else on the ground as he closed up the equipment storage. He stepped out of the dugout and looked over the field, his eyes dark under the brim of his hat, his clipboard and scorebook under his arm. He half expected Brandon to have bolted. They'd both had a lot of time to think about what they had started in the heat of the moment, and Jake quite frankly wouldn't have blamed the man for running scared. He turned to look over the right side of the field, and his stomach jumped as he saw Brandon leaning against the fence. Taking a deep breath in an attempt to calm himself, he turned and began to walk slowly over to him.

The early afternoon had been tense. Not bad tense, just tense. As the kids started arriving it got easier, and time passed. Then the game ended, and now Brandon could feel that banked tension transforming into butterflies as he watched the sun sinking in the early evening sky. He wondered if Jake would invite him back over to finish what they started. He wondered if Jake would leave without even speaking to him. He squeezed his eyes shut and made his own wish, though it would make his life much more complex. God help him, he wanted Jake.

Jake's footsteps were silent as he came up to Brandon, and he looked around them carefully before leaning his elbows against the fence. Their arms barely brushed as he turned his head to watch the last few cars leave the lot.

The fence gave slightly and Brandon knew who it was. Every

nerve in his body jumped to attention and nearly screamed, thinking about Jake being this close. He drew in a shaky breath and opened his eyes, turning his chin to look at the other man, hoping his face was composed. He knew he couldn't do anything about the desire in his eyes.

Jake licked his lips and then turned his head to meet Brandon's eyes with a raised eyebrow and a slight smile. When he was nervous he immediately sank back into his comfort zone, and his comfort zone was smiling and joking. "I hear you have a hot date tonight," he drawled to the man with a glint to his black eyes.

Brandon blinked and chuckled, his nerves popping. "Yeah, well, I got lucky, I guess."

"Not yet you didn't," Jake snickered as he leaned into Brandon and nudged him a little. Lips pursing, Brandon's eyes flashed with heated amusement, and he stuck the tip of his tongue out in comment. "Don't tempt me," Jake growled as he leaned closer. He was all too aware that they were not anywhere near being in a private place, and he wanted to get to one. Now. "Care for a beer?" he asked in a low voice as he met Brandon's eyes with a little glint.

Brandon really didn't want to wait that long. "How about a shower first?" he suggested as he pushed himself away from the fence, walking backward toward the gym, eyes locked on the other man. He didn't know how he found it in himself to be so bold, but something about the heat Jake infused in him gave him unusual courage.

That anticipatory twist of nerves hit Jake again, and he found himself following Brandon as if the man had latched a hook through his nose. "Getting clean is begging for trouble," he warned in a low voice, his big shoulders rolling as he practically prowled forward.

Successfully getting Jake to follow, Brandon's breathing picked up as his arousal returned in full force. He swallowed and licked his lips. "Didn't say anything about getting clean," he taunted before turning and jogging across the parking lot to the doors leading inside.

Jake growled under his breath and looked left and right, assuring himself that no one was left in the back of the campus before starting off across the lot after Brandon. Was he actually considering doing something on the school grounds? Yes. Yes, he was. The fact that they could easily be caught seemed to only make it more arousing.

Brandon pushed through the double doors and made directly for the visitors' locker room, turning at the door to wait, just long enough to see if Jake would continue to follow. He had no idea how he thought they could do this – this, whatever it would be. More kisses? And more, he suspected and hoped. And right here at school. Dear God, he *was* a total slut. He swept into the locker room and checked around, making sure it was empty. Jake stalked in after him, trusting that Brandon had cleared the room ahead of him, and he grabbed Brandon as soon as he stepped through the door and kissed him hungrily.

The heat flared out of control and Brandon clutched at Jake. The only thing that would have made it more intense would have been Jake pushing him against the lockers. And he wasn't sure that still wouldn't happen.

Jake knew on a basic level that they couldn't fuck in here. But holy hell, that was what he wanted just then. He let his hands travel over Brandon's body shamelessly as he kissed him and it just wasn't enough. He yanked at Brandon's jersey, hearing a seam rip somewhere and not caring as he continued to pull at it and kiss the man messily. It still wasn't enough, and he pushed Brandon toward the nearest hard surface, slamming him brutally against the empty bulletin board.

Brandon thought he'd died and gone to heaven when his back hit the wall and his choked cry of approval was lost in Jake's voracious mouth. He could feel the coach's hands all over him, and Brandon wanted to do the same. His fingers dug into the waistband to drag Jake's jersey and Under Armour free so he could slide his hands up onto hot skin.

Jake growled in response, pushing Brandon harder against the wall and sliding his hands up the man's body to tangle in his hair. Brandon wailed softly and clutched at him, spreading his legs to a wider stance so Jake could push closer. And Jake did, insinuating himself between Brandon's spread legs and growling ferally as he reached down to hitch Brandon up off the ground. He pressed him against the wall hard, holding him up more with the force of his body than with any strength in his arms.

"Oh God, yes," Brandon hissed, head thrown back as he held onto Jake's shoulders and wrapped his long legs around him, and he moaned aloud as their groins rammed together. He spared a thankful prayer for neither of them wearing a cup today and squeezed his legs tighter.

"Wildcat," Jake teased breathlessly as he licked at Brandon's neck and nipped at the tender skin.

Brandon laughed desperately, moving to catch Jake's face between his hands and dropping his head to kiss him, unable to get enough of the taste of him. It was as if that first tentative kiss had unleashed all the longing and desire inside Brandon, and now it was boiling over uncontrollably. Jake groaned into the kiss, a plaintive sound that spoke of the desire to get Brandon naked and in bed with lube and condoms so he could do all kinds of dirty things to him.

Lips sliding apart, Brandon dove back in, sliding his tongue over teeth into Jake's mouth to tangle with his tongue. It was sloppy and hurried and hot and Brandon couldn't imagine it being any different. He was pinned against the wall with Jake grinding against him, and it was the best he'd felt in he couldn't remember when. A goddamn wet dream come true. He pulled back, panting. "We staying here or not?" he rasped.

"I dunno," Jake panted in answer, "I can't think. What are you thinking?" he asked breathlessly before diving back in for another kiss.

Brandon's words disappeared into Jake's mouth before they pulled apart again. "Jesus, can't think of anything but you," he swore, biting his lip and moaning as Jake rubbed against him again.

Jake moved back slightly and eased Brandon back to his feet. His hands began to tug at Brandon's belt, easily getting it loose and unfastening the pants underneath. "We'll go back to the house," he breathed as he pushed Brandon's pants down, then slid his hands under the man's briefs and began to push them down as well. "As soon as we take care of this," he murmured, wrapping long fingers around Brandon's erection.

Brandon choked on a gasp as a strong hand covered him, and his eyes rolled back into his head. "Jake, damn!" he hissed, jerking helplessly into his fist as he clung to the taller man's shoulders. Any remaining lucid thought dissipated.

"Keep your feet," Jake ordered in his coach's voice as he began to sink in front of Brandon. Brandon's eyes flew open, huge, and all he could do was whimper. Jake's knees hit the cheap locker room carpet, and he gripped each of Brandon's hips with his hands and looked up at the man. Without waiting for any sort of response he pulled slightly at Brandon's hips and opened his mouth wide, letting the motion essentially force Brandon to thrust into his mouth.

"Unnghhhh!" was Brandon's response as his head banged back against the cork board. This was so far above and beyond what he'd ever imagined that he was swiftly losing control – this was going to be embarrassingly short. But fuck all if he cared! He was gonna go off like a fucking rocket at this rate. "Jake…" he gasped, voice deep and needy.

Jake smiled around the man's cock and plunged his head deeper. His hope was that Brandon would come quickly, and he could drag him home and spend the rest of the night doing more unseemly things to him. He also gave a passing thought to wishing he had locked that door when he'd come in, but soon he was overpowered by the erotic joy of sliding his tongue around the head of the man's cock. He hummed long and loud and wrapped his arms around Brandon's hips.

"Jesus!" Brandon yelled before slapping one hand to his mouth, biting on the heel of his hand as he thrust forward. Almost ... almost ... The world spun around him, and the only thing holding him down was Jake. The orgasm threatened suddenly and he pawed at the other man's shoulders. "Jake – Jake!" he tried to warn.

The rasping calls only spurred Jake on, and he lifted up slightly, tilting his head and sucking as he wrapped one hand around the base of Brandon's cock.

Looking down at Jake was the wrong thing to do if Brandon wanted to stave off the explosion, and with a snap of his hips and a gasping mewl he came so hard he saw spots. It seemed to go on and on, and he had to remember how to breathe when it finally ended.

Jake swallowed as his fingers dug into Brandon's hips. He was breathing heavily through his nose, and his heart was racing as his body throbbed needily. One last lick and he pulled his head back, looking up at Brandon in fascination as the man tried to regain his breath.

The cold air on his hot skin got Brandon's attention, and he opened glazed eyes to peer down at Jake, speechless. He truly couldn't string together two words at this moment, much less two sentences.

Jake grinned up at him and kissed his bare hip sloppily, then licked his lips and settled down on his heels. "You're gonna have to help me up," he told the man with a laugh.

Brandon stared at him blankly for a few seconds and managed a weak laugh. He braced his ass against the wall and leaned over to slide an arm under each of Jake's to help him to his feet.

Jake took the opportunity as soon as he was on his feet to fall into Brandon's arms, pressing him against the wall again and kissing him roughly. He wanted more, but he knew waiting until they at least got to his house would be well worth the five minutes it would take to get there. He hoped it would, anyway, because it was very plausible that he wouldn't make it that far.

Totally pliant, Brandon relaxed completely against Jake, smiling against the mouth that practically ravaged his. Replete, he purred and rubbed against the coach sinuously.

Jake groaned wantonly and gripped Brandon tighter. "I can't fuck you here," he practically whined.

Brandon would have fallen over right then and there if it weren't for Jake holding him up. "Then take me somewhere you can," he urged, already reaching to pull up his briefs and pants. Jake continued to kiss him as he fumbled to help with his clothes, finally reaching down to yank his belt off so he wouldn't have to deal with it.

"Come on," he breathed as he grabbed Brandon's hand and tugged him toward the door. "Whichever car's closest, I don't care," he growled. "We'll steal one if we have to," he declared, pushing Brandon ahead of him through the door.

Brandon laughed in disbelief, but let Jake push him along before digging in his heels. "Wait, keys, I need car keys!" he exclaimed.

Jake growled in frustration and flopped his hands around. "Well!" he demanded impatiently. "We'll hotwire it," he exclaimed with eyes that sparkled mischievously.

Brandon laughed again, a richer, fuller sound. "Just hang on a sec." He loped back to the locker room, turned the corner and snagged his back pack, emerging with it while digging for the keys, which he held up with a triumphant, "Ah ha!" Jake watched the man light up and grinned at him, wanting him even more. "Come on!" Brandon said, grabbing Jake's arm and pulling him out to the parking lot and toward the Jetta, where he threw the bag in the back seat and climbed in.

It was the shortest mile on record. They hit that damn stoplight just right and got to Jake's house in 96 seconds, a new land-speed record, and Brandon barely had the car in park before Jake was out the door. Brandon grabbed the keys and his backpack and launched out of the vehicle, following the other man up the front steps.

It took Jake a bit of fumbling with the key before he remembered that they'd left the door unlocked, and he shoved it open and pulled Brandon into the house. Once again he was tugging at the man's clothing, tearing the jersey even further as he yanked at it and pushed Brandon toward the staircase. "Nice driving," he grunted as his hands wandered, slowing their progress but enjoyable all the same.

"Thanks," Brandon said breathlessly as he tried to unfasten the buttons on Jake's jersey. But he finally stopped and forced Jake's arms up so he could pull both the jersey and Under Armour over his head, knocking his cap to the floor as well. The sight of all those muscles made Brandon get aroused again. He had no problem figuring out what it was about Jake that was driving him wild – his forcible nature, his strength, his hard body, his passion. "I was motivated," he added, starting in on Jake's belt before his hands got smacked.

"I'll show you motivated," Jake growled, herding Brandon up the stairs and down the hall. "Faster," he snarled as he shoved Brandon into the bedroom and pushed him toward the bed.

Brandon's face flushed and his eyes glazed again as Jake took control. He stumbled back to the bed, kicked off his shoes and pulled his jersey and shirt over his head, tossing them to the floor. *Christ.* He wanted this so badly he could taste it, taste Jake on him and in him and around him. *We're totally nuts to be doing this*, some residual voice of reason told him. Brandon pretty much kicked it aside and ignored it.

Jake stood at the end of the bed and watched Brandon get rid of his shirts hungrily. He was waiting until he could really pounce on the man, just like he had wanted to do that day in the locker room. He pushed his own pants down and stepped out of them, sliding his briefs down next and kicking them away as he stalked closer.

Focusing on stripping off his pants, briefs and blue socks, Brandon straightened to see Jake walking toward him, face set and eyes flaming. He was stunned by the other man's body - he'd known it was muscled and firm and big all over, but he'd had no idea. "Christ," he breathed. "You're fucking gorgeous."

Jake barked a laugh, the tension in his shoulders easing a little as he got closer. "Quit talking about yourself," he scolded as he slid his hands over bare skin and shivered in anticipation.

Making note of how Jake played off his words, Brandon slid his arms around the other man, bringing their bodies into contact. All over. He moaned. "I believe you mentioned fucking?" he said weakly against Jake's ear.

Jake made a noise that he wasn't sure he'd ever made before. Something between a whimper and a moan that ended up just sounding pitiful. "Yes," he groaned softly, pressing his lips to Brandon's neck and sliding his hands experimentally down the man's back. "Does that interest you?" he asked cheekily, his voice gusting over Brandon's skin.

Brandon jabbed Jake in the ribs. “You said it first, Thundercat,” he prodded. “You gonna make good or not?”

“Oh Christ, not if you keep calling me that,” Jake groaned as he pressed himself hard into Brandon and toppled them both to the bed.

Laughing all the way down, Brandon wrapped his arms and legs around Jake and clung close. “Why not?” he mock-whined. “If you don’t like it, tell me something else I can call you to ‘crank you up’,” he teased, invoking one of the popular cheers.

“Are you trying to kill the hard-on?” Jake asked incredulously as he pinned Brandon’s elbows. “Is this some sort of long-term revenge for something I did to you in high school? ’Cause I have to say,” he murmured, kissing along Brandon’s jaw, “bravo for patience.”

Brandon snickered and shook his head, shifting under Jake to press up against the thick, hard length digging into his thigh. “You have *no* problem with this hard-on,” he said. “And my highly vaunted patience is quickly waning. I can’t imagine what state yours must be in.”

Jake pushed up and looked down at Brandon with a grin. “Are you saying I’m impatient?” he asked as he reached for the drawer in the side table. His fingers brushed the handle, and he growled and stretched harder.

Hard put not to laugh again, Brandon pressed his lips together and instead gave Jake an apologetic look.

“Shut up,” Jake huffed as he bent his head to kiss him again, a brief refill before pushing back up and reaching again for the drawer. “Dammit!” he swore, finally letting go of Brandon and crawling the tiny bit more he needed to open the drawer.

He couldn’t hold it back. Brandon convulsed with laughter as Jake climbed over him. And since he had the opportunity, he groped.

"Now you’re laughing at me!” Jake cried as he got his hands on the lube and the box of condoms and then smacked them down on the mattress beside Brandon’s head.

Brandon sat up and pushed his way into Jake’s arms. “Sex is supposed to be fun, Jake. Enjoy it,” he said with an honest smile.

"Enjoy it, damn, but don't laugh," Jake muttered with a grin, nuzzling against Brandon's cheek. "You could injure my manhood," he purred into Brandon's ear as his hands slid over Brandon's skin slowly.

Humming with pleasure, Brandon moved to close a hand around Jake's considerable 'manhood'. "I'll just nurse it back to health," he drawled, stroking the thickened cock slowly. "Feels healthy enough to me." Somewhere inside, Brandon was stunned by his forwardness in this whole encounter. All he could think of to explain it was how right it felt. Exciting, explosive and right.

Jake groaned and pushed his hips against Brandon's hand. "Oh God," he moaned against Brandon's cheek, all desire to joke gone as the lust overpowered him. He panted and moved to kiss the man again, murmuring, "I've wanted you for weeks now."

Brandon kissed him back, their mouths open and wet, digging the fingers of his free hand into Jake's shoulder while his other hand continued to move. "I'm here now," he said in a voice shaking with desire.

The words sent another shiver through Jake and he reached down to grab Brandon's hand before he got carried away. He reached for the lubricant and hovered over Brandon, looking down at him seriously as he spread his legs further apart with his knee. "I'm going to fuck you now, Brandon," he murmured, "unless you stop me."

Brandon looked up into dark, serious, hungry eyes, not even trying to pull loose. "Not stopping you. I want it too," he breathed.

Jake kissed him hard, the hand holding the tube traveling down to tug at Brandon's thigh. He pushed up again, breaking the kiss regretfully, and squeezed out a line of the clear lubricant onto his finger as his eyes devoured Brandon. Without giving him time to second guess, Jake adjusted his position and kissed Brandon again, slowly this time, using a well-practiced finger to massage tense muscles.

Sighing long and low, Brandon pulled his legs further apart, one folding up against Jake's side. He kissed Jake, hard, not wanting him to stop. *Ever*. "More, please, more," he gasped against warm lips.

Jake practically snarled against Brandon's lips and pressed his fingers inside, roughly. Brandon jerked under him with a cry of approval, tilting his hips up closer to Jake's hand. Jake bit lightly at Brandon's lower lip and twisted his fingers brutally, tangling his free fingers in the man's hair when Brandon started to shift under him, trying to snap up his hips. Brandon shifted both legs even further apart, heels digging into the mattress as his body took over, leaving him to pant and make rasping cries with each plunge of Jake's fingers.

Jake's breaths came in painfully short gasps as he ran his tongue along Brandon's teeth. Any inclination he possessed toward going slow flew completely out the window with Brandon's cries. After another brutal twist of his fingers, he grunted demandingly and thrust his hips forward. If Brandon wasn't ready, Jake wasn't sure he cared at this point.

Shaking all over, Brandon dragged his eyes open as he practically wailed under Jake's ministrations. "Oh fuck..." he bit off, voice gone dark and low. "Do it, for God's sake! *Please*!" he urged, convinced he was about to go insane, and it would only get better.

Jake made another whimpering sound that he hoped at least sounded a little bit like a growl, and he pulled his fingers out and swiped them through the rest of the lube on Brandon's thigh. "Roll over," he breathed as he pushed back to kneel between Brandon's legs and wrapped his lubed fingers around his own cock.

Dragging in deep breaths, Brandon pulled up one knee so he could move, and he climbed to his knees, bracing himself on his forearms near the headboard. If this went as he hoped, he'd be hanging onto that headboard very, very soon. He looked back over one shoulder, arrested by the sight of Jake – absolutely fucking gorgeous, built and very well-endowed Jake – moving behind him.

Jake shivered involuntarily as he watched Brandon move. Christ, was he really preparing to fuck him? Jake shook off the slight misgivings and placed his hand on the small of Brandon's back and edged forward behind him. His fingers dragged across the skin, leaving behind red trails as Jake guided himself closer. "Ready?" he panted.

Brandon nodded, meeting Jake's eyes. "Yeah," he said, arching to press harder against Jake's hand. He wanted this *so much*.

Jake pressed the head of his cock against Brandon and watched the line of his shoulders as after a couple of tries he pushed slowly in. He groaned softly and his fingers curled against Brandon's skin. Gripping Brandon's hips, he flexed his own forward slowly, groaning again and unable to stop himself from rocking deeper.

Brandon gasped, tensing for a long moment, then relaxed, letting Jake in. It was an incredible feeling. Pleasure and pain because Jake was certainly the biggest he'd taken. He moaned Jake's name and shifted back, trying to ease the ache and burn.

Jake gripped Brandon's hips harder and pushed further into him, finally groaning out loud as the throb in his groin increased from the tightness. "If you keep moving this won't last long," he groaned roughly as he pushed his hand up the back of Brandon's spine and leaned over him.

"Oh God – not the 'move; don't move' thing again," Brandon groaned, digging his fingers into the sheets as he tried to stay still.

"I didn't tell you not to move," Jake responded in a tight voice as he thrust forward slowly. "Just that it'll be quick," he groaned, reaching around to glide his fingers over Brandon's balls.

Brandon arched and shoved back in response to his touch, crying out as Jake was pushed deeper. "Jesus," he said weakly. "It's gonna be quick and it's still gonna kill me." He could feel his cock aching, just barely brushing the bed below him with each of Jake's pushes. It wasn't enough stimulation yet.

Jake closed his eyes and breathed out deeply, knowing this felt incredible and different, but not sure why. He began to rock his hips slowly, his fingers digging into Brandon's hip as his other hand encircled Brandon's cock and squeezed. "Oh God," Jake growled as he rubbed his thumb over the head. His stomach coiled and his groin throbbed pleasantly. "I see no reason to extend this past the few fucking seconds it'll take for me to come," he ground out as he pulled out, little by little. He rocked there as the pleasure continued to coil, and then he slammed into the man with a powerful snap of his hips.

Brandon's ecstatic yell echoed off the walls as he quivered under Jake, all the clenching and knotting in his groin pulling tighter and tighter. Jake's hand around him was just that much more working to tip him over the edge. "A few seconds," he gasped out. His voice was thinned and borderline wild.

Jake's free hand gripped Brandon's ribs, slid down his side and back up to grab his shoulder and hold him still as Jake hit his rhythm. His hips rolled against Brandon's ass and he thrust deeper and harder, working himself closer to completion, his hand massaging Brandon in the same punishing rhythm. His body flushed with heat and he bit his lip as he pounded into the other man even harder. "Fuck!" Jake shouted, his fingers digging in at Brandon's collarbone. "Brandon," he gasped, lowering his forehead to the man's sweaty shoulder and whimpering as his orgasm rushed through him.

He'd remember the sound of his name on Jake's lips for a long time, Brandon thought as he slid into orgasm with a deceptively soft gasp, moaning with each pulse as the fingers wrapped around him kept moving, extending the sensations until he trembled all over.

Jake's body convulsed violently as he emptied himself into the man, his teeth sinking lightly into Brandon's shoulder while he rode out the waves. He stayed like that for a long moment as his ears buzzed and head swam, until he pushed up and carefully pulled out of Brandon's body. He flopped to his side with a groan and sprawled.

Once Jake moved, Brandon collapsed in place and fell to his side, curled up facing Jake and breathing hard. He was still seeing stars and he could still feel where Jake's cock had been inside him. He moaned, stretched, and shifted his hips, feeling wet warmth trickle out, and he turned his face into the sheets to moan again, fingers clutching in the quilt. *Fuck* if that wasn't the sexiest result of an incredibly hot fucking. It was nearly enough to get him hard again.

Jake lay next to him, breathing hard and utterly spent even though his mind was telling him to get up and do something. Preferably that, again. Eventually he turned his head to look at Brandon, chest rising and falling heavily as he tried to recapture his breath. "Fuck," he groaned, raking his eyes over his partner. God, Brandon looked incredible; stretched out and glistening with sweat, face pressed into the sheets, hair loose and a mess, practically writhing from their fucking. "Fuck," Jake offered again, this time a little more reverently.

Brandon opened hooded, dazed eyes to see Jake next to him, and the hunger that swamped him anew was inhuman. How was it possible for him to be so intensely attracted to this man? He lifted a shaky hand and reached out to touch Jake's chest with his fingertips, just to make sure. He didn't think there was any way this was a dream, not with his ass aching, his head spinning, and slick, warm come leaking between his thighs.

Jake folded his hand over Brandon's and closed his eyes as he tried to slow his breathing. "Fuck," he repeated for a third time. "God, you're incredible," he murmured without opening his eyes.

Brandon's pulse slowly ratcheted down, and he gazed at the other man in wonder, a slightly amused smile tilting his lips at the continued profanity. He didn't know what he'd done to catch Jake's attention, but he hoped like hell he could keep doing it. He felt Jake's heart beating under his fingers, and the time seemed to stretch as he lifted that hand, taking Jake's with it, to lightly trace the other man's cheekbone and jaw. The tenderness almost seemed out of place, but he couldn't help himself. It occurred to Brandon that he'd really like to be held right about now, but he didn't know if Jake would go for it after the rough, frenzied, and mind-blowing sex.

Jake's eyes opened as Brandon began to move, and he turned his head to the side to meet Brandon's eyes as the man's warm hand slid over the lines of his face. He gripped Brandon's wrist hard, stopping the motion, and he gave the arm a little tug instead. "C'mere," he growled, stretching his other arm out to the side and under Brandon's neck.

Startling when Jake's hand tightened, Brandon wondered if Jake was reading his mind. He scooted over close to Jake's chest, curling his arm over his waist, laying his head on Jake's shoulder and sighing. Jake rested his chin on top of Brandon's head, wrapping his arms around the man as if they had done this a thousand times before. His thumb slowly slid back and forth over the side of Brandon's wrist as he held it, and he wedged his foot in between Brandon's ankles, burrowing his toes under the warmth of the other man. The fingers of his other hand slowly stroked up and down Brandon's shoulder.

The warmth of Jake's body lulled Brandon into a doze. He felt very safe and very comfortable, and he was sure he didn't want to move anytime soon. Although he knew he had things he could – even should – be doing, none of them held any appeal. He sleepily mused that they had not only tonight, but tomorrow, and it seemed too good to be true.

Jake lowered his head slightly to breathe in the scent of sex and dirt and shampoo. Finally adjusted and comfortable, he sighed heavily and opened his eyes again.

Sitting unobtrusively on the corner of the mattress was the little box of condoms.

Jake lay there staring at the box for a long while, too comfortable to actually move anything to reach for them. He wasn't all too concerned, if he were honest with himself. He should be, he knew. Jake had truly forgotten them, overcome by lust that had apparently sucked his brains out of his ears. But Brandon had forgotten them, too, and Jake didn't want to cut this short by pointing it out and sending the other man into a panic. Panic could come later, maybe. Along with the other panics that their little tryst would no doubt produce in them both. Until then, Jake closed his eyes and rubbed his cheek against Brandon's forehead, practically purring as he held the man.

The quiet rumbling made Brandon smile, and he turned his chin slightly to press his lips against Jake's throat. He floated in a pleasant haze he knew would end, but for now he would soak up as much of it as he could get, just in case. Jake tilted his head and rolled slightly, catching Brandon's lips with his own and kissing him gently. Brandon sighed against warm lips, the languid kiss pushing away the wakefulness that approached. It was so easy to just push everything away while he was in Jake's arms. His chest began to tighten as he had the thought that this might be it. One time to get it out of their systems. Brandon already knew once wouldn't be enough for him.

Jake fought with himself over whether to bring the issue up now or to leave it until they weren't happily tangled together in bed. He wished his better senses would have told him to speak out with it as soon as possible, but Jake didn't really have better senses. He pulled Brandon closer to him and kissed him harder before murmuring a teasing, "Wake up, Sleeping Beauty." Brandon mock-whined in protest. Jake kissed him again and rolled until he was on top of the man once more. He pushed up onto his elbows to look down at him.

Brandon opened his eyes as he rolled and looked up at Jake, the last of the lassitude draining away. Time to face the music, he thought regretfully.

Jake smiled slightly and settled back down, his thumb gliding over Brandon's lower lip as he slid his other fingers into his hair. "Hi," he offered softly.

Brandon blinked. That wasn't what he'd expected. He smiled tentatively. "Hi," he whispered back, placing his hands along the small of Jake's back.

Jake bent his head to kiss Brandon slowly, one last time, and nuzzled his nose against his cheek briefly before whispering, "We have a small problem."

Tensing, Brandon wished, wished, *wished* this didn't have to happen. "We do?" he murmured.

Jake nodded and lifted his head, looking up at the corner of the bed and reaching slowly to snag the edge of the box. He settled back onto his elbows, Brandon still securely beneath him, and waved the box through the air with a little flick of his wrist.

Brandon frowned as Jake shifted, and he followed the other man's movement until he could focus on the box. He stared at it for a moment, connected it with the stickiness between his legs, and his brows shot up. He pressed his lips together to stifle a laugh. "Um," he offered. "Some health teacher I am."

"I've found that you laugh at rather inappropriate times," Jake observed with some amusement. He chucked the box over the edge of the bed and bent to press a kiss to the side of Brandon's neck before flopping to his side again.

The science teacher chuckled and covered his face with both hands before groaning in resignation. "Do I need to be worried?" he asked calmly after pulling his hands away. He really didn't think so, but you never knew. He also wondered how the hell he'd keep a straight face when he gave the standard safe sex lecture at school.

"No," Jake answered immediately, not asking the question in return. If the answer had been a yes then Brandon wouldn't be quite so calm, he reasoned. "I'm sorry," he offered sincerely. "I don't usually get carried away like that."

Brandon smiled. "Well, I'm rather glad I inspired it, actually. You don't need to worry, either," he added. It had been far too long and too many standard checkups ago to even think about, he added silently.

Jake couldn't help but smirk slightly as he snaked his arm across Brandon's waist. "So, Mr. Health Teacher," he teased in a low voice. "Practice what we preach, huh?" he snickered, pulling himself closer to nuzzle Brandon's neck. The relief over it not being a big deal was enough to make him a little giddy.

Brandon rolled his eyes and groaned, but he still hugged Jake close. "I'm going to hear about this for awhile, aren't I?" he drawled before thinking. He stiffened. What if there wasn't awhile?

"Oh yeah," Jake laughed gleefully. "If I'm still Thundercat after fifteen years, you'll be hearing about this for at least as long."

Brandon's pulse raced again at the implication, and he just looked at Jake's smile until he couldn't resist kissing it.

Jake groaned in surprise and tightened his hand in Brandon's hair. They kissed for a long moment that stretched on and on, and Jake found himself in serious danger of enjoying it just a little too much. "Stay here tonight," he requested impulsively.

Brandon gazed at him, recognizing the fact he wanted nothing more. He was already in so, so deep. There wasn't going to be any way to save himself anyway. "Okay," he agreed quietly.

Chapter 8

IT was a long while before Jake decided he was too sticky. A shower and some more groping later, he stood in front of the refrigerator staring at the meager offerings within. He held his pills in his hand, and his eyes strayed to the beer on the top shelf.

Brandon padded into the kitchen, dressed in more of Jake's clothes. He stopped next to the other man, glancing into the fridge and raising an eyebrow. "I'm guessing you didn't find anything." It was certainly different from his own fridge. While he didn't cook, Brandon ate a lot of fresh food, and he kept the larder stocked.

"I need to go to the store," Jake grumbled as he reached in for a soda and popped the pills into his mouth while opening the can.

Brandon rolled his eyes and pushed the fridge door shut. "Ya think?" he asked sarcastically. "So are we ordering in or do you want to go to Publix?" He glanced to the clock; it was late, but not too much so for a Saturday night.

"Store, I think," Jake answered after downing the pills. "What are you wanting? Anything specific?" he asked as he set the can down on the counter and reached for Brandon's hips, pulling and turning him just a little to put Brandon between him and the refrigerator with a smirk.

Brandon smiled as he allowed Jake to maneuver him where he wanted him, and he settled his hands behind Jake's elbows. "I mostly eat sandwiches, fruit, fresh vegetables, things that don't require cooking." He narrowed his eyes and looked pointedly at the other man. "I've eaten more pizza in the last month than in my entire life, I think." His face scrunched in distaste.

Jake pressed himself closer and bit his lip to stop his smile. "Well, we order it with vegetables on it," he reasoned.

"Only after I threaten Jonathan within an inch of his life," Brandon retorted.

"You were quite sexy doing it, though," Jake purred teasingly, leaning in to brush his lips over Brandon's. "I've got some pasta," he offered. "I accidentally made this shrimp scampi with alfredo sauce once and it was really good," he admitted with a small laugh.

Brandon shrugged slightly, still smiling, warmed by the continuing affectionate gestures. How so much had changed in a single day. "If you're brave enough to cook, I'm brave enough to eat it," he said. "But the store is fine, too."

"I'd rather brave the cooking than the store," Jake declared with another kiss. "Mainly because of the whole getting-dressed thing," he growled before pushing away from the refrigerator. "But I bet you want like fruit and stuff, though, huh?" he laughed with a grin. "You want to come with me or stay here and snoop through my things while I'm gone?" he asked playfully, his hands drifting down Brandon's sides before taking another step back.

Eyes bright, Brandon chuckled. "No preference. Unless there's something really interesting I'll find if I 'snoop'," he teased. "Besides, you don't know what kind of 'fruit and stuff' I like," he pointed out.

"Point," Jake conceded with a grin. "Let me get my shoes," he huffed as he turned away and headed for the hall closet. "You'll have to drive!" he called over his shoulder as he climbed the stairs.

Brandon looked down at the running shorts and T-shirt he was wearing and figured they were fine for the store. He headed back upstairs to the bedroom where his shoes had been tossed two different ways. He sat on the edge of the mussed bed to pull them on, pausing after to look at the sheets where he'd laid in Jake's arms.

Jake rummaged through the upstairs hall closet and found his flip flops, thwapping them down onto the floor noisily and sliding into them. He peered down the hall and saw Brandon sitting on the end of the bed, glancing over his shoulder. "You okay?" he asked lightly, not letting the sudden flash of worry show through.

Brandon turned to look at him, unaware of the soft, endearing smile on his face. He'd been thinking about how he couldn't have asked for a better first time with Jake. Followed by hoping it wasn't the last, although he was feeling pretty damn good about that. Jake was being amazingly affectionate and it made Brandon happier than he had expected. Just that simple affection *meant* more, although he certainly wouldn't want to give up the incredibly passionate sex. "Yeah, I'm good," he said softly.

Jake raised an eyebrow and closed the hallway door. "You're not going all mushy on me are you?" he asked teasingly as he flip-flopped down the hallway toward the bedroom. He leaned against the doorway, and his lips twitched in amusement. "I don't wanna talk about my feelings," he told Brandon sternly with a wag of his finger.

Brandon again quashed a laugh. Despite his tough words, Jake's actions didn't back them up at all. "Oh, heaven forbid," he said drolly as he stood up. "C'mon. Food so you can feed me after you used me so mercilessly."

"You know you liked it," Jake shot back with a cocky jerk of his head. The little rush of heat that shot through him at the thought said that he had liked it too. A lot.

Brandon stopped right up against Jake's chest rather than continuing into the hall. "Yeah," he rasped. "I did."

The heat billowed, and Jake's smile faded as he met Brandon's eyes. "Me too," he whispered in a low voice.

Brandon leaned forward to kiss him gently on the lips, then his cheekbone, then the very corner of his eyes. "Offsets the mush, then," he murmured. Jake growled softly and enjoyed the kisses like a puppy being petted by his master, his eyes closed and a small smile on his face. Pulling back to look over Jake's face, Brandon whispered, "You really are gorgeous."

Jake opened his eyes and cocked his head. He had heard such things before. Coming from Brandon, though, he wondered why they sounded more sincere. He smiled softly and shook his head. "I thought I told you to stop talking to yourself," he murmured teasingly as he pulled him closer and kissed his chin.

Brandon's eyes fell mostly closed and he rubbed his cheek against Jake's chin. "Would you rather hear that you really are addictive?" he asked, sliding his hands around Jake's thighs to grope his ass. "Can't keep my hands off you now."

"That might be a problem come Monday," Jake drawled with a little laugh.

Brandon pulled back, eyes wide. He cleared his throat. "Ah, well. I guess I'll have to figure out how to rein myself in," he said, wondering how in the world he had become the subtle aggressor between them.

"You do that," Jake responded sternly. "I'll just stay close to the showers myself."

Narrowing his eyes, Brandon poked Jake in the ribs. "I'd hope I have the same effect on you that you have on me. Certainly seems like it anyway," he said.

Jake grabbed Brandon in a lightning-quick movement as soon as his ribs were jabbed, and he slammed the man against the wall and kissed him brutally. Brandon barely had time to get in a breath before he was gasping into Jake's mouth, going achingly hard as Jake manhandled him. He'd never have thought he'd be so turned on by being thrown around, but God help him... He tried to kiss Jake back just as firmly, grinding against his thigh. At this rate they'd never get dinner, and Brandon just didn't care.

Jake grinned as Brandon responded to him, and he nipped once more at his lip before pulling back. "Like that?" he asked innocently.

Sucking in breaths, color high on his cheeks, Brandon paused, then nodded quickly. "*Jesus,*" he hissed, eyes dilating with desire.

Jake's eyebrows shot up. "Yeah?" he asked with a smirk as he slid his hands down Brandon's ribs. Trying to get in enough air to calm down, Brandon gave Jake a helpless look. "You're so cute when you're flustered," Jake laughed impulsively, taking Brandon's face in both hands and kissing him.

Brandon's "Cute?" came out muffled, but he really didn't mind. He slid his arms around Jake's neck and held close, distantly amused that they were standing in the doorway necking like kids. He smiled against the kiss. Yeah. Jake was *very* affectionate.

It was another moment of languid kisses before Jake pulled back and licked his lips, fingers trailing through Brandon's hair. "Dinner?" he suggested a little breathlessly.

"Yeah," Brandon agreed. "Store?"

Jake let his eyes rake over Brandon's body as if he were considering getting dinner *there* instead, but then he smirked and looked up to meet Brandon's eyes again with a mischievous little glint. "Yeah," he answered. "You're driving." Brandon nodded and started down the hallway. Jake watched him go before following him, hopping a little as he walked to catch up to the other man.

Brandon snagged his keys off the hall table where he'd thrown them earlier. "We ought to pick up your truck while we're out," he said as they walked down the front steps.

"Good idea," Jake answered and spun on his heel toward the kitchen and the hook where his keys lived. He'd put them there after picking them up off the living room floor just a while ago. "We're going to have to be careful," he warned seriously. "You know how rumors make it around a high school." He practically groaned.

Brandon was composed and appropriately sober. "Yeah," he said, stopping at the bottom of the porch stairs. Each time Jake said something like that, he felt like it meant Jake was going to be interested in something more than the occasional fuck. But he figured Jake's tease about not talking about feelings was grounded in fact. Hell, he didn't know how he felt himself, other than mushily swept off his feet.

"What?" Jake asked as he came back into the entryway. "You keep looking like I kicked your puppy," he observed with a slightly worried smile. He took a step closer and looked Brandon over carefully. "I didn't hurt you, did I?" he asked suddenly, horror creeping into his tone.

"No!" Brandon exclaimed, startling himself with the

vehemence of his answer. "No," he repeated in a modulated tone. He actually shuffled in place, wishing he could hide, even a little bit, and expressively he closed up. "I just don't know what to expect," he said, unable to look up at Jake in case he saw annoyance or amusement.

"Expect?" Jake echoed in confusion. "Out of what?" he asked a little tentatively. "Going out in public?" he asked with a little smile.

Sighing, Brandon shook his head. "No. In public, in school, I get it. I understand and appreciate discretion. I mean..." he fumbled for words. "I don't know what you want out of this," he admitted. "It's disconcerting."

Jake blinked at him and inclined his head a little, taken by surprise. "Oh," he responded stupidly. "Well, I hadn't really gotten further in the thought process than wanting to get you naked, so I guess I'm a little behind," he told Brandon with a slight blush and a smile to ease the tension he felt creeping back in.

"Yeah, well," Brandon tried a smile, hoping to defuse the sudden edginess between them. "I'm always overthinking things, brain in overdrive, that sort of thing," he offered, hoping to play it off, starting to walk toward the car. While he appreciated Jake's comment about wanting him, he hadn't gotten a reply to his admission. How could he have said something like that, anyway? Wanting to know what was happening next when they'd only kissed for the first time about ten hours ago?

Jake watched him go down the walk with a frown, but smiled slightly as he had an idea. He reached down, took off his flip flop, and chucked it at Brandon as he walked away, hitting him right on the back of the head.

Brandon's eyes bugged out, and he whipped around to look at Jake in amazement. "Did you just do what I think you did?" he exclaimed.

"Depends on what you think I did," Jake shot back with a signature grin as he thumped down the front steps and strolled forward to retrieve his flip flop. "That's what we do. You think and I throw things," he explained. "So I'll make you a deal. You stop thinking," he drawled, bending to pick up the shoe and wave it around threateningly, "and I'll stop throwing things."

The laughter was unstoppable. Brandon bent over for balance he laughed so hard, and when he looked up at Jake's fake angry face, he just pealed into near giggles until he got short of breath and had to brace himself against the car. "Oh God. Are we total opposites or what?" he asked, calming down enough to get in the driver's seat.

"Hmph," Jake offered good-naturedly as he flopped into the passenger side. "Since we're opening up with our feelings and all, I feel the need to tell you that this is the gayest car I've ever been in," he told Brandon.

Brandon looked at Jake in surprise. "It's a green Jetta. Why is that gay?" Jake threw his head back and laughed merrily in response. Brandon looked even more confused as he started the engine.

"It'll be okay," Jake chuckled, reaching over to pat Brandon's knee.

"What the hell are you on about? Or are those pills finally kicking in?" Brandon asked suspiciously as he started driving to the Publix he knew was a few miles away.

"Yeah, they are," Jake admitted with a content nod. "Sorry," he offered as he looked over at Brandon with a smile.

Brandon chuckled. "Well, I guess I'll have to make an allowance for that," he said. Then he glared at Jake. "My car is not gay," he asserted. "It's practical."

"It's practically rainbow-colored!" Jake giggled.

Looking at the hunter green paint, Brandon shook his head in exasperation. "What kind of pills are those?"

"Good ones," Jake practically purred as he slouched down in the seat. He glanced over at Brandon and laughed softly. "Your car's not gay, Brandon," he cooed, "I just like to see you get all ruffled."

Brandon rolled his eyes, but inside he was grinning madly. "Great," he said with a faked aggrieved sigh. "And I know I'm easy to tease. So I guess you'll be seeing me ruffled a lot."

"Hope so," Jake growled mischievously as he slid further down in the seat and rested his foot on top of his knee. His foot bounced in the silence, and he idly watched the scenery pass by as the very brief high and relief from his aches hit him.

Slanting a glance to the side, Brandon looked over Jake, seeing the effect of the drugs. He tried to recall what the options could be in the way of prescriptions, but he really had no idea. It had been ten years and so much had advanced since then. He pulled the car into the grocery lot, not bothering to look for a closer spot. “You okay to walk?” he asked politely.

“Yep,” Jake huffed. “Unless you’d like to carry me?” he offered.

Brandon looked at him in disbelief. “Me? Schlep around a lug like you? You’d squash me!”

“Hmph!” Jake offered that with a bigger grin as he opened the door and groaned getting out of the car. “People my size don’t belong in small cars,” he complained as he shut the door.

“So you drive next time,” Brandon said absently, locking the doors before they walked toward the supermarket.

Jake muttered in response and shuffled along after Brandon, trying to get his flip flops on straight as he did so before jogging a few steps to catch up. “You’re a bit of a bastard after you get laid,” he murmured to the man with a smirk as they walked.

Brandon snorted. “Insults won’t get you a repeat.” He grabbed a basket as they walked in, entering the fresh produce section first.

“I suppose you want like juice and milk and stuff, too, huh?” Jake looked around the market in distaste.

“How do you keep your girlish figure if all you eat is pizza, Hostess cakes and Doritos?” Brandon asked, bagging an apple and an orange.

“I don’t eat Hostess cakes,” Jake argued sulkily before smiling again and winking at the man. “I’ll get the liquid stuff,” he offered as he headed off to the left.

“Liquid stuff,” Brandon agreed, tossing ready-to-eat carrots in the cart before pushing toward the deli.

Jake strolled toward the other end of the store in search of milk and orange juice. He turned the corner into the last aisle and practically skidded to a halt as he saw a woman slowly pushing a cart up the other end of the aisle. It was too late for Jake to bolt out of sight, and he stood there for a moment mentally whimpering as Misty looked up and caught sight of him.

Her eyes flared with pleasure and cunning, and she started prowling down the aisle toward him, her heels clacking on the floor. "Why, Jake, imagine catching you out so late," she drawled, leaving the cart to approach him. "And all by your lonesome?"

"I got cut from the herd, apparently," Jake answered as he looked over his shoulder and craned his neck as if looking for someone – anyone – to save him. "Misty," he finally greeted with a barely concealed grimace.

Tossing her curly brown hair over her shoulder, Misty walked right up into Jake's personal space. "What are you looking for this late on a Saturday night, hmmmm?" she said in a seductive tone.

Jake resisted the urge to back up and instead looked down at the woman he towered over. "Milk," he answered helplessly, trying desperately to think of a way out of the innuendo she always threw at him, but unable to do it with his head floating merrily like it was.

Misty smiled and reached up to place her small hand on his chest. "You can't tell me you're just out grocery shopping when you could be out having a good time," she purred.

Having gathered meat from the deli and some Kaiser rolls, Brandon pushed the cart along the back of the store, blinking when he looked down the length of the aisle to see Jake just standing there, a smaller woman in front of him practically crawling up his chest? Blinking again, Brandon wished he could see her clearly. His eyes were pretty good, really, they just fuzzed out some, up close and at a long distance. But he could make out the slightly panicked look on Jake's face as he towered over her, and Brandon had to bite his lip not to laugh out loud.

Jake's eyes caught movement at the end of the aisle, and he looked up to see Brandon watching them with amusement clearly written on his face. He had to repress the urge to growl, and instead he smiled politely and reached up to carefully pluck her hand from his chest. "You know, you're right," he responded as if the thought had just occurred to him. "I'm just going to go find a good time," he said as he backed away from her. "See you Monday," he added once he was far enough to get to the end of the aisle and turn to dart away.

Nearly collapsing against the cart as he tried to keep his laughter quiet, Brandon scooted away from that aisle and down the next two, looking to catch Jake. Who the hell was that woman? He'd not gotten a clear look at her.

Jake turned down the row two aisles over and practically jogged down it, sliding his feet to make sure his flip flops didn't slap against the tile floor. It was pretty easy to lose someone in a grocery store, right? Right. He practically bowled Brandon over at the end of the aisle, and he grabbed the man, holding him in front of him like a shield.

Brandon broke into laughter as Jake wrapped an arm around him, using him like some kind of human wall. "Who was that?" he asked.

"Misty," Jake hissed. "Spawn of Satan. I feel dirty," he added with a grimace as he looked around furtively. "Let's get the hell out of here," he pleaded.

"Misty?" Snickering, Brandon let Jake pull the basket and subsequently him to the front of the store so they could check out. "I'm guessing she wondered why you weren't shacked up somewhere with someone since she didn't have you?"

"Something like that," Jake grumbled with a glance over his shoulder. He cleared his throat and looked at Brandon with wide eyes. "I'll wait in the car," he declared abruptly.

Stifling another laugh, Brandon dug the keys out of his pocket and held them out to him. Jake snatched the keys and gave Brandon's arm a quick pat as he stepped around him. "Good luck out there, soldier," he offered as he retreated to safety.

Shaking his head as he watched Jake practically flee from the store, Brandon pushed the basket forward and started pulling stuff out of it and putting it on the conveyer belt. He heard the heels clacking before he saw her, and he straightened to see Misty get into line. Brandon doubted she would speak to him. They certainly weren't friends. And now that Brandon got to thinking about it, he didn't like her trying to get at Jake. He swallowed down the boil of possessiveness. "Evening, Misty," he said.

Her eyes barely registered Brandon as she scanned the front of the store and the windows that showed the parking lot out front. "Brandon," she finally sighed in greeting, looking away and placing her items on the rolling belt. "Hey, did you happen to see Jake Campbell come through here?" she asked as she rounded on Brandon and put her hand on her hip petulantly.

Brandon's lips twitched. "Yeah, actually, he went through the express line and took off," he said, slowing to pull items out of the basket.

Misty huffed in exasperation. She looked away and shook her head, eyes narrowing as she thought about Jake and how fucking difficult he was being. Everyone could see how perfect they would be together. She glanced at Brandon and again and raised her eyebrow. "You're coaching baseball, right?" she asked as she turned toward him and leaned against the counter, close enough to him that she knew it would make him nervous. Brandon had always been the jittery type.

"Yeah," Brandon answered cautiously, edging away when the cashier started on his groceries.

Misty took another step closer and leaned toward him. "So you see a lot of Jake, right?" she inquired cagily. "Is he seeing anyone?"

"Ah, well," Brandon drew back, already scared of the predatory look in her eyes. He suddenly felt a lot more sympathetic toward Jake. "Yeah, we're with the team all the time. But I only see him after sometimes. For, you know, meetings." Brandon swallowed, somehow proud of the fact that he hadn't lied yet. But he thought he would, if he needed to.

Misty sighed and tilted her head impatiently. "Is that a no?" she demanded with a raised eyebrow.

"I don't know how to answer your question, Misty," Brandon said a little desperately, tapping his foot, trying to hurry the cashier.

Misty huffed and turned away, clicking her heel loudly as she did so. “Well, if he’s spending all his free time on baseball and meetings then he’s probably not got much time for a personal life,” she reasoned out loud, shooting Brandon a sideways glare. Something seemed to click in her mind as she looked at him, and she turned her body toward him again. “How rude of me, Brandon, how are you?” she asked sweetly. “We don’t talk nearly enough,” she said, placing a hand on his elbow.

Now Brandon got really nervous. “Well, we’re in different departments,” he said weakly, pulling his debit card out to pay. Now that he was pinned under those eyes, he really wished Jake was here to help. Brandon was never going to tease him about Misty again. He felt trapped.

Misty hummed in response and removed her hand slowly. “So, when’s your next game?”

“Away at North on Monday,” Brandon said, figuring she could find out herself anyway. He watched her apprehensively, wondering what she was up to. There was an odd glimmer in her eyes.

“Well,” Misty responded as if that were good news. The cashier handed Brandon a receipt to sign, and Misty stepped away from him again. “Maybe I’ll see you there,” she told him with a sparkling smile.

Brandon offered a really fake smile while he gathered his two bags. “Sure thing, Misty. Night!” And he escaped out the door, feeling like he had the hounds of hells at his heels. Getting to the car, he dropped the bags in the back seat and flopped behind the wheel, clutching it like a life preserver.

“Heh heh heh heh heh,” Jake offered from where he lay flat in the passenger seat.

Looking down at the other man, Brandon was going to say something snarky, but he thought better of it and started the car to get them out of there before Misty came out. When they reached the stoplight a few streets away, he finally said, “I feel for you, man.”

“Mm hmm,” Jake responded, rolling onto his side. He smiled in the darkness as the car began to move again. “I was thinking,” he murmured as he tried to get comfortable, "as I was hiding in the floorboard of your car," he added with a wry smile, "that we have all day tomorrow."

Brandon glanced down at Jake before he got them moving again, turning toward Jake's neighborhood. "Yeah?" he said, trying to keep it light. "Did you have something in mind?"

"Maybe," Jake grinned as he looked up at Brandon from his side. "I'm thinking a trip to your place to get your stuff for Monday might be in order. 'Cause I don't intend to let you leave tomorrow night."

Startled, Brandon stared out the front window, hands gripping the steering wheel. "Is that so? What about the whole being careful thing?" he answered almost evenly as he made the turn into Jake's subdivision.

"You get to school at like 6 a.m. anyway, right?" Jake asked, pulling the seat to an upright position. "Ah, dammit; we forgot my truck," he muttered as they pulled into the driveway.

Brandon shut off the car. "We can get it tomorrow," he said. Then he tilted his head, eyes slightly amused as he thought of something a bit out of place. "You know, you just told me I'm staying tomorrow night. What about tonight?"

"You already agreed to that," Jake reminded as he reached over and grabbed Brandon's shirt, tugging him closer and leaning over to kiss him.

Jake's lips on his, hot and demanding, made Brandon's head spin again. "Umm..." he mumbled as Jake only slightly pulled back and Brandon discovered both his hands were clutching the front of Jake's T-shirt. "I forgot?"

"My feelings might be hurt," Jake responded with a smirk.

"I'm thinking every time you kiss me I forget what we were talking about," Brandon corrected.

"I'll keep that in mind for when I get into trouble," Jake laughed as he popped open the door and swung his legs out of the car. Brandon swallowed hard and got out as well, snagging the bags of groceries and following Jake up the stairs and into the house.

JAKE awoke with a groan and flopped onto his side, throwing his arm and leg over the man in bed next to him and dragging him closer to wrap around him like a big blanket. He growled contentedly and then began fading back to sleep.

Dimly aware of being moved, Brandon roused enough to shift more onto his side from his stomach, where he usually sprawled. It was much warmer that way, he thought sleepily. Warmer? He slowly pulled one eye open, becoming aware of the limbs weighing him down. *Oh... Jake*. Brandon drew in a slow breath and sighed contentedly.

Jake floated for a while in a pleasant state, barely awake. He was aware enough to feel the body next to his, but asleep enough that his mind wasn't yet wandering into the rest of the day. Finally the call for the bathroom was strong enough to rouse him, and Jake buried his nose in Brandon's hair and inhaled deeply before raising his head and looking around. It was barely light outside. "Urgh," he groaned. Still mostly asleep, Brandon answered with an inquisitive grunt, face still buried in the pillow.

"It's too early," Jake responded as he rolled onto his back and then kicked the covers off his legs. "What day is it?" he asked sleepily, rubbing his face to stifle a yawn.

"Mmmmmm." Brandon didn't move, much too lethargic to wake up without his alarm clock jarring him from sleep.

"That, too," Jake groaned as he swung his feet out of the bed and sat up. He got up without another word and went to take care of what had dragged him from sleep. Soon he was padding back out into the bedroom and cocking his head at Brandon with a smirk. He took a few steps, leaped back into the bed, bouncing the man on the mattress, and then crawled on top of him and kissed the back of his shoulder happily.

Brandon sucked in a shocked breath as the bed suddenly rocked, and he jerked his head around to see Jake climbing over him. He closed his eyes, trying to swallow his heart back down. "What the hell?" he muttered, voice rough with sleep.

"Grumpy," Jake murmured with a smirk and a kiss along Brandon's shoulder blade. "I thought you were a morning person?" he teased as he laid himself down on top of Brandon.

"Ehhhh," Brandon whined, trying to hide his face in the pillow. The rest of his words were mumbled. Jake sighed long and loud and pushed up onto his hands and knees, then flopped heavily onto his side and rolled onto his back. Brandon pushed himself up from the pillow and looked at Jake blearily. "You keep me up 'til 3 a.m. and you expect a morning person before dawn?" he asked mildly.

"I didn't hear you complaining last night," Jake reminded with a sideways glance at the man.

Brandon gave him a silly grin. "True," he admitted.

Jake reached his hands above his head and pressed both palms upside down against the headboard, then stretched until it arched his back and made his toes curl. Brandon looked up and down the other man's body, licking his bottom lip as he raised a brow in appreciation. Jake's body twisted as the stretch wound down, and he turned onto his side and rested his head in his hand as he looked down at Brandon. "I vote for staying in bed the rest of the day," he said with a smile.

Still comfortably lying against the pillow, Brandon smiled. "Nice thought. But I imagine you'll be hungry soon," he predicted.

"A minor problem," Jake growled as he slid his arm under Brandon and scooted closer to him suggestively.

Brandon's smile grew, and he shook his head in wonder. "You're a big teddy bear," he accused playfully.

Jake gave an insulted huff and pushed at Brandon's shoulder to roll him over. "Better than Thundercat, I guess," he murmured, bending his head to begin kissing along Brandon's collarbone.

Brandon just purred and slid his hand down Jake's body to cup his ass. "I like it when you go all Thundercat," he drawled. Jake bit the man in retaliation and then continued on with his languid morning groping. Brandon chuckled and squeezed, arching into Jake's hands with a hum of approval. Jake raised his head to press his lips to Brandon's demandingly, his hand splaying out over the man's stomach in a possessive manner while he scooted even closer. "You afraid I'm going somewhere?" Brandon murmured, slowly writhing under Jake, trying to touch his body all over.

"Not really," Jake growled in response. "If you do I'll start throwing things again," he warned, shifting enough to slide his knee between Brandon's legs.

"Mmmmm, that's quite a threat. I've seen you throw a flip flop recently," Brandon said, starting to move his hips to drive his rousing cock against Jake's firm thigh.

Jake snuffed in response and bent his head to nip at Brandon's neck, then began moving down Brandon's body.

Eyes rolling up to the ceiling above him, Brandon dragged his hands up Jake's back, sighing happily. "Hell," he whispered. "Best morning I've had in a long while."

Jake grinned and looked up at him, giving his stomach one last kiss before pushing up. "Oh good," he responded with a grin. "Time for breakfast," he announced cheekily as he rolled off Brandon and to his feet.

"You bastard!" Brandon threw his pillow at Jake at he sat up, pulling his feet free of the tangled sheet and quilt. Jake bit his lower lip and grinned, hands on his hips as he watched Brandon expectantly. Eyes narrowing, Brandon shifted to his knees and crawled to the edge of the bed, reaching out to grab Jake's arm and yank him back toward the bed. "C'mere," he growled.

Jake shuffled forward obediently and grinned wider. "Hmm?" he asked in an innocent tone.

"Don't give me that angel act," Brandon said, rising up on his knees to bump his chest and other parts against Jake. "You *really* want breakfast now?" he purred, sliding his hands up Jake's sides.

"That depends on what you're makin'," Jake drawled as his hands came to rest on Brandon's hips.

Brandon leaned forward to lick his way up Jake's throat to his lips. "How about a protein shake?" he rasped before kissing him.

Jake laughed softly, the sound turning into a low growl as he lifted his chin up and smiled contentedly. Slowly he began to sink against the edge of the bed, fingers holding to Brandon's hips as he got lower.

Shivering, Brandon felt his cock go fully hard at the thought of Jake's very talented mouth. Jake kissed at his sternum and then gently pushed at his hips, standing up again to urge him to lay back with another, slightly more heated kiss. Brandon wrapped his arms around Jake's neck and let the other man lower him to the mattress. He kissed him back, licking along Jake's lips before deepening it.

Jake indulged himself for a long moment, enjoying the kissing before tearing away and making his way down Brandon's body. He placed one large hand on each of Brandon's hips and pressed down into the mattress, bending his head to lick at him experimentally.

Brandon hissed and moved slightly, hips lifting. "Jake, c'mon," he encouraged. "Sooner I'm done, sooner you get attention."

"Impatient, too," Jake observed with another slow lick.

"Yeah, well, we established last night that neither of us are that strong in the patience area," Brandon replied, but his voice was teasing. Jake responded by plunging his head down and humming deep in the back of his throat. "Oh *shit*," Brandon breathed, shuddering, his hands sinking into Jake's hair as his head fell back.

Jake's back arched and one arm slid under Brandon's hip to lift him up, his movements sinuous and animalistic as he aimed for more of Brandon's cursing.

It didn't take long before Brandon sucked in a breath and obliged. "*Fuck*, Jake... ohhh *fuck*..." Brandon's voice got quieter and his language got dirtier until he was practically hissing with each thrust into Jake's mouth.

Jake's arm tightened around Brandon's hips, his fingers digging into the skin as he swirled his tongue and plunged his head repeatedly. He groaned at Brandon's words and shifted his weight, tugging Brandon with him until they were on their sides and Brandon was able to truly thrust into his mouth.

Hips now able to move freely, Brandon moaned as he fucked Jake's mouth, muscles straining. Then he shivered and started to come, chest hitching. "Baby," he breathed, eyes squeezed shut, fingers clutching Jake's shoulder.

Jake's grip tightened, and he swallowed as Brandon emptied into his mouth. His free hand clutched at Brandon's chest as he did so, his toes curling with Brandon's obvious pleasure. Brandon wailed softly before melting back against the bed, panting, fingers loosening, and he petted Jake's arm absently. The bigger man rolled Brandon again until he was flat on his back, and then crawled up his body until he could rest his chin on Brandon's chest. "Now I know what gets you up in the morning," he quipped with a smirk as he watched Brandon try to breathe again.

Brandon groaned and covered his eyes with one arm. "You don't need any help," he muttered. It was true. At this point, all Jake had to do was look at him and he was hard. Jake touching him was gravy. Jake blowing him was indescribable, and then there was still the fucking...

Jake laughed softly and crawled the rest of the way up Brandon's body to kiss him again, disregarding the arm covering his eyes. "Now," he purred, "what would you like for breakfast?" he asked. "It's the only meal of the day I can make."

Laughing low and grinning, Brandon took advantage of Jake's movement to grab him and roll them over, settling his weight on him. "Yeah, but it's really delicious," he drew out, leaning to lick Jake's lips.

"Mmmm," Jake responded as he stretched like a large cat under Brandon's weight.

Grinning, Brandon dragged his hands over Jake's chest, following them with his mouth, licking along the defined muscles and abs before kissing at the crease of Jake's legs, his chin rubbing against the hard flesh nearby.

Jake tensed and finally jumped and gasped as Brandon moved lower. "I was actually offering real food, but okay," he groaned in a rough voice, beginning to squirm.

"This is 'real' food," Brandon said before licking him from balls to cock head. "Protein, fructose, amino acids, vitamin C," he recited between teasing licks, taking longer with the lick each time.

"Fructose?" Jake groaned distractedly as he arched his back and his fingers dug into the sheets.

Brandon purred as he lapped up a cloudy dot of liquid. "Fructose. A simple sugar found in many foods, one of the three most important blood sugars." He mouthed the swollen head, sucking lightly before pulling away to lap again. "Found in honey, berries," he said throatily, "and some root vegetables..."

"God, shut up," Jake moaned, his fingers sliding into Brandon's hair.

Brandon smiled and sucked Jake into his mouth, dipping his head rhythmically with a purr of pleasure. He loved Jake's reactions to what he did to him.

Jake writhed, letting his body take the lead over his mind, as he so often had in his life. It was shamefully easy to get him to whimper, but he knew that if he didn't come soon Brandon's jaw would probably lock or something. He opened his eyes and looked up at the ceiling for a brief moment before pushing onto his elbows to watch what Brandon was doing to him. Watching the head of his cock disappear between those full, wet lips was the surest way of getting off, Jake decided. Hell, just the memory would work in the future, he realized as his gut tightened.

Feeling Jake shift and tilt, Brandon moved to his knees to slide more of Jake into his mouth, and when he heard a low gasp, he looked up at Jake.

Jake breathed out heavily as he met Brandon's eyes. "Brandon," he murmured helplessly, then bit his lip and let his head fall back. His hips lifted just enough to make him moan softly.

Brandon redoubled his efforts, wrapping his palm around Jake and focusing his sucking toward the head, listening to Jake's breathing pick up. He hummed again, sliding his free hand between Jake's legs to rub there as well.

Jake cried out and arched his back again, fingers digging into the sheets and toes curling as Brandon's talented mouth sent him spiraling. He didn't even have time to call out a warning.

The hot seep of thick liquid on Brandon's tongue made him

swallow convulsively as he kept sucking, and he could feel the large body under him quaking. When it stilled, he pulled away, licking his lips and wiping his mouth with the back of his hand.

Jake's tense muscles all relaxed as he forced his eyes back open. "God," he murmured stupidly.

Brandon chuckled. "You keep saying that," he teased, rubbing one hand over Jake's chest in a soothing fashion. Although it and many of his other touches qualified as intimate to him, Jake didn't seem to mind.

"You're killin' me," Jake groaned with a smile that said it was a wonderful way to go.

"Nope," Brandon said, shifting out from between Jake's thighs to kneel beside him, where he leaned down to kiss him gently. "Physical therapy," he joked.

Jake groaned and rolled his eyes. Brandon laughed and lightly slapped his belly. "C'mon. We're awake, might as well get some things done." He climbed off the bed and offered Jake a hand. "We can always nap later," he pointed out.

"Things?" Jake asked incredulously. "Done?" Brandon put his hands on his hips, trying not to laugh and not having a lot of success. "Shut up," Jake muttered as he rolled onto his stomach and began to burrow under the sheets.

"Awwww, baby," Brandon said, crawling back onto the bed. "C'mon. You said we'd go out to my house so I can get clothes for tomorrow," he reminded.

Jake rolled quickly and grabbed him, yanking him down and wrapping around him in a classic wrestler's hold while pulling the sheet over them.

"Jake!" Brandon yelped, pulled down and engulfed by the other man's arms and body, struggling and finding he could hardly move.

Jake snickered evilly and tightened his grip. "What's the problem?" he asked in an innocent voice, muffled by the sheets.

Brandon stopped moving and closed his eyes. *Aw hell. This is wonderful*. He inhaled deeply, wallowing in Jake's heat and scent. "Nothing," he said, starting to move his hands over whatever skin he could touch.

"No getting frisky," Jake growled in a warning. "I need my beauty sleep," he preened.

So instead, Brandon just curled his arms around him and squeezed him close. He could almost believe this connection he felt between them had been there for months instead of hours. *It just feels right*. He pressed his lips to Jake's shoulder.

"Exactly," Jake murmured with a smile as he closed his eyes and settled in, holding Brandon closely. "You know," he sighed after a moment. "This feels pretty good."

Brandon didn't move a bit. Although Jake's words were thrilling, he didn't sound exactly all that thrilled about it. Almost like he didn't know what to think about it. Brandon wasn't sure he did, either. "Yes. It does," he murmured.

Jake opened his eyes, unable to think of what to say now. He had always been a little too impulsive for his own good. He had always worried his loved ones with his decision making, throwing all his heart into things before they were on solid ground. He bit his lip on any of the things he wanted to add to what he was saying. Brandon relaxed utterly, letting Jake support him, content to wait until the other man moved. Jake laid there holding him until his stomach rumbled, demanding food. He huffed and smiled slightly, lowering his head and hiding his face against Brandon's cheek in embarrassment. "Guess we should get up before I start starving."

"Don't want you wasting away," Brandon said, but he smiled against Jake's shoulder.

"Hmph," Jake offered as he forced his way between Brandon's cheek and shoulder and bit lightly at his neck. Brandon's response was a low moan and a wiggle. Jake snickered and lifted his head to kiss him slowly. "Any requests for breakfast?" he asked.

Brandon smiled against Jake's lips and murmured, "Here we go again." *I want to eat you alive,* he wanted to say. *I want to sink into you and stay*. God, how did this happen so fast? He was dizzy with it, with Jake's passion, his laugh, his growl, the deep brown eyes that darkened with hunger when they looked at him. Brandon shivered and wrapped his arms around Jake's neck to hold on tight.

Jake jabbed at Brandon's ribs with his knuckles, huffing a bit.

Brandon sighed regretfully. "All right. Breakfast out? Couple of places we can stop at on our way to Mountain Park, if you still want to go, that is. I ... I could drop you off at your truck." Now faced with going back out into life, away from the bedroom, he felt his nerves quiver anew. He told himself not to worry, but it sure didn't help.

"I'll have to get dressed for that," Jake practically whined.

"Jake," Brandon said.

"Hmm?" Jake asked with wide eyes as he looked down at Brandon.

Fulfilling a hidden want, Brandon reached up to place long fingers upon Jake's forehead, sliding them down over his eyes and cheekbones with a feather-light touch until they rested on Jake's lips. Jake's eyes closed automatically and his lips formed a smile. He opened his eyes to look up at Brandon and kissed his fingertips.

And Brandon knew without a doubt. He was in love. *Oh. Fuck. A. Duck.*

"Okay?" Jake asked with a small smile as he gave the fingertips a nip.

No. Not okay. Not okay by a *hell* of a long way. But what could he do about it now? So Brandon just nodded as his heart swelled in the quiet of the moment. "I'm afraid you will have to get dressed," he said apologetically. "Would be quite the stir if you were mobbed nude in the Waffle House."

"Waffle House," Jake echoed dubiously. "Ooh! Waffles!" he beamed as if the idea had just occurred to him. "Yeah, okay," he grunted as he pushed up and kissed Brandon before climbing out of the bed.

Brandon looked after him incredulously. Where did Jake hide all this when he was at school? Was it a case of every action having a complete and opposite reaction? Sure seemed like it. He sighed and swung himself out of bed and headed for the bathroom.

Jake slid into a comfortable pair of old track pants and rummaged for a T-shirt and sweatshirt as Brandon disappeared into the bathroom. "You need more clothes, right?" he called as he pulled out another pair of pants and searched for more.

"Yeah," Brandon shouted back from the bathroom as he took the time for a decent cleanup, deciding to skip a shower because he didn't want to wash Jake's scent off. Then he froze, staring at himself in the mirror. "Man. You have it *bad*," he told himself aloud.

"I have what?" Jake called, straining to hear while yanking out an old sweatshirt that had his worn fraternity symbols on the front.

Brandon's eyes bugged out. "Ah. Nothing important," he said back, tossing the washcloth he'd been using into the nearby hamper.

Jake ducked his head around the corner of the bathroom door and grinned. "I thought you said I had a nice ass," he teased with a wink, throwing the man the clean clothes.

"You *do* have a nice ass," Brandon agreed, catching the clothes against his chest and starting to put them on. "Maybe I should get to know it better," he chanced. He'd been more than happy to be fucked several times so far, but he was curious whether Jake would want the same. Better to hint or ask outright than be shot down in an attempt.

Jake laughed and ducked back out of sight. Brandon heard a few rummaging sounds and soon Jake reappeared and tossed a little tube of 'travel-size' lubricant at him, grinning widely. "Put that in your knapsack for the trip to your place," he snickered before disappearing again.

Brandon looked at the bottle he'd bobbled to catch and got a wide, silly grin on his face.

Chapter 9

DRIVING into Mountain Park, Brandon turned onto one of the few roads and up through the woods to his house. He felt overfull after eating waffles, but not too badly. He looked over at his passenger, who was studying the scenery as it went by.

"Beautiful place," Jake mumbled. "You said you grew up here? How were you in Parkview's district?"

"My mother worked at Central Office, so they paid for me to transfer districts," Brandon answered. "More challenge and opportunity at Parkview. More students, too. She was worried I wouldn't adjust well to college if I wasn't used to other kids. I was home schooled until then."

"Oh," was all Jake could think to respond. He couldn't imagine how horrible being home schooled would be. Never getting out, no friends, no sports, nothing but home and work all the time. He repressed a shiver and looked back out the window.

Catching the pinched look on Jake's face, Brandon grinned. "It wasn't that bad, Jake. I had friends. And I went to the middle school here about an hour a day for P.E. and music."

"Ugh," Jake offered that bit of information. "I'm sorry, but that's just cruel," he stated with a shake of his head.

"Cruel? Explain, please?" Brandon asked as he turned onto a smaller lane that ran along the lake.

"It's cruel," Jake shrugged. "Kids don't understand that kind of thing, and we both know kids can be mean. And I'm sorry, but thinking you know enough to teach a kid everything he could learn from a variety of teachers and experiences and peers is just arrogant."

"Oh, you mean the home schooling. I thought you meant the P.E.," Brandon said. "I can't argue, really. While going to Parkview really threw me at first, I think it made me focus on what was important. It was easy to be lackadaisical at home when it was just me. I could study when I wanted, take off to explore in the woods, fiddle around. There wasn't much structure."

Jake nodded and sniffed a little. The topic was one of his major tender spots, and he couldn't help but get a little ruffled by it. Hell, if Brandon's mother had sent him to real school when he was younger, his life could have been completely different. He could have played sports – he certainly had the physique for it – or joined clubs. He could have had friends who were loyal instead of just wanting help with their homework, and he could have been part of something instead of being on the outskirts. Jake shook his head angrily and pressed his lips together, trying not to get worked up.

Brandon frowned. Jake seemed to be really upset. "Jake?" he asked as he pulled into the driveway beside the white bungalow surrounded by wildflowers and trees. "What's wrong?"

Jake shrugged and shook his head. "Sorry," he offered sheepishly. "I get pissy about that kind of thing. Nice house."

Turning off the car, Brandon murmured a thanks. But the rest of what Jake said bothered him. "What do you mean, pissy? About the home schooling?" He didn't get why Jake would care about that.

"Yeah," Jake answered, leaving it at that. He had belatedly realized that bitching about it would imply bad things about Brandon's dead parents, and he really didn't want to go there. "Do I get a tour?" he asked with a smile toward Brandon.

It was obvious Jake didn't want to elaborate, so Brandon let it go. "Sure," he said, smiling a little as he climbed out of the car. "Inside or outside first?"

"Inside," Jake answered mischievously as he practically crawled out of the car. "Where's the bedroom?" he asked innocently, looking up at the house.

Brandon rolled his eyes. "One-track mind," he muttered as he jingled the keys, walking around the house to the back door. The front walk was overgrown with a colorful mesh of early spring flowers, blocking the walkway.

"Well, yeah," Jake responded with a huff as he followed obediently. "My brain is tuned continuously to ESPN, the Food Network, or porn. Sometimes two. Sometimes all three at the same time," he told Brandon studiously.

Brandon stopped in his track and looked over his shoulder, eyes dancing. "The Food Network?" he asked, voice a bit strained.

"Yeah," Jake answered defensively, pursing his lips and frowning. "*Food*, man."

Biting his bottom lip, Brandon shook his head and turned around to walk to the back door. He unlocked it and pushed it open. "*Entre vous*," he said with a sweep of his hand. Jake grinned and let his hand glide across Brandon's stomach as he passed him into the house. Brandon sucked in a breath at his body's response, flooding him with heat. Jake's every touch turned him on like crazy, and he *really* needed to get a handle on it before they went back to school and baseball practice. Not that they touched much then, but the temptation would be there. Brandon had discovered that Jake was a very tactile person. And Brandon had discovered he really, really liked it.

Jake inhaled deeply when he stepped into the house, smiling as he glanced back at Brandon. "Smells like you."

Brandon laughed. "If you say so," he said. "So, here, obviously, we're in the kitchen. Over there," he pointed to the left doorway, "is the laundry room and pantry." He walked around the small kitchen island to stand in the juncture of three rooms. "That's the TV room," he said, waving at the room ahead of him, "And this way two bedrooms and a bathroom." He shrugged. "Not much, I guess. But I don't need this much room, even." He looked around wistfully, obviously seeing memories everywhere.

"Isn't it hard, living here?" Jake asked after a moment of

watching Brandon.

Eyes clearing, Brandon looked over at Jake as he crossed his arms and leaned back against the wall. “Sometimes,” he said quietly. “I’ll look at something and just....” He looked hurt for a moment, but then the emotion was hidden away. “It’s all good memories. I just miss them.” Jake was silent, watching him expectantly. Brandon’s eyes moved through the room, but he didn’t really see it. Brandon was seeing the past. “Yeah, it’s hard,” he murmured. “But it’s all I have left.” His lips pressed together hard. “I didn’t get to say goodbye.”

“I’m sorry,” Jake offered quietly. “You’re stronger than I would be.”

Closing his arms around himself, Brandon gazed over at Jake. “You never know,” he smiled a little, shrugging off some of the seriousness. He felt a little silly now, babbling about his parents like that. “I think you’re awfully tough. You could handle it. But I hope you won’t have to, not for a long, long time.”

“Tough?” Jake echoed with a small smile, intending to veer away from an obviously painful topic.

“Tough,” Brandon repeated with a nod. “And don’t try to deny it. I’ve got some idea of the hell you go through with your shoulder, knee, and ankle. And you still go out and coach year-round.”

“You’re talkin’ ’bout two different things,” Jake pointed out as he moved slowly closer to Brandon, stalking him.

Brandon’s brow furrowed. “I am?” He watched Jake approach, anticipation curling in his gut. He had that look in his dark eyes, the look that Brandon knew meant the other man would soon have him begging. But in an oh-so-good way.

“Oh yeah,” Jake murmured, moving closer. “Takes a lot to face your past,” he said seriously as he cornered Brandon in the kitchen and stepped up to him. Jake sounded serious, so Brandon just waited as he felt the heat of the other man’s body come into contact with him. What did he want him to say? Jake took his face in his hands and kissed him gently.

Brandon’s chest tightened, the ache of memories brought into focus by the tender kiss, but Jake's words and having him close were a great comfort. He'd never talked to anyone about losing his parents. He relaxed against Jake, their foreheads touching as he kissed him back. To him, it was intensely emotional and painful. He couldn't admit to Jake how he felt about him. It was just ludicrous. Although he'd known of him for almost fifteen years, they'd only become acquainted a month ago. They'd only found common ground a day ago. How was that possibly enough to fall in love? Brandon sighed.

"You wanna get your things together?" Jake asked him softly, letting his fingers slide into his hair as they remained pressed together.

Brandon nodded, rubbing their cheeks together, breathing in Jake's scent and finding it calming. But he wasn't ready to move. Not until Jake did.

"We could just stand here," Jake murmured with a smile, sliding his hands down and around Brandon's waist.

Closing his eyes, Brandon gave in, moving to wrap his arms around Jake's neck and lay his head down on his shoulder. He didn't know what Jake would make of it. He didn't want to think about it. He just needed to be close.

Jake understood the urge. He lived in the house where he'd grown up, and even with his parents alive and just a state away, Jake sometimes found himself overwhelmed with melancholy. Memories of better times and crowded rooms that were now empty were just too much to bear sometimes. He held Brandon tighter and turned his head to rub his cheek against his.

Brandon drew several long, slow breaths, almost clinging, before he started loosening his hold on the other man. "Thanks," he murmured, kissing Jake's neck.

"Mm hmm," Jake responded with a rumbling hum, his hands moving up and down Brandon's back.

Brandon started smiling again as Jake didn't release him. "So, gonna let go of me anytime soon?" As soon as the words were out, Brandon wished he hadn't said them. Too easily misinterpreted.

"No," Jake answered with a smirk, letting his hands drift under the loose waistband of Brandon's borrowed pants. "Why, did you have something to do?" he asked innocently as he kissed at Brandon's neck.

"No," Brandon said, nuzzling Jake's throat, his smile huge now. "Not besides you."

"Now that sounds fun," Jake growled as he nipped at tender skin and gave Brandon a little tug away from the kitchen counter.

Brandon gasped when he felt the little bite. "I'm all for fun," he said, letting Jake move him as he liked.

Jake murmured back to him and continued to nibble as he dragged him further away from the counter. "Sure you're not bored with me yet?" he asked teasingly.

"I don't know how you could ever think that would be possible," Brandon answered, breathless.

"Oh, you'll get there soon enough," Jake assured him with a laugh, "after I pounce on you every time I see you for about a week."

Brandon raised a brow, giving him a disbelieving look. "And you think I'm going to get tired of *that*? Think again, Thundercat."

Jake growled dangerously and picked Brandon up off the ground by the backs of his thighs, letting his toes drag. "What was that?" Laughing aloud, Brandon taunted him some more by singing the chorus of the hated song. "Oh, you are asking for a beating," Jake laughed, dragging Brandon toward a bedroom.

"Oh baby, oh baby," Brandon exaggerated, "give it your best shot," he managed between chuckles as Jake pulled him down the hall. Jake slammed him against the wall as soon as they got to the hallway and kissed him roughly. Just like that and Brandon was hard as a rock. Moaning and whimpering against Jake's lips, Brandon responded with the same fervor, curling his hands into his shirt and grinding against him.

"What did you do with that lube?" Jake asked as he pressed him harder into the wall.

"In my ... my pocket," Brandon managed to get out, hand shifting to dig into the track pants he wore, fingers grasping the small tube and pulling it free. Jake took it from him and stepped back, tugging him forward and pushing him toward the bed. Brandon landed on the mattress on his side and rolled to his back, shoving the loose track pants off his hips and kicking them to the floor.

Jake followed him onto the bed and kissed him again, wondering if Brandon would take control over the encounter since he had expressed an interest in doing so. And apparently the other man was reading his mind, because as soon as Jake settled against him, Brandon rolled them over to land on Jake's thighs and rub against him while capturing his mouth again. Jake groaned and arched his back, enjoying the pressure on top of him.

Brandon growled and bit down on Jake's collarbone before kissing the same spot, all the while rocking their erections against each other. "Jake?" he rasped.

"What?" Jake panted.

"I want you," Brandon said intently. "Can I..." He licked his lips nervously, voice hitching. "I want to fuck you 'til you lose it and scream."

Jake gasped out a heavy breath and shivered under Brandon. "You better get started then," he breathed.

Brandon squeezed his eyes shut for a moment, then climbed off Jake and urged him to move to the center of the bed as he popped the tube open. He settled between Jake's thighs with slick fingers and leaned over to lick along his abs before shifting his mouth downward. As his tongue lapped at the head of Jake's cock, he carefully dipped his fingers inside Jake until the other man shivered uncontrollably.

Jake dragged his short nails over Brandon's shoulders and then scrambled for something else to hold onto when he realized that wasn't going to cut it. He reached up and placed his hands flat against the headboard, body arching and whimpers sounding at Brandon's touch.

Pushing one of Jake's knees back, Brandon started pushing his cock in, groaning as he got the slightest bit inside. He dropped his head and grasped for his dwindling control. "Now I know why you said it would only take seconds the first time," he said through gritted teeth.

Jake hitched his hips up higher, fighting against the burn and yet trying to pull Brandon closer with his foot wrapped around the man's hips. "Stop talking," he gasped with a smile, reaching for Brandon's shoulders again.

Sucking in a deep breath, Brandon pushed harder, looking down to see his cock disappearing into Jake. "Fuck," he whispered before he started rocking his hips. Jake curled in on himself, gasping as his fingers dug into Brandon's arms. Shuddering, Brandon kept moving slowly. "Okay?" he breathed.

Jake's back arched again, his body writhing against the intrusion while still begging for more. "Yes," he managed to groan in a strained voice. He pulled again at Brandon's shoulder, urging him to go faster. Grunting quietly, Brandon drew back and thrust in with more force. Jake called out a wordless cry and reached up to press his hands against the headboard again, pushing back against the thrusts and curling his knees closer for a better angle.

Brandon closed his hands on Jake's hips, sliding to cup his ass as he began thrusting in earnest, breaths getting harsh as he used more force. He knew he was repeating himself, but he couldn't help it. "Fuck, you're gorgeous," he hissed.

Jake barely heard him, all his considerable concentration resting solely on the pressure inside him and the fucking fantastic feeling. He made a sound in response though, something between a whimper and a grunt, and he tightened the grip of his knees on Brandon's waist.

Seeing the other man's focus, Brandon settled into a fast, pounding rhythm. He wanted to knock Jake right out of that daze. He wanted to hear him scream, just once.

"Oh fuck," Jake gasped desperately, throwing his head back as the muscles of his arms flexed against the headboard in a pounding rhythm. "Fuck, Brandon!" he cried out, pleading.

Squeezing his eyes shut to help cling to his control, Brandon kept up the punishing thrusting, pathetically grateful for the years of running that gave him endurance now, although the slick pressure around his cock was swiftly driving him to the edge.

Jake finally let go of the headboard, unable to resist the desperate need to wrap around the man inside him. He dragged his hands down Brandon's back and pressed his face against his shoulder, yelling out uncontrollably and writhing as his orgasm hit him.

The wild sound ripped the last of Brandon's control away, and after a few more hard thrusts, he threw his head back in a nearly silent sob and came in several pulses, each time sapping more of his strength until he leaned over and held Jake protectively. Jake was gasping for breath by the time Brandon's motions ceased, and he curled around Brandon like a large cat with a prized plaything and nuzzled him as he tried to regain some air.

Brandon shivered, panting and clutching at the man who held him so close, and he felt a sting in his eyes that he had to push away for his own sanity. He turned his chin to press a soft kiss to the crown of Jake's head, allowing himself that one outlet of tenderness until he knew Jake would welcome more. Jake raised his head into the contact and practically purred as he nuzzled against Brandon's mouth and chin. It was all too easy to capture Jake's lips in a soft, wet kiss, expressing with actions what he didn't dare say in this vulnerable moment. Brandon knew it would pass, and he'd find his composure again. For now, he needed to be careful, and it tore at him as being so, so unfair.

SITTING at his desk, ostensibly grading essays as his class worked in groups to plan their semester projects, Brandon stared at a paper, outwardly the picture of studious focus. But inwardly he was thinking nothing about grading papers and everything about biology. It had been terrible dragging himself out of Jake's bed and Jake's arms at 5:30 this morning; it had been even worse to gently kiss the sleeping man's forehead and leave the house to head to school.

It was easier to get back to work than he'd expected. He wasn't too distracted; it was like his memories and thoughts about the weekend just receded. They were no less important, but they didn't jockey for attention unless he deliberately focused on them. Like now.

The sex last night had been equal parts rough passion and tender touching, enough of a dichotomy that it would drive Brandon's analytical mind over the edge if he let it. He was trying hard to not give Jake reason to throw something at him. Now, away from Jake, he was fighting the urge to go out to the gym and find him. He was undecided about eating lunch in the teachers' lounge in about an hour. He wondered if he would see the man he was now thinking of as "My Jake" rather than "Coach Campbell." His lover really was two separate people.

His lover. What a thought. Did two days make that appellation true? Or did it have to last longer? Jake's actions and even words indicated he was interested in keeping Brandon around, and Brandon wasn't going to disagree. How Jake held him when they drifted off to sleep convinced him that the other man had to feel something for him, even if it was just friendly affection colored by heated desire.

One of the girls trying to get his attention pulled the science teacher out of his thoughts. Brandon set aside the essays and got back to work. But Jake was right there, on the edge of his awareness.

The real Jake stalked through the crowded cafeteria, glaring at kids who got too loud and stealing fries off the plates of kids he knew. He was able to keep all thoughts of what had gone on the past weekend cleanly out of mind. It was the game-face advantage, honed over many years. He'd taken a brief moment to be disappointed when he woke alone, and a slightly longer time smiling uncontrollably as he remembered the night before. And he'd spared a few moments of thought to wonder how they would treat each other if they saw each other before practice. Jake honestly didn't know how he would react. Would he be friendly and familiar with the man? Or would his other instincts kick in and make him hide behind his newspaper like he always did?

Jake prayed for the former and quietly dreaded the latter as the bell rang.

Brandon was still undecided about lunch. His normal plan was about 50/50, depending on what work he wanted to accomplish. Considering how little work he'd gotten done over the weekend, he should have been more behind, but his classes were in a lull between tests. He looked down at the essays, not at all interested in reading them. He was more interested in going to the lounge on the off chance that Jake might be there.

But what would he say? How would he act? What if other people were there and Brandon retreated into his turtle shell while Jake went back to brash and boisterous? What if there were *no* other people there besides Jake? Would he be the easygoing guy he'd been with Jake or would he turn back into his quiet, withdrawn self?

Finally he rolled his eyes at his fretting. Christ. He was acting like a high school kid with a crush. *You do have a crush*, he reminded himself with a wince. Time would tell how much of one, but right now it felt pretty damn serious. He decided to go to the lounge. He didn't want to hide. Brandon grabbed his planner, an apple and the sandwich he'd made at Jake's the night before, and left his classroom for the trek to the commons area.

Jake stood in the middle of the hall, towering over the sea of kids coming and going for the third lunch period with a long walking stick held over his shoulders like a water carrier. He was essentially on Brute Squad duty, and as soon as the kids filtered out of the halls he could see to his own lunch.

Brandon turned the corner, walking with one eye on his planner and one on the kids in front of him, heading around the circle to the wide hallway that led to the commons, occasionally jostled by the kids on their way to lunch. It didn't bother him, and he murmured a hello and pushed up his glasses when a few different students greeted him.

Jake turned, recognized the telltale bowed head of his weekend lover, and smirked, his stomach flipping quite inappropriately. He began to ease his way through the thinning crowd of kids, setting his large body in Brandon's path as the man came toward him with his eyes on his planner.

Brandon glanced to the side when a group of girls pushed past him, hitting his elbow and apologizing as they kept walking. He shook his head and barely came to an abrupt stop just before he walked right into a very recognizable chest. Both Brandon's brows flew up as he juggled the planner, the apple and the sandwich while chancing a look up at Jake.

Jake grinned at him and winked. "Watch where you're walkin', buddy," he murmured in a voice low enough that none of the kids would hear him and mistake it for anything but teasing.

Brandon's lips twitched into a smile, and he realized it was going to be okay. Now that he was with Jake – it was all okay. "Hey, Coach," he greeted. "Have a good weekend?" he asked evenly, but his eyes sparkled. No one would think anything of the two coaches talking in the hall.

"Coulda been better," Jake answered with a shrug and a twitch of his lips.

Amusement clear on his face, Brandon just nodded. "Well, that's too bad," he sympathized, nodding to one of the varsity players who walked by. "My weekend was spectacular. Going to lunch?" he asked, holding up the apple.

"Yeah," Jake answered with a huge grin as he reached out and took the apple with a cheeky "Thanks."

Brandon didn't even try to swipe it back. "Lounge?" he asked, turning to continue down the hall.

Jake jerked his head in that direction and made one more sweep of the hallway. Most of the kids had filtered into or out of the lunch rooms, and his duty was now over. He lowered his stick and walked alongside of Brandon, discreetly using it as a sort of cane. "How's your day been?" he asked with a smile he couldn't seem to repress.

"Not too bad for a Monday. I'm only a little behind on my grading," Brandon answered. "How's your knee?" he asked in a casual tone.

"Hurts like a bitch," Jake answered candidly, still smiling in an almost serene way as they walked. "My ankle's kickin' it up again, too. The tendon's tight," he said, not realizing that that was more information he ever gave anyone about his aches and pains, even his closest friends.

Brandon made a noncommittal noise. They'd gotten too wrapped up in each other yesterday for Brandon to try a treatment, and Jake had claimed he wasn't hurting at all. "I'm sorry to hear that," he said sincerely as they entered the noisier commons area. "Do they always make you hobble down here for hall duty?" he ribbed, a smile flitting around the corners of his mouth.

"I'm the only teacher not afraid to beat a kid with a stick," Jake joked as he waved his makeshift cane around. "I get it three times a week unless there's a game," he answered more seriously.

"That's a lot; I only draw it once every two weeks or so," Brandon said as he pushed open the door to the lounge.

"Welcome to the world of P.E.," Jake responded with a smirk as he followed Brandon into the room. A careful glance showed the room was empty, and Jake placed the end of his stick at the base of the door as soon as it had closed and pulled Brandon to him to give him a quick kiss. "Hi," he said as he let Brandon go.

Brandon's eyes widened as he was quickly kissed and just as quickly released. His features softened as he looked up at Jake. "Hi," he replied.

"I don't like this you leaving at the crack of dawn arrangement," Jake growled.

Brandon's heart skipped a beat. "You don't?"

"No," Jake sulked until he heard a shuffle of feet outside the door. He waited for a moment as they passed and then grinned widely. "You giving me a ride home?" he asked softly.

"I'd like to," Brandon murmured, stepping away from the door and Jake. He immediately felt cooler away from the coach's body heat.

Jake spared a moment to give Brandon a predatory once over, and then smiled and nodded. He took the stick away from the door and his "Coach" mask fell back into place. He took a bite of his stolen apple and nodded at the table in the corner. Brandon wandered in that direction after greeting the two teachers who came in. He stopped at the Coke machine for a diet soda while Jake went to the mini-fridge and retrieved his water. They'd actually done this a few times already, to talk baseball, so it wasn't new. But it felt new.

Jake took another bite of his apple and grinned as he chewed.

The door to the lounge opened, but Jake didn't turn to see who entered.

"Brandon, aren't you checking your messages? I called you this weekend about the A.P. paperwork," Rhonda said, moving to stand at their table, where she flipped her shoulder forward seductively. "Hi Jake," she said with a pretty smile. "I don't think we've actually been introduced." She turned an expectant look toward Brandon.

The science teacher cleared his throat. "Rhonda, this is Jake Campbell, P.E. teacher and head coach for football, weightlifting and baseball. Jake, this is Rhonda Anderson, chemistry teacher and academic team coach."

Rhonda stuck out her hand. "Jake," she practically gushed. "Brandon has told me so much about you." Brandon gave her a clear look of disbelief.

"Has he?" Jake responded with a glance at Brandon and a barely restrained smirk as he took the woman's hand. Brandon resisted rolling his eyes.

"Oh yes. And the kids love you as a coach. I'd love to know some of your secrets," Rhonda cooed.

Jake smiled as he extracted his hand and cleared his throat. "Then they wouldn't be secrets," he told her, leaning back in his chair, away from the table and from her.

Brandon pressed his lips together as Rhonda's face fell. "Well, maybe another time. See you, Jake." Rhonda turned away and fled, so embarrassed she didn't even say goodbye to her fellow science teacher.

Jake lowered his head a little, watching the door close out of the corner of his eye. When it shut he rolled his eyes and sighed. Brandon bit his lip and looked at Jake apologetically. Jake just shrugged and leaned forward again, resting his elbows on the table and taking another bite of his stolen apple.

Unwrapping an overstuffed roast beef sandwich, Brandon set half on a napkin and nudged it toward the center of the table. "Remember what I said about that girlish figure?" he murmured before taking a bite.

"Not really," Jake answered dubiously, sniffing at the sandwich. "What, you want me to eat that?" he asked in an incredulous voice.

Brandon frowned at him. "I *have* seen you eat."

Jake waved his apple around in evidence of the fact that he was eating and raised an eyebrow. "I ate about three dozen fries in the lunch room, too," he snickered before taking another loud bite of the apple.

Brandon turned up his nose. "Girlish figure," he muttered. "I can't eat that shit. I'd gain ten pounds."

"Well, lucky for me, I ain't a girl," Jake returned with a cheeky shake of his head and a grin. Knowing it was an insult, Brandon picked a grape up and chucked it at Jake, hitting him right on the nose. "Oomph," Jake muttered as the grape bounced off his nose and rolled across the floor. "Foul! I call foul!" he shouted as he stood up and pointed at Brandon.

Brandon cackled and leaned back in his chair, not even thinking about the teachers across the lounge who looked at them in surprise. Although it was becoming more common to see Campbell and Bartlett working together, this was new. Jake reached his walking stick across the table and poked Brandon in the shoulder with it. "Bully," he sulked as he sat back down.

Laughing harder, Brandon swung his hand ineffectually at the stick and took another bite of his sandwich. "Wuss," he poked, knowing it was anything but true.

Jake gave an outraged little squeak and held his hand to his heart as if he'd been wounded to his very soul. "I'm going back to my office," he huffed as he stood up again, poking Brandon with the stick once more and grinning. "Don't forget to bring your pocket protector to the game," he told Brandon as he made his way to the door, noticeably not limping in the presence of the other teachers.

"Funny, Campbell. Ha ha," Brandon sniped, but he watched him all the way to the door before going back to his sandwich, sighing silently. Huh. That went well. They'd managed to be together in public without jumping each other; they'd even had normal conversation. Relieved, Brandon turned his mind to the next class period.

BRANDON groaned and covered his eyes as he leaned against the dugout fence. Another error. What a nightmare. They were down 9-1, 7 hits to 1, zero errors to 4. The kids were dejected when they jogged in from the field for the last inning. Brandon glanced to Jake. His jaw was visibly grinding and his left eye was twitching.

There wasn't much a coach could do for a team in a game like this. Jake leaned against the dugout wall in the far corner and stood glaring out at the field, the kids giving him a wide berth.

Watching as the terrible game ended, Brandon urged the players out to walk the line to offer the other team congratulations, and he had quiet words with their senior pitcher, who was about to have a shit fit in the dugout. After a minute or so of Brandon's reasoning, the kid nodded and joined the end of the line before mutely returning to pack up his gear. The assistant coach directed them to the bus immediately, knowing none of them wanted to stick around any longer than they had to.

Brandon stood at the door to the bus as the kids climbed in, and blanched as he saw Misty and a passel of cheerleaders approaching as Jake loaded gear into the bus storage compartments. Shit. This had disaster written all over it.

Jake chucked the bat bag into the compartment and straightened, reaching up to close the heavy door when he saw the woman coming toward him out of the corner of his eye. He growled under his breath and pushed the door down and shoved his shoulder into it to shut it, pretending he didn't see her.

Brandon swallowed hard. This was likely to be very, very ugly. For Misty, anyway. He jogged over to Jake, speaking loudly enough that the woman approaching could hear. "Hey, Coach, Jeremy needs to talk to you on the bus, some kind of minor meltdown," he said, voice deep with concern. For Jake, but hey, it worked. He glanced up to see Misty faltering. At least she had some decency where the kids were concerned.

"Coming," Jake grunted in relief, turning his back on Misty as if he had never even noticed her.

Raising a hand to wave at Misty as though he'd just seen her, Brandon took a few seconds to shut the other storage compartments and shoo the last couple of players onto the bus. He climbed in last and sat in the front seat across from where Jake sat in the driver's seat. "Let's get out of here before she decides to climb on and ride back with us," he muttered.

Jake closed the bus doors quickly and then glanced over his shoulder at Brandon. "We got a count?" he asked.

Brandon nodded, still counting caps back through the bus. "Eighteen, nineteen, twenty, twenty-one. We're good, Jake," he answered in a low tone.

Jake put the idling bus in gear and nodded silently, driving out of the parking lot without saying another word. The kids all knew they were going to get an earful at some point. The bus was sedate, almost silent, and when the kids did speak, they did so in hushed tones. Finally when the bus was on the highway, Jake glanced over his shoulder at Brandon and muttered, "Thanks for that back there."

"You didn't need to deal with her shit after this afternoon," Brandon answered, sitting on the edge of the front seat closest to Jake, voice raised just enough to be heard over the road noise.

"It always worries me," Jake murmured in return, his eyes still on the road, "when she's followed by the girls. It usually means she's come up with something official-sounding. Last time it was a date auction to raise money."

Brandon blinked. "A *date* auction? Like a date with a *student*?" he asked in disbelief.

"Students bidding on students, community members bidding on teachers." Jake practically shivered as he spoke.

Stunned, Brandon stared at Jake's profile. "How did I miss this? When was it?"

"It never happened. Apparently I wasn't the only one horrified by the prospect," Jake answered wryly.

Relaxing in relief, Brandon shook his head. "Students bidding on students. Yeah, that would have been a *wonderful* idea. Why not do a slave auction instead?" he asked cynically, remembering such a fraternity function in college.

Jake just shook his head and pulled his right hand off the big steering wheel of the bus, resting it in his lap as he drove. It was days like this that he began to wonder if maybe quitting would do him more good than sticking with it.

Sitting back again, Brandon shifted to lean against the window so he could look at Jake without turning his head. He looked tired and upset, and it was no real surprise. Sighing, Brandon rubbed his eyes with one hand. He had more grading to do tonight, and a couple of tests to make, and he really, really needed to get a run in after skipping the last couple of days. He glanced out the window. Maybe another half hour and they'd be back at the school. He could be home by 10 p.m., go for a run, make the tests and do a little grading, crash about 2. He could do the rest of the grading during tutoring in the morning.

Unless he didn't sleep at all, too busy thinking about Jake.

BRANDON pulled the Jetta into Jake's driveway. It was 9:10, about what he'd figured, and he had no idea what to say. On one hand, he certainly wanted to stay. He should just come out and ask, but after the depressing tone of the last few hours, he found he couldn't be that bold. So he turned to look at Jake, whose face was shrouded in darkness. "Get some rest," he murmured. "We'll pick the game apart tomorrow."

Jake turned his head just slightly, not quite looking at Brandon, but not looking away either as he sat in the passenger seat. Well, that was a pretty good indication that Brandon wasn't planning on staying the night, he thought. He gave a little nod and reached for the door handle, dreading when opening the door would turn the overhead light on.

He wanted to lean over and kiss Jake, and he even reached

out, but Brandon stopped his hand and dropped it to the gear shift. Jake wasn't shy. Surely if he wanted him to stay, he would say something.

Jake hesitated a moment, closing his eyes and telling himself to just ask Brandon to stay. He hurt all over, and he was tried and cranky and pretty damn miserable, and all he wanted was someone warm to hold him tonight. He gave a glance back and saw Brandon's hand on the gear shift, waiting for him to get out of the car so he could head home. Jake sighed to himself and gave another little nod. "Thanks for the ride," he said before opening the door and climbing out of the car gingerly. "Have a good night," he added, leaning over to grab his bag, then closed the door before Brandon could see how torn he was over letting him go home alone.

Brandon almost blurted out something, anything, to stop him, but then Jake was walking away from the car and climbing up the steps to the house. Waiting until he saw Jake was inside, Brandon backed the car out and started driving, on autopilot the whole way home as the scene played over and over in his head. When he got there and stopped in the driveway, he lowered his head to the steering wheel and thwapped it a couple times. He got inside with his backpack and papers, tossed them all on the table and looked right at the phone. *Right at it.* Resisting, he went to the laundry room, stripped down and pulled on running shorts and a T-shirt. And he looked at the phone. He headed back to the bedroom for his trainers and stopped dead in his tracks. The bed sheets were still a mess from their romp yesterday.

Brandon couldn't resist any longer. He snatched up the cordless and dialed Jake's number. As the line buzzed, he berated himself for acting like a middle school girl, but he couldn't bring himself to hang up.

The phone rang just as Jake stepped out of the shower. He'd already done his nightly pills and beer regimen, and the shower was just hot enough to make him languid and sleepy. He took his time getting to the phone, a towel slung over his shoulder as he dripped on the floor.

"Hello?" he answered sedately, not even remembering to

check the caller ID first.

Brandon's eyes immediately fell closed as arousal ripped through him. He'd last heard that tone in Jake's bed, in Jake's arms, before they'd fallen asleep last night. "Hey," he rasped.

Jake blinked in surprise. "Brandon?" he asked in confusion, looking at his wrist to see what time it was and belatedly realizing he didn't have a watch on. Had he even had time to get home? "Are you okay?" he asked worriedly.

No. No, I'm not. Not when I'm here and you're there. "Yeah, I'm okay. I just wanted to, ah, check and see if your knee was okay." Brandon winced. What a stupid thing to say. He turned and pushed his face against the wall.

Jake blinked stupidly again, frowning at the odd tone of Brandon's voice but not able to figure out quite what was wrong with it. "Uh," he answered as soon as he realized that he needed to say something, "it's doing about the same as usual."

"Right," Brandon answered, then he caught himself. "I mean, sorry about that. I guess you've taken the painkillers and all." He was standing there shuffling in his own bedroom. God. Could he get any *more* pathetic? He'd been just *fine* when they were together.

"Yeah," Jake answered guiltily, blushing a bit as he drip-dried beside the bed. He'd never felt guilty for his nightly painkiller regimen before; why should he now?

"Okay," Brandon said, at a loss for what to say but unwilling to give up the tenuous connection over the dead air.

Jake waited, frowning harder now and wishing he had just kicked himself into asking Brandon to stay. Even if Brandon hadn't wanted to, he probably would have, right? And if he was calling now, maybe he hadn't wanted to go home after all. "You should've stayed," he blurted.

Brandon's stomach rolled and he squeezed his eyes shut. "I wanted to," he admitted.

Jake was silent, the missed opportunity curling in his chest painfully. "We really need to work on our communication skills," he finally said flatly.

"I agree," Brandon said, voice strained. He turned and leaned against the wall, sliding down until he squatted, face turned down to the floor. "I just haven't got the greatest confidence, I guess," he murmured.

"Me either," Jake muttered as he rubbed the back of his neck and looked down at his still wet body. He sighed heavily and pulled the towel off his shoulder to begin patting at his skin. "Sorta stupid considering what we did all weekend, huh?"

Brandon groaned. "As much as I appreciate the thought, don't remind me, okay?" He sighed. "I thought about you all the way home, how I should have said something, how I should have at least kissed you good night."

Jake's lips twitched, and he lowered his head. Telephones made some people say things they wouldn't normally say. For Jake, though, he was probably less likely to say what he wanted if he was saying it to a mouthpiece. He bit his lip, sliding his toe across the floor as he tried to force his tongue to form a response. "You should have," he eventually replied.

Fuck. Brandon wanted to get right back into the damn car and drive there right the hell now. "I'll keep that in mind," he said in a hoarse voice. He was never going to sleep now. Not without a massive jerk-off first.

Jake smiled slightly at the sound of Brandon's voice. "I thought about you until the water went cold," he said on impulse, blushing even as he spoke.

"Jesus Christ, Jake!" The voice that rasped was obviously strained. "I'm not going to be able to run with my cock this damn hard."

Jake's lips twitched into another smile, and he licked his lips. He really enjoyed the idea that just a phone call had excited Brandon. "You should have thought ahead," he scolded, his voice just a bit lower than normal.

Brandon groaned audibly. "The *wrong* head is doing all the thinking," he muttered. "But I'm still glad I called."

"Me, too," Jake responded as he dropped his towel and

shivered involuntarily. "You really going running?" he asked, not even sure why he asked. What, did he want Brandon to stay on the phone with him until he fell asleep? Jesus.

Sighing, Brandon sank the rest of the way to the floor. He wanted to lie. He didn't want to expose himself so much. But "I'd rather stay here and talk to you" was what came out.

Jake shivered again as he sat on the edge of the bed. He shook slightly now, but he wasn't certain exactly why. He considered asking if Brandon was willing to drive back to his house and stay there. He had to make the drive in the morning anyway, right? But he didn't dare admit how selfish he really was. "I'm not sure how long I'll last," he murmured instead, rubbing his eyes as he said it. "I'd feel guilty for keeping you."

Brandon felt flushed all over. "You sound really tired. I'm going to go for a short run, then grade some papers," he said, though he felt rather resigned about it. Maybe he'd just curl up in the sheets and see if he could still catch Jake's scent. "Get some sleep, okay?"

"My pillows still smell like you," Jake told Brandon with a small smile. "Should be easy to sleep."

Aw. Hell. "Bastard," Brandon muttered. "Good night."

"Night, Brandon," Jake murmured, his knee bouncing nervously. "I'm glad you called," he added with a tinge of relief.

"Me too," Brandon said, then forced himself to pull the phone away from his ear and push the button to end the call. He clutched the cordless between his hands and pressed it to his forehead, feeling more alone than ever. Dragging himself up, he looked at the bed. Within a few seconds' time he had decided, dropping the phone and crawling into the sheets to curl up there and just remember and dream.

Jake heard the line go dead and sighed heavily as he looked down at the receiver and shut it off. There was something about Brandon's voice that always left him feeling empty when it was no longer there.

Chapter 10

IT was a gorgeous day for running. Low 70s, a nice breeze, just a bit overcast. Brandon had settled into a solid run seven laps ago and was about to finish the second mile. A glance at his watch told him he had plenty of time for a couple more and a shower after. He could feel the stress sloughing off and told himself again that he *had* to make time for this. It cleared his mind, and he felt much better for it as his long legs ate up the track. Distracting himself, he composed a test in his head, working out essay questions. It would be simple to type it up later. He'd gotten a decent amount of grading done during tutoring this morning, and he thought he might try that more often to free up running time at night.

Striding past the press box, Brandon was oblivious to anything else but the asphalt. Kids began to filter out of the gymnasium complex in twos and threes, some carrying soccer balls or footballs and chattering happily, some looking around for a way to escape class today. The coach was the last one out of the building, his clipboard under his arm and his whistle in his teeth as he counted the kids. Not many were brave enough to try and escape Jake's gym classes. He was one of the few teachers spiteful enough to track them down when they did.

Jake caught sight of the lone figure running the track around the field, long and lean and eating up the distance with graceful strides. He blinked at the unexpected pang of lust that shot through him and looked away quickly. Jesus, what was wrong with him? Another glance that he just couldn't help, and an uncomfortable flutter of relieved emotions went through him as Jake realized that it was Brandon running.

The scattered sound of voices caught Brandon's attention and he looked up to see students crossing the track to the football field, some already kicking soccer balls around. A gym class. Which meant Jake couldn't be far behind. Despite the rise in his pulse, Brandon forced himself to keep drawing slow, easy breaths, never breaking stride as he raised a hand in answer to some of the students' greetings.

Jake headed over to the benches that lined the football field and thunked down, his eyes barely ever leaving Brandon's running form. He had to pass behind Jake on the track, and when he did Jake lowered his head and bit his lip, watching the disorganized soccer game intently. As Brandon hit the top of the track again and came into view, Jake's eyes followed him. He had never seen him run like this. He had known he could, obviously, but sometimes only seeing was believing. He swallowed heavily and tried desperately to pay attention to the class.

Finishing his third mile, Brandon was aware of Jake's presence, and he thought he might have caught the coach watching him. It was easy to keep going. He'd long ago perfected the art of staying in gear while his mind went other places. Now he was well warmed up, and he added a bit of speed as he started into the fourth mile. He wanted to finish strong so he'd be pleasantly tired tonight. Brandon wondered, idly, what Jake was thinking about if he was watching him.

If he had known exactly what Jake was thinking, he likely wouldn't have been able to finish his lap.

Another seven minutes passed and Brandon finally slowed to a jog for half a lap, then a rolling walk, hands extending over his head in a cooling stretch, feeling much better than when he'd awoken that morning. He stopped to grab the towel he'd tossed over the fence so he could wipe away the worst of the sweat, and when he turned, it was impossible to miss Jake sitting inside the fence on the sideline bench. Brandon ambled in that direction, hanging the towel around his neck, arms dangling from each end.

Jake turned his head slightly to see Brandon walk up. He

couldn't help but smile when their eyes met. "I see you never got your run in last night," he greeted in a knowing, intimate voice.

Brandon would have blushed if he wasn't already flushed. He leaned on the fence, about ten feet away. "No, no, I didn't," he admitted. "Had other things on my mind, actually," he said pointedly. To him, keyed up from his run, warm all over and now fighting the urge in his gut, Jake looked positively edible. *Bad idea to have a hard on in running shorts, Bartlett.*

"Oh yeah?" Jake responded innocently. "Have a hard night, did you?" he asked in the same tone, craning his neck to peer up at Brandon through the bright sunshine.

Eyes narrowing, Brandon's answer was designed to hopefully make Jake feel the same way he did. "There were some things hard about it, yes. For a while, anyway. Then it was easier to sleep."

Jake pressed his lips together to restrain the smile and nodded. "I had a hard night, too," he countered, resting one ankle on his knee and holding his foot to keep his knee from bouncing.

"I'm sorry to hear that," Brandon said, deliberately playing it up, although he'd really rather stop talking so vaguely. He sighed. "I need to go shower. I've got about thirty minutes until class," he said regretfully.

Jake looked down briefly before glancing back up at Brandon. He was no longer smiling, and his eyes had gone black and glinting. "You giving me a ride home today?" he asked in a low voice, mindful of anyone close to them.

Rather than waffling like yesterday, Brandon knew exactly what he wanted. The shine in Jake's eyes was almost a promise. "Yes."

"Good," Jake murmured, lips curving crookedly in a pleased, slightly evil smile. "I look forward to it."

Brandon knew he would think of that smile the rest of the day. "Good," he said playfully, walking backwards away from the fence before turning to jog back to the gym and the shower.

Jake was careful not to turn and watch him go. Instead he turned his attention back to the kids and silently wondered how he would get through the rest of the day.

Confirming his thought, Brandon did indeed think of Jake's smile through classes, lunch and practice. He packed up equipment along with Jonathan, thinking about that smile. He waited as Jake finished up, leaning on the fence as usual, contemplating how caught up he was in the other man. He felt like he wanted to change his whole life around just to keep Jake in it. Brandon was pretty sure it wasn't transitory on his part. He wouldn't tire of being around Jake's frenetic energy and schizophrenic behavior. No, he was more concerned about Jake deciding he'd had enough of the admittedly geeky and focused science teacher who was taking a flying leap by trying to at least act like a coach.

Jake took one last look around the empty field before strolling over to the fence where the other coaches were all waiting for him.

"Whatcha think, Coach? You ran them hard enough. Have they got that defeated mindset out of their heads?" Troy asked seriously.

"No," Jake answered, kicking the fence in frustration. "They will, though," he added determinedly watching the last tired kid straggle out of sight. "Let's go home," he huffed. "I'm tired."

Jonathan and the college guys said goodbye and wandered off, and Troy zipped off in his golf cart, leaving Jake and Brandon walking across the parking lot toward the Jetta. It was a quiet drive to Jake's, even more so when Brandon pulled into the driveway.

Jake cocked his head to the side and looked up at his house. "So what am I doing wrong?" he asked out of the blue. "What am I doing different this year that's fucking them up?"

Brandon glanced at Jake, a little surprised. "I'm not sure I can even come close to answering that, Jake. But I can tell you what I think," he offered.

"Okay," Jake responded with a nod, still looking up at his house.

"I think they're nervous. They want to please you. They're so tied up in knots about it that their focus is shot."

Jake flinched and glanced over at Brandon. "That's never been a problem before," he argued weakly.

"They've never been this close before," Brandon said in a quiet voice. "They want it, and more so, they know you want it. It's not a bad thing, Jake. They're just, well, they're trying too damn hard. They need to relax and enjoy it."

Jake was silent again, thinking. He would have to turn more of his concentration to this than he had been. He hadn't even realized he had begun to slack until it was too late.

"Jake. You have got to relax. Every time you tense up, they tense up. The tighter you get, the tighter they get. Hell, the more you stress, the more they stress!" Brandon shook his head, seeing the dark look on Jake's face. "Am I getting through at all here?"

"Yes," Jake answered tightly.

Closing his eyes as Jake's tense voice cut through him, Brandon tried to shrug it off as much as possible. "Okay," he whispered, just sitting there. He didn't know what else to say or do.

"Thanks," Jake whispered, feeling guilty. He swallowed and nodded at the house with a small smile. "Care to come in?" he asked wryly.

Brandon's eyes blinked open, and he relaxed a little as he looked over at Jake. "Yeah," he agreed.

Jake had been watching him and he sighed. "I make you nervous, too, don't I?"

"Sometimes," Brandon admitted evenly, but he added a playful grin after. "It's usually in a good way, though."

"Is it?" Jake asked.

The moment tensed, and it felt like a turning point – like Brandon's decision now would turn him right or left. One road steered him on his way alone. The other.... He nodded, meeting Jake's eyes, purposefully letting the emotions he usually quashed shine in his eyes. This was his chance. "Yes."

Jake felt an unusual flutter in his chest, and he frowned at Brandon in continued silence. Then he leaned over the console between them and pulled Brandon closer to kiss him impulsively.

It was like the first time, that nervous kiss on the couch.

Brandon's surprise held him aloof for a few moments before he relaxed into Jake's arms and returned his kiss whole-heartedly. Maybe Jake had glimpsed what Brandon felt.

When Jake finally pulled away, just a little, and rested his nose and lips against Brandon's cheek, his chest was tight and his breathing was coming in slow, quiet gasps. "I could really get used to this," he murmured.

Aching and swirling with heat, Brandon nodded his agreement. "Car's probably not the best place," he murmured, but he made no move to uncurl his hands from Jake's jersey or pull away.

"You're absolutely right," Jake answered, kissing him again.

Brandon literally whimpered into Jake's mouth, sliding one hand up to cup the back of Jake's neck. He was swiftly losing any sense of propriety. "Jake," he breathed as their lips parted for a bare moment.

"Inside?" Jake breathed in response, not removing his lips from Brandon's as he spoke.

A moan caught in Brandon's throat. "Inside... inside!" he urged, deliberately acknowledging the double meaning, and he crushed his lips to Jake's again for a heated kiss before pulling back and lurching out of the car.

Jake was left sitting in the car and swallowing hard when the door slammed shut. He sat for another moment, blinking and trying to clear the fog of lust in his brain, then he followed Brandon out of the car and caught him as he came around the front end. Jake grabbed him and threw him against the hood of the car, flattening him there and kissing him again feverishly in the semi-privacy of his large, wooded front yard.

Brandon's breath whooshed out of his chest as he hit the hood, Jake's weight atop him and around him and eating him alive, feeding the hunger that flared inside him. He clung to the other man, arms closing around wide shoulders and one leg curling around firm thighs, his other knee propped up so that Jake ground their groins together. He was only dimly aware of the light breeze blowing through the trees as the sun set.

Jake all but devoured him, pressing him against the hood of the car and kissing him as if he had been deprived of the privilege for years. His hands roamed over Brandon's body, depending on the sheer force of his body weight to keep him from getting away, and he rocked against him, demanding more.

There was no way Brandon was going to summon the strength to resist this. It was everything he wanted to be reassured. Wanted. Craved. *Oh God.* His cock was rock hard and practically screaming at him, and he didn't doubt for one second that if this went on much longer he was coming right then and there.

Somewhere in the distance a dog began barking, but Jake didn't even lift his head as he continued to kiss Brandon with everything he had. He didn't even part for air, instead forcing them both to breathe noisily through their noses as Jake's hands dragged over Brandon's body.

Brandon arched up against him, needy sounds garbled by their kiss. His hands gripped strong shoulders and started pulling the jersey from the back of Jake's pants, then the Under Armour, digging for warm, smooth skin.

Jake growled aggressively and lifted Brandon up off the car just enough to slam him back into the hood with a clang and a rattle, pushing closer to him and insinuating himself between his legs as he did so.

"Jesus *fuck*!" Brandon cried out roughly in response, his hands sliding into the form-fitting pants to grip Jake's bare hips as he went spiraling towards orgasm, desperately wrapping his legs around the other man and forcing his hips upward. He was *so fucking close* to losing his mind.

Jake rocked against him, one hand coming up to tangle in his hair and pull his head back to give Jake access to his neck. He pressed the length of his entire body down against Brandon's and began to suck and nip at the most tender spots under his ear and chin.

A soft wail ripping from him, Brandon gasped wildly. "Jake–Jake!" he grated, teetering on the edge.

Jake moved his mouth back to cover Brandon's with more

hungry kisses. "Shh," he urged, the sound muffled by Brandon's mouth as Jake rocked into him rhythmically.

Brandon shivered hard in Jake's arms. His fingers flexed and dug in as his vision went out of whack and he climaxed hard with a grunt against Jake's lips, hips jutting upward with each pulse washing through him.

Jake finally lost his grip on himself and moaned against Brandon's lips when he realized the other man was coming. He gasped into the kiss, hand tightening in Brandon's hair. Under Jake, Brandon shuddered, head hanging back so that his neck arched as he sucked in breaths. His head was spinning. Jake's movements finally slowed as Brandon's breathing began to calm, and he kissed Brandon's neck up and down in a random, almost frantic manner; following his jaw line and moving suddenly to his mouth again before nipping at his neck once more.

Squeezing Jake a little closer, Brandon sighed and tried to find some composure. "Jake," he said softly. "Take me in the house. You can't fuck me out here."

"I bet I could," Jake argued in a low growl before kissing him again.

Brandon's exhale was a soft moan as desire continued to zip through him. "Ohhhkaaay," he answered weakly, eyes rolling back into his head as he clung to the other man.

Jake kissed him again and slowly eased up on the pressure he was exerting, letting Brandon slide to the ground carefully while he backed up a step. Brandon reopened his eyes once his cleats touched the ground and he looked up at Jake with glazed eyes.

Jake licked his lips and cracked a smile through the haze of lust he was still battling. "You just gonna stand there or should I carry you?"

Brandon pushed himself up on his elbows, still bent back over the hood, chuckling. "You're gonna carry me?" he asked in obvious disbelief.

"If you don't move your ass inside I will," Jake threatened with a point to the door, his voice taking on a decidedly impatient and hungry edge.

Not wanting to risk it, Brandon pushed himself off the car and wavered a little, having to catch himself against the fender for a second. Then he made purposefully for the stairs. Jake followed him, practically vibrating, and as soon as he made it through the unblocked front door Jake tackled him again. Literally tackled him, landing them both on the sofa as Jake began pawing at him yet again. Brandon yelped and turned just in time to catch Jake around the middle before he hit the couch on his back. "Damn, Jake!" he laughed, trying to help the other man get into his clothes.

"You asked for it," Jake argued as he yanked at Brandon's uniform demandingly.

"I asked for it?" Brandon repeated, pushing on Jake's chest to get enough room to pull his own jersey and shirt off. "Tell me how you figure that," he breathed.

"I'm not sure," Jake huffed impatiently, pressing Brandon into the couch as soon as he had the shirts off and kissing him hungrily. "But I'm sure I'm right," he murmured distractedly, tugging his own jersey over his head.

Brandon really didn't care. He moaned instead as his hands came into contact with hot skin, and he worked on toeing out of his cleats, each one thumping to the floor so he could spread his legs for Jake to get closer.

And Jake took advantage of the invitation, grabbing Brandon's thighs and tugging him until he was on the edge of the couch. Jake laid himself out over him, one knee propped on the frame of the sofa as he dove into another series of heated kisses. Thinking he might just melt, Brandon met each touch, each kiss with enthusiasm, arousal spiking through him again with a slow, simmering heat. He couldn't imagine what Jake was feeling. He apparently had a hell of a lot more control than Brandon did. He groaned and bit Jake's lower lip as one hand slipped around the back of Jake's neck to hold him in place.

Jake actually whimpered, sliding his hands under Brandon to bring their bodies closer. "I didn't exactly think this through," he whined as he pulled back and looked up at the stairs, estimating the distance they had to travel to get to the bed.

Brandon grinned up at him. "Get off me, ya big lug. I promise not to run away," he said. Jake stood and held out his hand to help Brandon to his feet. His entire body was practically vibrating. Brandon slid his hand into Jake's and used the leverage to push himself off the couch to find himself standing chest to chest with him. It was difficult to resist kissing again. "C'mon," he said. He could see how Jake shook. He pulled the bigger man behind him up the stairs and into the bedroom, where he started pulling off his socks.

Jake started on his belt and pushed down the baseball pants, only remembering when they pooled at his feet that he'd not yet taken off his shoes. He shuffled to the bed and began yanking off items of clothing haphazardly, tossing them to the floor and growling with each one that came off.

Shucking his baseball pants, Brandon grimaced at the damp, sticky mess of his briefs. "Look at this mess you caused," he accused playfully.

"Better get even with me," Jake told him with a smirk as he divested himself of the last of his clothing. Brandon huffed and shoved the briefs over his hips and down his legs, pulling them off and using them to wipe up a bit before throwing them to the floor and stalking toward Jake on the bed.

Jake's entire body flushed with warmth and anticipation as Brandon got closer, and he found himself, for once, unable to move. Brandon stopped right in front of him and reached out to run his fingers through Jake's hair. "You gonna be a good boy and clean it up?" Brandon rasped, curious as to what Jake would do; Brandon wasn't usually this forward, mostly content to let Jake be the aggressor.

Jake's shoulders stiffened and his eyelashes fluttered as he tried to maintain eye contact. He never knew which Brandon he was going to get, and *God*, there were two very different Brandons inside the man he was beginning to think of as his lover. After a brief, tense moment of pondering this, Jake reached out and dug his fingers into Brandon's hips, sliding himself off the end of the bed to his knees in front of the man.

Swallowing hard when Jake got to his knees, Brandon petted

his hair reassuringly. Hell, he'd have been thrilled if Jake stayed sitting to do this. The few times he'd taken the lead, Brandon had braced himself for Jake's refusal, but it hadn't come yet. Jake tilted his head into the strokes of Brandon's hand and licked at the head of his cock slowly, closing his eyes and humming as he took it into his mouth. Brandon hissed and kept petting, caressing the curve of Jake's skull as his hips shifted slightly.

Jake raised up a little, taking him further into his mouth and sliding his hands slowly around to pull at Brandon's hips. He knew he couldn't stay down there long enough to make Brandon come again. That wasn't really his goal here anyway. He wanted Brandon to know that Jake wasn't the only one in the relationship who should feel free to toss the other around. To be in charge.

Brandon groaned as the wet heat of Jake's mouth moved on him, an interesting counterpoint to the soft hair that ruffled under his hands. But as good as it felt, he couldn't let Jake stay on his knees. He didn't want any part of them being together to be painful. He gradually pulled back, the sight of his half-hard cock sliding out of Jake's lips enough to help him harden a little more. "C'mon," he said, leaning over to slide his arms under Jake's to help him to his feet. Instead of standing up, though, Jake pulled Brandon down with him, reaching up to him and tugging in an oddly sweet gesture.

Surprised, Brandon went down on one knee, pulling back a little bit, a slight frown on his face. Jake reached for him without a word, taking his face in his hands and kissing him. The gentle kiss kept Brandon off-balance, and he leaned into Jake's arms as they kissed tenderly, *oh Christ*, almost lovingly. He had to stop thinking this way. It was a sure road to disaster, though he'd enjoy the ride. One of his hands sprawled across Jake's chest, just touching.

Jake moved until his hand covered Brandon's resting on his chest, and his other hand stayed at Brandon's face, his thumb sliding over Brandon's cheekbone. His entire body thrummed with the need for release, but he ignored it. This gentle kiss intoxicated him. For his part, Brandon was terrified of moving. He didn't want to do anything that might end this moment. It was so unlike anything he'd felt before, his chest aching as he trembled under the gentle attention.

Several times Jake pulled back from the kiss, intending to end it only to tilt his head the other way and delve back into it for more, still gentle. His heart raced, but he didn't know why. His breath was gone like it had been sucked out of him by a cold wind, but he didn't know why. All he knew was that this felt incredible. Familiar. Right.

"Jake," Brandon whispered in an aching voice. He wanted to know where this was coming from; he wanted to ask if Jake felt like he did. But the words wouldn't come. He didn't want to move an inch from Jake's arms.

Jake pulled back just far enough to rest his forehead against Brandon's, and when he spoke he was still close enough that their lips brushed. "Are you asking me to stop?" he asked quietly, heart in his throat.

"Never," Brandon breathed without hesitation. They were so close that Brandon's eyes were still closed, and his fingers clenched on Jake's shoulder. Jake responded by merely pressing his lips to Brandon's again, whimpering a little as the lust finally began to overpower whatever magic this surreal kiss had created. Brandon's voice was almost inaudible between kisses. "Please don't stop."

Jake gasped out a breath and dragged the air back in, barely able to breathe as Brandon begged him. "I want you," he rasped between kisses.

"I'm yours," Brandon sighed against Jake's lips.

Jake groaned against the gust of the words, surprised at the rush of emotion they caused in him. He hesitated, not wanting to end the moment, but his desire won out, and he urged Brandon to stand with him as he struggled to his feet.

Brandon shook so hard he had to hold onto Jake for balance once they got their feet again. He curled his arms around Jake's neck, sliding close against him, clinging for all he was worth.

Jake simply turned them both, laying Brandon out on the bed beneath him; then began to commando crawl up the bed, sliding Brandon with him until they were close enough for Jake to stretch across to the bedside table. As he reached for the handle his fingers shook.

Feeling drunk on Jake's scent, Brandon moaned and nuzzled his neck before he moved, hands sliding along his arms and back, pulling his eyes open to watch him longingly.

Jake grabbed the bottle and looked back down as he ran his free hand along Brandon's chest. "When I saw you running," he said before he could think twice about it, "I didn't even know it was you and I wanted you."

Brandon lifted his hand to slide his fingers along Jake's chin. "Hmmm. Might make me jealous, wanting some stranger running around the track," he murmured.

"I felt guilty for it," Jake admitted breathlessly as he turned his head into the touch and closed his eyes.

"Guilty? For wanting a stranger?" Brandon asked, caressing Jake's cheek with his knuckles. Jake nodded, not opening his eyes as he blushed slightly. His hand dragged down Brandon's side, sliding under his hip. Brandon raised an eyebrow. "And when you figured out it was me?" he fished.

Jake breathed out heavily again and lowered his head, one hand working under Brandon's thigh to lift his leg slowly and wrap it around Jake's hip. "I was relieved," he answered in a hoarse gust of breath.

Brandon tightened his leg around Jake, one arm sliding around his neck. He wanted to beg for clarification – relieved it wasn't someone else? Or did that mean Jake felt something for him? Instead, he tried laughing it off. "Well, that does a lot of good for my ego," he poked, smiling a little.

Jake turned his head and pressed his lips to Brandon's demandingly, shifting his hips to settle between his legs. "Means that some time between Friday and this morning I fell pretty damn hard for you," he breathed, his heart pounding.

Sweet Jesus. "Fell for me– me?" Brandon asked in surprise, fingers gripping Jake hard as he hoped with everything that was in him.

"Hard," Jake breathed with a nod, his face pressed against Brandon's cheek, unable to look at him.

Brandon moaned sharply as he clasped Jake's face between his hands and pulled him up to kiss him, ever so lightly, gentle, like before. "Me too," he whispered.

Jake's breath left him in a little rush of air, and he kissed Brandon yet again, reaching between them with his other hand to slide a lubricated finger into the man little by little .

Shuddering, Brandon's breath hitched, then relaxed utterly as he fell into the kiss. This was not 'just sex' anymore. Not to him.

"Christ, what have we done?" Jake panted as he kissed Brandon urgently and prepared him as quickly as he dared.

"Don't know, just don't stop, please," Brandon begged as soon as their lips parted, writhing under him. Jake nodded obediently and lifted himself up, covering his cock in the slick lubricant and then lowering himself back down to capture Brandon's lips as he guided himself in.

"Jake, oh *God*, don't let me go," Brandon whispered, closing his eyes as he welcomed the other man into his body, hitching both legs up around his waist. "Oh please..." He was out of his mind with what Jake had admitted. It exploded in his head and burned through him like wildfire.

Jake responded by rocking his hips and groaning as he slid his hand under Brandon's shoulders to pull their bodies closer together. Brandon wrapped around Jake like a limpet... he thought distantly that this was getting totally out of hand, echoing Jake's most recent question. But he couldn't bring himself to focus on it, not when he wanted this so much. "Now, Jake, now," he breathed.

Jake pulled back and slammed into him, rocking deep inside before repeating the motion and falling into a punishing rhythm, whimpering and moaning Brandon's name as he tried to keep the pace. Brandon's abandoned cries of pleasure only served to encourage Jake further, and he gave up on any pretense of gentility. Brandon bit his lip against even more inappropriate words as the thrusts jarred him, almost as if each snap of his body was emphasizing what he felt.

Jake gasped now with each thrust into Brandon's body,

groaning as if the effort of not coming was too much for him to take without a struggle. He pulled almost entirely out of Brandon after every thrust, wanting to make damn certain Brandon enjoyed it. The pleasure and effort began to make him lightheaded, and with that came a complete loss of his considerable control. He cried out suddenly, pushing up to his knees and dragging Brandon's hips up into his lap as he tried desperately to fight back his orgasm and fuck Brandon at the same time.

The lost sound wrenched from Jake made Brandon arch up against him. He gave a rough yell of strained pleasure as his entire body stiffened, and Brandon threw back his head and cried out his lover's name as he slammed into orgasm, the proof of it marking them both with hot slickness. Jake's body curled over his, hips losing their rhythm as his fingers dug into Brandon's skin, and he came with a tortured shout.

His muscles twitched and clenched through the orgasm and Brandon was afraid he'd break out crying at the gorgeous pleasure of it, God help him. He squeezed his eyes shut and rode it out, wrapped around Jake as his shout echoed in his ears.

It felt like hours before Jake stopped shivering. He pushed up and looked down at Brandon finally, panting slightly, eyes screwed shut, skin glistening with sweat. Without a word he carefully pulled out, gasping at the over-stimulation of the friction, and lowered himself to his side next to Brandon.

Brandon didn't even wait. He rolled over to wrap his arms back around Jake's neck, curling as close as he could get while still trying to catch his breath.

Jake held him close, shutting his eyes as he tried to remember why in the *hell* he'd told Brandon what he had. And what was more, it was true. And Brandon had reciprocated, something Jake had never expected. "We're in quite a mess now," he murmured affectionately.

Tightening his arms, Brandon nodded against Jake's chest. He didn't trust himself to speak just yet. He was quite afraid of what might come out.

Not getting any response, Jake frowned, worried, and lowered his head to press his lips against Brandon's forehead. "Did I hurt you?" he asked softly.

"No," Brandon murmured, shaking his head to reinforce his response. After a few moments, he had to say something. "A mess, huh?"

"I'm a mess," Jake responded with a nod.

Brandon smiled a little and chuckled, keeping his head tucked against Jake's neck. "No, you specifically said *we're* in quite a mess."

"Well, now, we are," Jake argued sensibly. "Doesn't mean the inner Jake isn't doing a Snoopy dance, but it's still a mess."

Pulling back to look at Jake incredulously, Brandon just *barely* held back a guffaw. "A *'Snoopy'* dance?"

"You can't tell me you don't know what I'm talking about," Jake insisted haughtily, raising his chin to hide the smile that played at his lips.

"Ah, okay," Brandon said. He was more interested in the rest of what Jake said anyway. "I'm glad I could make you dance inside," he murmured, pressing a soft kiss to the corner of Jake's mouth. Jake responded in kind, pulling Brandon closer and turning his head into the kiss.

Brandon sighed, but didn't want to let the question slip away. It would bother him all night. "Jake. Mess. Talk," he murmured against swollen lips.

Jake groaned plaintively and sighed as he rested his head back on the pillow. "If we're ever found out," he murmured in answer, "it could ruin us. And now we've got the added bonus of getting our hearts broken if something goes wrong."

Brandon drew in a slow breath. He really hadn't expected Jake to put it so plainly. But there it was, clear as day. "So now what?" he murmured, huddling in closer with his forehead against Jake's shoulder, afraid to look at the other man's face. "Do we just stop?" His voice broke at the end, reflecting how very much he did *not* want that. Jesus. They'd been 'together' for three days. *Only three days*.

"Pfft. I'm cynical, not masochistic," Jake answered with a small laugh, squeezing Brandon tight.

The breath audibly stuttered out of Brandon as he tightened his arms around Jake. "I'm glad," he murmured against warm skin.

Jake ducked his head to nuzzle against Brandon's temple and sighed. "I need to go get my pills," he whispered regretfully. He didn't want to get up, but he knew if he left it much longer he wouldn't sleep at all.

Brandon sighed too and started to move. "Stay here. I'll get them," he murmured, rolling out of the bed and padding out toward the kitchen.

"Don't forget the alcohol!" Jake called out as he lay in bed shivering at the sudden loss of warmth.

"Don't get your hopes up!" Brandon yelled back from the stairs. Wincing a little at the cold tile in the kitchen, he opened the cabinet he'd seen Jake get into, frowned at all the little bottles, and started reading labels.

Thinking about the cabinet, Jake huffed and rolled out of bed, wincing as he stood. Adrenaline was a wonderful thing. After the fact was when it hurt to move. He padded through the hallway, down the stairs, and into the kitchen to slide up behind Brandon. Reaching into the cabinet for the large prescription bottle on the bottom shelf, he kissed the back of Brandon's shoulder, then turned to the refrigerator.

"Jake, most of these are expired; why do you keep them? These types of drugs don't keep their efficacy, you might as well be taking sugar pills," Brandon said with a frown, poking around through the bottles. "And some could be dangerous if mixed."

"The labels don't mean shit," Jake answered as he reached in for a beer and straightened back up to lean against the island.

Brandon threw an annoyed look over his shoulder. "Please tell me you don't mix and match these. Really," he asked.

Jake shrugged noncommittally and popped the two pills into his mouth before twisting open the beer cap.

Brandon looked nervous and on the edge of scared. He glanced back to the cabinet, then back to Jake. "If I quit giving you the eye about the muscle relaxers and the beer, will you let me throw the rest of this shit out?" he asked seriously.

"Maybe."

"Jake," Brandon protested, voice pained. "I really, really would like to know you're going to wake up every morning."

Jake sighed and his shoulders slumped. "It's not that big a deal."

Brandon literally flinched, and he turned his chin sharply away, unable to verbalize anything after what felt like it might as well have been a punch in the gut. He twisted his body away from Jake's, gripping the edge of the bar to keep from reaching for him.

Jake watched Brandon's reaction and his stomach turned as he stood there. He sighed softly and looked away, shaking his head as he tapped his finger on his beer bottle. "Brandon," he finally said.

Forcing himself to take a breath and blink burning eyes, Brandon turned his chin just enough to acknowledge him. Jake took a step forward and slid up behind him, wrapping his arms around him and setting the bottle on the counter. He rested his chin on Brandon's shoulder and looked up into the still open cabinet. "What do you want me to do?" he asked quietly.

He suspected Jake meant the pills, and Brandon did make his eyes focus on the several rows of bottles, but what he had inside had to come out. "I want you to wake up each morning," he said in a fragile voice. "With me."

Jake turned his head just enough to press his nose against the side of Brandon's neck. There were a lot of different meanings he could take from that, he knew. Was Brandon still talking about the pills and the possible danger of taking them, or was he talking about something more personal? Either way, it was a tricky subject, wasn't it?

"Then stay here with me," Jake responded finally, not giving himself a chance to think it through.

Brandon relaxed back against Jake, sliding his hands over strong forearms to settle over Jake's fingers. How they'd gotten onto such shaky ground, he didn't know. Brandon cursed himself for getting too serious too fast, although Jake seemed to be right there with him. "I want to," he whispered. Then his voice strengthened. "And I want to flush most of this shit down the toilet," he added.

"That would make me mighty cranky," Jake muttered with a sigh. "You do realize most of those aren't even prescription pills, right? I've put over the counter stuff in the smaller bottles because the shelves are so small. And the prescription stuff I do take is the only thing keeping me moving at all," he argued, trying not to get defensive.

Brandon's eyes softened, and he turned his chin to rub his forehead against Jake's chin. "I want you to take care of yourself," he said helplessly, still frowning at the bottles. "I hate that you hurt."

"So do I," Jake laughed wryly, reaching out to pluck a bottle at random off the shelf. He opened and dumped several of the pills out onto the counter. "Tylenol Arthritis," he said as he turned one of the huge white pills so that the name could be read. He reached for another and repeated the action, revealing a mound of little bitty pink Benadryl pills. Another container held blue and white Tylenol PM tablets. And another Jake pulled out revealed several Tylox. He pointed at them and said, "I'm allergic to those, but they're stronger. If I'm hurting real bad I take one of those and two Benadryl with it."

Surprised, Brandon watched in silence as Jake went through several of the bottles with him. It was more than he could have hoped for, considering. Matching up the number of surgeries with the pain and looking over the medicines spread across the bar, Brandon's gut cramped uncomfortably. "I think I understand the beer a little more now," he murmured. He didn't like it. But he understood it. He was also more upset, because this revealed just how much pain Jake must be living with daily. Just living with. His hand curled into a fist.

Jake smiled a little, his chin still on Brandon's shoulder. "And," he held his breath for a moment, sighing heavily and pushing at the bottle of Vicodin. "If you really want me to give those up, we're talking a few weeks of withdrawal. I'd rather wait 'til summer if it's all the same to you."

The anger drained away as Brandon comprehended what Jake was offering. His fist relaxed, and he reached up behind him to curl his arm about Jake's neck. It was a hell of a peace offering. "How about we talk about it when school's out?" he posed, knowing he was making several large assumptions based on Jake's words.

"And until then you stop worrying?" Jake countered.

Brandon licked his bottom lip, looking across the counter and the host of pills. "I'll try," he promised in a hoarse voice.

Jake sighed again and nodded as he lifted his head off Brandon's shoulder and kissed the warm skin gently. "I've been doing this for over ten years," he murmured, "I'm okay. I'll be okay." His voice, although the tone was reassuring, sounded slightly bitter and tinged with sadness. It was obvious that Jake had long ago resigned himself to pain every day. He was willing to give up the prescription pills because the reality was that they *didn't* help all that much.

Sighing and trying to push away his worry and uncertainty, Brandon looked over at the clock. "We didn't have dinner and it's still early. Want something to eat?" he asked.

"Yeah," Jake answered, kissing Brandon's neck one last time for good measure before he stepped back to let him move. He looked Brandon up and down appraisingly and smirked. "Want some clothes?"

Glancing down at himself, Brandon rolled his eyes. "What's the matter?" he asked, his voice slowly going back to normal. "Don't like the free show?"

"Mystery can be alluring," Jake countered with a wag of his finger. "And cooking while naked is not recommended," he added with a serious nod.

Brandon laughed at him. "You need to get yourself some clothes then, Thundercat. Because whatever I attempted to fix would not be edible. I wasn't kidding when I said I couldn't cook."

Jake muttered and then took a long gulp of his beer. "Pasta?" he suggested after swallowing.

Nodding, Brandon leaned over to kiss him sweetly. "I'm getting in the shower. Want some clothes?" he asked, eyes brightening at his joke.

"Hmph," Jake answered as he wrapped one arm around

Brandon and squeezed his ass in a blatant move.

A little over an hour later, they were back on the couch, Brandon with papers and pen, wearing more of Jake's clothes, Jake with the television remote and baseball. The science teacher glanced over his glasses in amusement each time Jake crowed or cussed, but held his tongue as he graded. It was comfortable. It was comforting.

When the game ended, Brandon glanced at the clock and groaned. 11:30. He started stacking papers and sliding them into his backpack in resignation. Jake had asked him to stay after Brandon had expressed his desire to wake up with him. But tonight it just wouldn't work. He had no clothes for work and his tests for tomorrow were on his computer at home.

"Spring training games can bite my ass," Jake grumbled as he clicked off the television. He looked over at Brandon and tried not to sigh. He knew Brandon had things to take care of at home.

Brandon chuckled and pulled off his glasses. "Opening day next week," he reminded as he closed his pack and stood up. Jake muttered disconsolately and sulked on the couch. "Christ, don't do that, Jake. I'll be driving home and back at 4 a.m.," Brandon said.

Jake glanced up at him in surprise and then huffed and stood up slowly. "You'd better get going if you're going to get any sleep," he said, stepping closer to slide his hands around Brandon's waist.

"You know I don't want to go, right?" Brandon murmured, leaning his temple against Jake's lips.

"Mm hmm," Jake responded with a little huff.

Brandon sighed. "I'll see you tomorrow. Wash my uniform, will you?" he asked. "At least the pants and briefs."

"Oh sure, leave me alone *and* make me do manual labor," Jake teased with a little kiss to Brandon's ear before he pulled back. "Yeah, I'll wash 'em."

"Thanks," Brandon said, smiling. Reluctant to leave, he made himself step back, pick up his pack, and start for the door.

Jake watched him go with his shoulders hunched and his hands deep in the pockets of his sweats. It wouldn't be fair to ask him to stay or come back. And since that was exactly what Jake wanted to do, he kept his mouth shut.

"Hey, Jake?" Brandon asked from where he stopped in the doorway, keys in hand.

"Yeah?" Jake answered, trying to keep his voice even.

Several things warred for the opportunity to be spoken, and for a moment Brandon was afraid it would all spew out. After a long pause, he settled on, "Miss you already." And he was out the door before he lost the nerve to do what he had to do. Life had to go on, after all. Never mind that it hurt like hell to leave his lover.

Jake frowned as the door closed and sniffed loudly. He shuffled over to the front door and stood by the side window, watching as Brandon drove away.

Chapter II

STANDING beside the bus with a clipboard, Brandon tried to give out assignments to the players, two to a room, usually by grade level. He and Jonathan had spent the better part of the evening a few days ago thrashing out who could safely bunk with who. The guys stacked the gear and bags all around, blocking a big chunk of asphalt in the corner lot of the Holiday Inn Holidome in Tampa Bay, and the assistant coach sighed as he tried to get their attention again, finally losing his temper.

"Shut your traps and line up or you're all sleeping on the damn bus!" he barked over all their chatter, drawing huge eyes and silence. Coach Bartlett *never* yelled.

Jake raised his head and peered down from the window of the charter bus at Brandon, just as surprised as the kids seemed to be. He watched the boys all calm down and gather their things, and the other coaches began handing out room keys and checking off names.

The players didn't even peep as a disgruntled Coach Bartlett read off names and room assignments, and soon they scattered, heading into the hotel, glad to be free of constant supervision for awhile – not that Coach Campbell hadn't put the fear of God into them about leaving the premises without permission.

Sighing, Brandon muttered a 'yeah' to one of the college guys' question if he was okay. He wasn't okay. He was fucking exhausted. He'd slept all the way down here and felt worse. He couldn't remember the last time he'd been this cranky. Jonathan whistled in wonder and gave Brandon a wide berth as he climbed back into the bus.

"Hey Coach," Jonathan said quietly, approaching Jake. "What's with Bartlett? He's a bear today."

Jake shrugged and glanced back out the window. "No idea," he murmured.

"Well, I hope he works it out before this evening. I don't want to be in a room with him all night if he's in a snit," Jonathan said, picking up his duffle.

"I thought we each had our own rooms?" Jake asked as he straightened from repacking the bag he'd just been rifling through.

"Well, we did, until we got here and checked in. The hotel sold out too many rooms, so we had to double bunk. I put Troy in with you," Jonathan said and then he squinted. "Maybe that's why he's so pissed. He might have been looking forward to some peace and quiet on his own." He didn't sound offended, just thoughtful.

Jake swallowed, mind whirring as he tried to think of a way to fix this without being too suspicious. Finally he smirked and stuffed the last shirt into the bag. "I'll trade you Troy for Brandon," he offered playfully as he zipped up the bag. "Bastard snores like a freight train."

"How do you know... oh, yeah, from when he crashes at your place after away games. Well, hell, I won't turn down that offer. Troy's cuter anyway. Snoring doesn't bother me," Jonathan said with a laugh. "Here," he said, holding out a key, "trade me."

Jake reached out and took the key, smirking still. "You base your roommate choices on looks?" he teased.

"Nah, just my chances of getting laid," Jonathan shot back with a wide wink as he walked backward down the aisle. "And I was thinking my chances with Brandon were below nil, so even Troy's gotta be better." He laughed at his own joke as he exited the bus.

Jake raised his eyebrow and smiled, glancing back out the window at Brandon with a frown. He should know, after a month of being the man's lover, what was wrong with him tonight. But he was ashamed to admit that he had no clue. His chances of getting laid were probably pretty low as well.

Brandon knew he was being an asshole, but he was worn out, stressed, annoyed ... You name it, he felt it. He'd been looking forward to having his own room so Jake could be with him – or he with Jake – but then the room shakeup blew that all to hell.

The last week before spring break had disintegrated into utter hell: Two weeks of state testing, finishing up grading on annual tests, grades, A.P. exam prep, and baseball games on four out of seven nights. Brandon hadn't slept more than three hours a night, even at Jake's house. He was at the end of his rope, and he'd really been hoping this trip would make a difference.

He jerked his bag up onto his shoulder and slammed the storage compartment doors shut. Wasn't looking good.

Jake stepped out of the bus stairwell and glanced around to make sure the others were gone before he sauntered over to Brandon's side and gave him a shit-eating grin. "Cranky," he observed mildly.

Brandon gave him a very clear look that said 'don't push me.' "You have no idea," he muttered, feeling much worse about the room assignments now that his lover stood right next to him. Surely they could find some time somewhere, somehow. Or else Brandon was going to go absolutely fucking insane.

Jake waved his traded key and smiled even under the withering glare Brandon had given him. "I forgot to ask Jonathan which room it was."

"What room?" Brandon asked tiredly, patting his pockets, looking for the key card he'd stashed somewhere.

"Our room," Jake answered, watching Brandon closely.

Brandon looked at him blankly for a long moment. "Our room?" he whispered, something like hope flashing in his eyes.

"Jonathan begged me to take you because he didn't want to be eaten in his sleep," Jake informed Brandon primly, barely hiding the smile.

It was all Brandon could do not to drop all his bags and throw himself at Jake, and it was clear on his face. "Oh God, *thank you*," he whispered fervently.

Jake grinned and chuckled. "Maybe when we get in there you can tell me what's wrong?" he ventured as he turned and began to head for the hotel entrance.

Brandon sighed, shoulders sagging. "Yeah. Nothing major," he murmured. "Just letting it get to me." He led the way through the automatic doors, making for the entrance to the Holidome. The Parkview team had all the rooms on the left side of the pool, with the coaches' rooms dotted through the row. Glancing at his key card, Brandon made a face. It looked like they were all the way at the end.

Jake glanced around the hotel and grinned. "Hey, pool bar!" he cried happily, veering off like a little kid with a short attention span.

Glancing after him, Brandon rolled his eyes before following. Jake was already getting a beer when he got to the bar, and Brandon let his bags thump to the outdoor-carpeted floor. He scooted himself up onto a stool next to the other coach with a sigh. When the bartender looked to him, he requested, "Vodka twist. A double."

"Uh oh," Jake murmured as the man popped the top off his beer and slid it over the bar to him. "It's a *drinking* problem?" he asked, semi-worried.

Brandon rubbed at his eyes, thanking the bartender and taking a big swallow of the vodka, wincing before giving himself a shake and making a face. "I'm a mess," he muttered.

"Why?" Jake asked with a small frown.

And the rest of the double shot went down. "You remember how we talked about burnout at the beginning of the season?" Brandon asked miserably. He gestured for another.

"Yeah," Jake answered tentatively as he watched the glass drain. He'd offered to help several times, and Brandon had happily accepted, but he knew his various skills at grading and whatnot weren't nearly on par for the science teacher's high standards.

"I hit the wall this week. Hard." Brandon picked up the second glass and took another swallow. Jake merely nodded, wondering if he'd have to carry Brandon to the room. He'd never seen him drink more than a few beers.

Sighing, Brandon pressed the back of his hand holding the shot glass to his forehead. "I even had help. I still hit the wall," he mumbled. "Tom let me out of tutoring this week. Still didn't help. And here we make this trip, and I feel like utter shit."

Jake pursed his lips and looked off into the two-story lobby of the hotel, complete with indoor pool, hot tub, restaurant, and bar. "You could catch a flight home," he suggested with a careful shrug.

Brandon looked over at him, wishing he could say what he wanted out loud. He'd been wanting to say something for over a month now. He and Jake had been together about seven weeks, and to him, it had just gotten better and better. Except for working so much he didn't have time to sleep, much less get in anything else but a quickie with his boyfriend. Brandon winced. "Don't want to," he said.

"You could miss the game in the morning," Jake suggested. "Could say you're sick and just stay in and sleep. We've got plenty of extra coaches without the freshman team here."

Looking a little petulant, Brandon visibly suppressed the urge to pout. He didn't want to sleep unless he was with Jake. He'd found the last couple of weeks that he didn't really want to do much of anything without Jake. He threw back the rest of his drink and tossed a twenty on the bar. "How about we take a load off in the room? My ass is killing me from that damn bus."

"All righty," Jake agreed, taking his beer bottle with him. He had never even unshouldered his bag.

Brandon groaned and leaned over to drag his bag and backpack off the floor and start trudging down the walkway past the pool, reading off numbers under his breath. They got to the very end of the row, and no room. He frowned and looked down a little hall, and there off by itself was another room, a handicap-accessible one – right next to the vending machines. He checked the number. Yep. He keyed open the door and walked in.

"Snazzy," Jake muttered as he followed his cranky lover into the room.

Letting his bags drop to the floor, Brandon turned and

watched Jake close the door and step into the wide open room. Then he walked right over to him and wrapped one arm around Jake's neck, the other around his waist. He buried his face in Jake's shoulder and clung. Jake pulled him close and nuzzled against his temple as he hummed soothingly. He'd had these days before. He knew that sometimes you just needed to be cuddled and cooed to.

Brandon clutched him closer, letting himself ever so slowly relax, safe in Jake's arms. The soft sounds and touches helped, and after a couple of long minutes he asked in a small voice, "Would you hold me while I nap? Just for a little while?"

"Yeah," Jake murmured in answer, turning his head to kiss Brandon's cheek. "I've got to make the rounds first, though, okay?"

Nodding, Brandon squeezed him tight before letting go. He pulled his sweatshirt over his head, revealing the T-shirt Jake had given him forever ago. "I'm gonna unpack," he said.

Jake reached out and grabbed his shirt, tugging him closer to kiss him slowly. "Why don't you just crawl into bed?" he suggested in a low voice.

Sighing when Jake's lips pulled away, Brandon blinked at him sleepily. "Want to wait for you," he admitted.

Jake cocked his head in surprise and smiled slightly. "I'll be fast, then," he promised as he stepped away and turned to the door.

Brandon wrapped his arms around himself and watched Jake go. He was just wasted enough to think about going with him. Instead he grabbed his bag and tossed it on the dresser, then hefted up his backpack. He seriously thought about chucking it out the window. It would have been more impressive if the room wasn't on the first floor. But he stood there staring at the window anyway.

Jake made the rounds, going first to Troy and Jonathan's room to get the master list and then going to each room to check the kids. He took their IDs, including the fake ones, and the kids all handed them over readily because they knew Jake would give them back when they got home without a word about them. He gave each group the same warning he always did about being caught out of the rooms: buying a bus ticket home and turning in their uniforms were the least of their problems if they wandered.

It took nearly an hour, but Jake was certain that no one would be out of line tonight when he returned to the room he and Brandon shared.

Brandon managed to make it twenty minutes before sitting on the edge of the bed, another ten before he leaned back against the headboard. Five minutes after that he'd collapsed over to hug a pillow to him as he fell into a troubled doze. It was hard to sleep without Jake now. It felt wrong.

Jake entered the room quietly and stepped up to the end of the bed in his sock feet. With a small smile he began taking off most of his clothing. He didn't dare strip when it was possible that someone might knock on their door at any moment, but he got down to his boxers and crawled into bed behind Brandon. He curled around him and kissed the back of his neck softly.

Just the warmth of Jake close was enough for Brandon to start relaxing, and he sighed his lover's name, already mostly asleep. The furrows carved on his face smoothed as he turned up his chin to press his cheek to Jake's lips.

"Hey baby," Jake murmured in Brandon's ear, pulling him closer.

"Mmmmmm?" Brandon shifted to his back, turning toward Jake instinctively.

Jake pulled him closer and kissed him. "You drunk?" he asked in amusement.

Brandon's lips turned up slightly. "God, I wish," he mumbled, "'cept then I wouldn't be able to appreciate this." He kept turning until his chest pressed against Jake's, sliding his face into the curve of Jake's neck, pressing his lips to soft skin.

"One day I'm gonna get you drunk," Jake promised with a smirk, "and grope you."

Brandon groaned. "You don't want to do that. Really. I'm a silly-ass drunk."

"And that's different than normal how?" Jake chuckled,

cuddling Brandon closer to him.

A happy smile spread on Brandon's face. "Missed this," he murmured, opening his hands to splay his fingers over Jake's chest.

"It's been right here," Jake whispered as he ducked his head and kissed Brandon gently.

Brandon winced and sighed in apology. "Not been fair to you," he murmured, soaking up being so close.

"Don't worry about it, baby," Jake murmured with another kiss. "It's enough to do this every night."

Brandon pressed his face closer, deliberately inhaling Jake's scent with a low, slow breath. He was so sleepy, but he didn't want to give up enjoying this time close to Jake. "I gotta cut back," he murmured to himself. "This is more important."

Jake turned his head and brushed his chin against Brandon's hair, frowning at the words. *Cut back?* "Cut back on what?" he prodded.

"Mmm. Work. Running myself ragged," Brandon answered drowsily. "Rather be with you."

"Are you saying you want to quit coaching?" Jake asked evenly, though he wasn't sure why the thought upset him so much.

Brandon stiffened. "No," he said, waking up a little. "I was thinking more along the lines of shelving the doctorate and quitting the tutoring." He fell quiet for a few moments. "Do you think I should quit coaching?"

Jake hesitated, frowning thoughtfully. "Which do you enjoy more?" he finally asked in response.

Rousing himself to give it some serious thought, Brandon tried to separate the fact that coaching meant more time with Jake. He'd been doing the tutoring for five years now, and while he did enjoy it, it wasn't at all challenging. The doctorate just didn't seem to be coming together. And with the baseball team, for the first time, he was accepted. Included. Welcomed. He sighed. "The coaching," he murmured.

"Then that's what I think you should do," Jake answered, his voice betraying that he hadn't expected that answer.

Brandon shifted back so he could look at Jake. "You sound surprised," he said. Honestly, he was, too. But then a lot of things in his life had changed the past couple of months.

Jake shrugged a little guiltily and smiled. "A lot of things about you have surprised me," he admitted as he rested his head back down on the pillow.

"Like what?" Brandon asked, smile pulling into a grin.

Jake just shrugged again, blushing slightly and pulling Brandon closer to hide his face against his neck. Brandon laughed and poked Jake's ribs. "C'mon now," he wheedled. Jake swatted at him and rolled until he was on top, burrowing his face into Brandon's neck and growling playfully.

"Man, pulling information out of you is like pulling teeth," Brandon said, still laughing. "Fine. I'll just go with my current assumption that you're rather fond of me," he said as he slid his arms around Jake's neck.

Jake pulled back then and kissed him, smiling as he did so. "I *am* rather fond of you," he murmured cheekily between kisses.

"Well, I sure hope so. You up to seeing me more in the mornings and evenings? Wouldn't want to wear out my welcome. I've been spending a lot of time at your house already," Brandon's voice teased, and for the most part he felt that way. But buried underneath it was uncertainty.

"It's easier, right?" Jake asked with a frown as he propped himself up on Brandon's chest and looked down at him. "Staying with me?"

Brandon looked up at him evenly, the teasing gone. "I don't stay with you because it's easy."

Jake returned the serious look for a long moment before breaking into a teasing grin. "You stay with me 'cause it's hard?" he asked innocently.

Lips clamping on a smile, Brandon thumped Jake's chest with the back of one hand, shaking his head. "Yeah," he said wryly. "That's it exactly." He was slowly figuring out that he wasn't going to get words from Jake. But the actions were pretty damn incredible, and he told himself to be content with that.

"Is it?" Jake asked in a more serious voice as he leaned back down to brush his lips over Brandon's again. "Exactly?"

Sliding his hand into Jake's hair, Brandon contradicted himself. "Not exactly," he whispered against his mouth.

Jake grunted and kissed him again. "Tell me," he urged, the words gusting over Brandon's lips.

Brandon shivered and closed his eyes. "Tell you what?" he asked. "Why I stay?" His fingers clenched into Jake's skin, holding on tight. He was afraid he'd ruin it. Jake merely nodded, his nose brushing against Brandon's cheek.

Jesus. Brandon was so tempted to keep turning it around, each of them asking question after question as they banged the issue around like a crazed ping-pong ball, but he didn't think he could take it. Brandon was already so tired and out of emotional fortitude that he'd let the conversation stray to this. His heart pounded. "Because I want to. I want you. And I hope –" his voice faltered, and he had to swallow before he could continue, "hope someday you might want more."

Jake closed his eyes and smiled against Brandon's lips. "I do," he responded simply.

Three heartbeats. "*Christ*," Brandon choked out. "Why the hell did you make me go through that?" he asked, if possible clutching Jake closer.

"Go through what?" Jake asked, innocent and wide-eyed as he raised his head again.

Growling, Brandon shifted his hands and went for Jake's ribs and ticklish spots. "Bastard," he swore.

Jake squawked and flopped to his side, curling up like a cat to protect his belly. "What'd I do?" he cried as he fended off the jabbing fingers. Brandon kept at him, sliding one hand down to catch the sensitive skin behind one of his knees, muttering all the while as he tried to get Jake on his back. Jake flopped again and wrapped his arms around Brandon to hold him closer, close enough that he couldn't reach him anywhere. "Bad!" he scolded.

"Bad? Me? Bad?" Brandon huffed. "Son of a bitch, making me think I'm going to scare you off. Always teasing and making light of things."

"But..."

"No buts!" Brandon insisted as he took Jake by surprise, rolling them and straddling his hips. He grabbed at Jake's wrists. "You tell *me* now, Jake. If only this once."

"Tell you what?" Jake asked teasingly as he stretched out under Brandon and smiled. The smile faded and his eyes darkened as he looked up at his lover. "That I think I'm in love with you?" he asked seriously.

Brandon stared down at Jake with wide eyes, totally speechless. Then he shook himself. "Not– Not unless you mean it," he stuttered. He saw Jake's eyes change, change like they did when they were in the midst of driving each other crazy, and his breath caught.

Jake was silent, looking up at Brandon in the light of the single lamp. "I'm pretty sure I love you," he stated calmly.

Brandon thought his heart would give out before Jake said something else. And his comment was just as earthshaking as the one before it. Brandon slowly let go of Jake's wrists, lowering his hands to the other man's chest as he peered at him in wonder. Jake gave him a crooked, slightly self-conscious smile and shrugged.

Brandon studied him, drawing on the cues he'd memorized in Jake's behavior. "You're not teasing," he murmured, a statement rather than a question.

"No," Jake answered with a shake of his head. He was beginning to wonder if he'd been a little too hasty. He'd thought he'd read Brandon right, he usually did, and he'd thought he'd get a similar admission in return. Now he was getting a little nervous. And blushing harder.

Jake's reddening cheeks made Brandon smile, and he slowly bent over until their chests touched and their mouths rubbed together. His eyes closed, eyelashes brushing over Jake's cheekbones. Jake licked his lips and closed his eyes, raising his chin and humming. Brandon's tongue followed after his lover's, lightly skimming into a kiss, slow and easy. And when the kiss ended, he sighed, cheek to cheek with Jake. "Love you, too," he breathed.

Jake didn't move or speak. He simply kept his eyes closed and tried to remember to breathe. He'd never told anyone he loved them. And he'd never been happy to hear it before this moment. A shiver ran through him, and he turned his head against Brandon's, sliding his hands around the other man's back.

Brandon had nothing else to say. Nothing could top that one, he thought, feeling dizzy and warm all over. Jake said it first. *Amazing*. He drew in an easy breath, the vise around his chest giving way, and slowly levered himself up to look at his lover. Love, now. Not just lover.

Jake finally opened his eyes and looked up to meet Brandon's. "You still tired?" he asked after a moment of composing himself.

"I feel remarkably energized, actually," Brandon said, eyebrow quirking. "I'm sure I'll crash hard later, though."

Jake smiled briefly and then bit his lower lip, a frown creasing his forehead. He couldn't think of a thing to say. His heart was still racing.

Brandon's brow furrowed, and he reached to slide the pad of his thumb over the abused lip. "What's this for?" he asked in a soft voice.

Jake's eyes closed at the gentle touch, and he smiled again. "We've made me speechless," he answered with a little laugh.

Grinning, Brandon lightly nudged the tip of Jake's nose with a knuckle. "No witty comeback?"

Jake huffed and shook his head. "Kiss me," he requested softly. More than happy to obey, Brandon didn't hesitate, dipping his head to capture Jake's lips in a slow, open-mouth kiss that lasted for some time before he finally pulled away. Jake reached up as soon as Brandon moved and tugged him back down, moaning into the second kiss and tangling his fingers in Brandon's hair.

Heat tearing through Brandon's gut, he pressed his body closer to Jake's, starting to rock his hips slowly, a groan escaping from deep in his throat. Every touch and every sound took on a whole layer of meaning, and Brandon's hand shook as he cupped Jake's face.

Jake groaned and raised his knee to slide his foot over Brandon's calves, wrapping his legs around him as he did so. He jumped violently when a knock sounded on the door.

When Jake sat up suddenly, Brandon flailed and grabbed at his lover's shoulders to keep from flying backward. But his pulse spiked, and he closed his eyes, gasping for breath. "Fuck," he hissed, his denim-covered groin rubbing against Jake's boxers-covered one.

"Yeah?" Jake called out in answer to the knock, his voice only a little hoarse.

"Got some surprise visitors for you, Coach." Troy's voice came through the door.

Brandon lowered his forehead to Jake's shoulder for a few seconds before pushing himself back to crawl off Jake's lap.

Jake flopped back down and sighed as he willed his body to calm. After a moment he rolled off the bed and slid back into the track pants and T-shirt he'd shed earlier and then shuffled to the door to open it.

Brandon sat at the table, sliding on his glasses and shoving around a stack of papers. When the door clicked open, he glanced up to see Troy standing there with his head bowed, looking up at Jake guiltily . Beside him stood Misty and four of her cheerleaders, smiling pleasantly. Brandon's stomach turned.

"Uhh," Jake managed to comment.

"They've traveled all this way to support the team," Troy supplied in a tight voice. "But they didn't think to call ahead for rooms," he added. "We're going to have to double-bunk some of the boys."

Jake nodded in a daze and half-turned back into the room. Then he stopped and turned back uncertainly. If he went to get the clipboard, Misty would surely shoulder her way in. "We'll clear up two rooms for them tonight," he finally answered, annoyance over this development barely concealed. "The rest of the week you're on your own," he told Misty coldly.

Brandon watched Misty's face twist and he felt dread building. Misty was quick to confirm his fear. "You should help us out, Jake. We came all this way. Why, you've got two beds in this room; surely the four coaches could bunk together as well as the students," she said, her voice sickeningly sweet.

"Sure we could, if we had known you were coming," Jake answered coldly. "In fact, Troy, clear out *one* of the rooms for them. We'll call for a rollaway to be brought up," he added as he turned to go fetch the clipboard.

Eyes widening, Brandon flinched as Misty shrieked about calling Tom, and she just kept on yelling. Troy and the girls shrank back into the hallway, obviously embarrassed. Seeing Jake's shoulders tighten dangerously, Brandon scrambled a little to get up and walk up behind him – ostensibly to look at the clipboard – but he also placed his hand on Jake's shoulder, a touch that wouldn't be questioned between friends. But it was one he hoped would help keep Jake from going totally postal on the screeching harpy.

Misty indeed pushed her way into the room and despite the calming attempt by Brandon, Jake's temper flared. He shoved the clipboard into Brandon's hands and ushered him out of the room, slamming the door on all of them before rounding on Misty. The shouting could be heard but not understood in the hallway, and soon Troy shooed the four girls away and told them to go wait in the lobby.

He then turned to Brandon and asked, "Do you have your key?"

Brandon tore his eyes away from the door to look at Troy, patted his pockets, and shook his head. "Probably on the table," he said, looking back at the door in ill-concealed concern. Not for Misty.

Troy stepped forward and banged on the door. "Jake! We need you to help with the boys!" he called, knowing that would be the only thing to cut though the rage Jake was channeling. A moment and a few quiet snarls later, the door opened, and Jake stepped out into the hall and stalked down the little corridor without a word to them.

Brandon's eyes tracked Jake as he walked by and he hurt just looking at how upset and tense he was. And not ten minutes ago.... He sighed and walked back into the room after Misty dashed by, red-faced. He snatched up his room key and walked back out to join Troy, pulling the door shut behind him. "C'mon," he murmured as the other man fell in beside him. "We better follow him."

They caught up to Jake at the first door on the list. He was stood there fuming, waiting for the boys to answer his knock.

As Brandon walked up to Jake's side, Troy stayed well back, familiar with Jake's temper. "She's gone," Brandon murmured evenly. "Will you let me deal with this?"

"I'm fine," Jake answered through clenched teeth.

Brandon stepped back, slid a hand into his pocket, and forced a half smile, deciding on a calculated risk. "If you say so, Coach," he said, injecting a note into his voice that clearly said he was humoring the bigger man. Out of the corner of his eye, he could see Troy take another step back.

Jake turned slowly to stare at Brandon for a moment. Hoping his face looked as innocent as possible, Brandon just raised one brow and waited. Jake turned back to the door, jaw tight and eyes flashing as one of the tired kids opened it. Jake stared at him for a moment, trying to regain his temper.

The player's eyes got big as he saw the look on the Coach's face, and he looked to the other coaches, wondering what was wrong. "Yeah, Coach?" he asked in a small voice.

"We need to do some shuffling, guys," Jake finally forced himself to say. "Gather up your things. Just for tonight."

The kid nodded immediately and headed back into the room, leaving the door halfway open. While Jake spoke, Brandon backed up to stand next to Troy, who nudged his arm.

"What the hell, Bartlett? You trying to be six inches shorter? Cause that's what you'll be when he takes your damn head off," Troy muttered.

Brandon's face got pinched and he turned a glare on Troy. "You were doing so well helping, I saw," he muttered.

"I learned some time back *not to help*. He must like you," Troy said under his breath. "Otherwise you'd be out cold on the floor."

Brandon's eyes shifted back to Jake, who was now talking quietly with the two players who had packed up fast and vacated the room.

As the kids dragged their things down the hall to the next room, Jake turned and looked at his other coaches, meeting Brandon's eyes for a long, tense moment before turning and following to knock on the next door. Brandon couldn't decide if he'd done the right thing or not. He'd just reacted, really. So he stood there with Troy and kept his mouth shut as Jake cleared up the situation with the rooms.

When he had the boys double-bunked and had taken their keys from them, Jake continued down the hallway to the lobby, fuming still and unable to look back at the other two men for fear of growling at them. He found the girls, who were now hunched together and chattering nervously, and he walked up to them and handed two of them keys and told them the room number. "Where's your coach?" he asked flatly, and the girls all just pointed toward the bar area and skittered away to their rooms.

Troy took that opportunity to mutter a 'good luck, road kill' and take off. Brandon spared a very violent thought for him before glancing back at Jake, who was staring at the bar, anger still clear on his face. Brandon decided he wasn't helping – probably hadn't since he first left Jake alone with Misty – and started walking back toward their room without a word. His burst of energy was gone and then some. If he was going to get howled at, he'd rather it be after he'd gotten some sleep. A moment later and Jake materialized at his side, walking down the hall silently without ever having approached the cheerleading coach at the bar. Brandon wasn't tempted to say anything, even when Jake pulled out his key card, opened the door, and gestured for Brandon to walk inside.

Jake followed and stood at the door, staring into the dark room morosely. "Bitch," he finally grunted before beginning to take off his shirt.

Brandon pulled off his glasses and tossed them haphazardly

on the table, where they slid across the messy papers. He pulled off his own shirt and worked on unfastening his jeans. Once Jake spoke the tension he'd felt had melted, and now it was all he could do to remain upright.

"She's going to follow me around for the rest of my fucking life," Jake muttered as if he was just now realizing this. Brandon couldn't help but snort as he shoved his jeans over his hips and kicked them off. "It's not funny," Jake insisted seriously. "What are we gonna do if she ever shows up on my doorstep?" he asked.

Brandon's head snapped around to look at Jake in disbelief. *Holy shit*. "Uh." All he could think of was that if she touched Jake again, he might slap the hell out of her. But that probably wouldn't go over real well.

Jake licked his lips and stared back at Brandon. "What if she finally gets the hint and turns her energy toward revenge?" he posed quietly, his body going cold at the thought.

"What if? Jake, we can go on about what ifs until we're both blue in the face," Brandon said, upset and resigned in equal measures. "Can you tell me it's going to make a difference? Because if it does, I'd rather know now." There was no strength behind his question, because for him, it didn't matter. Despite how much he bottled it up, he loved Jake desperately. He wasn't sure how he'd react if something happened to tear them apart so fast.

"A difference?" Jake asked in confusion.

Brandon sat down hard on the edge of the bed. He rubbed both hands over his face. "If Misty figured us out and did something about it, is that going to change what's between us for you?"

"No," Jake answered in surprise. "No," he repeated as he walked closer, sitting on the end of the bed beside Brandon. "I just ... She scares me."

"I understand," Brandon said softly, head in his hands with his eyes closed. "If it happens, we'll deal with it. Somehow."

"*We* will?" Jake asked, looking over at Brandon sideways and smiling a little.

Brandon looked up and blinked at him. "Yeah?" he drew out,

wondering why Jake would question that. "You think I'm going leave you alone if she tries to get her claws into you?"

"You'd better not," Jake growled.

"Not gonna happen," Brandon said as he looked up, face softened. Jake leaned over and kissed him on impulse, turning and crawling onto him to pin him against the mattress and kiss him some more. Brandon wrapped his arms around Jake's neck and held on tight. "Please tell me you locked the door," he murmured.

"Hotel door," Jake growled, "It locks on its own."

"Right," Brandon moaned. "Get on with it then. We don't have to be anywhere until after lunch tomorrow, and I intend to sleep late in your arms."

"Get on with it?" Jake asked in a mockingly offended voice. "*Get on with it*?" he teased as he gathered Brandon up and pushed him across the bed slightly and kissed him again.

Brandon snickered against Jake's lips, sliding his legs apart and then hooking his feet over Jake's calves. "Mmmm hmmm. Don't you want me to soothe the savage beast?" he teased between kisses.

Jake actually ruined the kiss by snorting. "Oh Christ, now I can't do it," he groaned as he pushed himself up onto all fours.

Chuckling, Brandon just looked up at him. "I could have called you Thunder– " Jake cut the word off with another growling kiss. Brandon grinned somehow under the pressure of Jake's lips and pulled his body back down, lifting his legs to curl them over Jake's hips.

"Get on with it, he says," Jake muttered against Brandon's lips as his hands began to pull at Brandon's briefs.

"Uh huh," Brandon breathed, dropping his legs to help and pushing at Jake's shorts and boxers.

Jake huffed and yanked at Brandon's briefs roughly enough to rip the seam and kissed him harder, trying to instill a little more excitement in him than 'get on with it.'

Brandon's muffled laughter turned to a deeper moan, and his hands tightened on Jake as his cock twitched and his gut clenched.

Pulling back from the kiss to gulp for air, he choked on a whimper. "Want you," he said, helplessly arching up against Jake's body. "Need you."

"That's more like it," Jake rumbled as he moved back just far enough to remove Brandon's briefs. "Tell me you packed optimistically," he murmured.

"I packed optimistically," Brandon said, already breathless, pushing himself up onto his elbows. "I figured I'd have to drag you off somewhere out of the hotel to even have a chance at this," he said, pointing at the duffle bag to the side of the bed.

"Lucky me," Jake moaned as he kissed him. He pushed up and quickly rifled through the duffel bag until he found the tube, then shed the remainder of his clothing before climbing back on top of Brandon. "Just no screaming," he growled in a low voice.

"Screaming? Me?" Brandon objected, ruining it by yelping sharply as cool, slick fingers slipped between his legs.

"Hush," Jake hissed, pressing his lips to Brandon's to muffle his words. He twisted his fingers evilly and growled.

Brandon drew in a sharp breath through his nose and dug his fingers into Jake's shoulders hard. "Please," he said against Jake's lips. "Please please please please," he chanted raggedly, tilting his hips up with each push of Jake's hand.

"Shhhhh," Jake soothed as he removed his fingers and guided himself quickly inside with an impatient growl. Brandon whimpered and wrapped his arms and legs around him, and Jake groaned softly, one hand wrapping over Brandon's head to tangle his fingers in his hair as he quickened his pace.

"Oh yessssss," Brandon hissed, hitching his knees up further and burying his face in Jake's neck to muffle a long moan. This man was his – *his* – and Misty would never, ever have him. Possessiveness like he never expected swamped him, and he slid one hand up over the back of Jake's neck.

Jake pressed his face into Brandon's throat and moaned his name brokenly, his hips rocking into him, but nothing else moving. Brandon wrapped his hand about Jake's nape, fingers digging in as he rolled his shoulders forward to press his lips to Jake's ear and growled.

"Mine."

"Yes," Jake gasped almost desperately as he sped up his rhythm, jarring Brandon's body with his thrusts.

Gasping harshly, Brandon's head fell back and he bit his bottom lip to hold in the cries he wanted to loose as Jake set him afire. Jake moaned brokenly and pressed his open mouth to Brandon's neck, tightening his grip as his muscles clenched. He gasped and groaned as his orgasm tore through him. The feel of heat and Jake's body shuddering made Brandon snap inside, and with a stuttered gasp he came, the pleasure crashing through him in heavy waves.

Jake whimpered as the aftershocks rippled inside him. He pressed his lips to Brandon's sweaty skin and sucked in air noisily, holding him tight. "Mine," he murmured, the word barely audible.

If Jake hadn't been so close, Brandon would have missed it, and the single word thrilled him almost as much as Jake telling him that he loved him. He turned his chin just enough to press his lips to Jake's throat. "Yours," he whispered.

Chapter 12

AFTER scribbling a few more notes, Brandon tossed down his pen and sat back from the writing desk. Thank God that was done – end of the year grades. Summer break was a breath away and he could hardly wait. Graduation was the day after tomorrow, he'd have one administrative day left, and then he could pack James into the closet and escape. The state tournament was next week and after that things would really calm down.

Brandon *really* looked forward to some uninterrupted time with Jake. They'd even talked about a week's vacation, the farther away the better. Brandon had suggested Denver, where they could watch the Braves against the Rockies in a three-game stretch. Jake had countered with San Francisco and a four-game stretch, plus San Diego not so far away. They were still undecided on anything except that baseball would be involved.

Remembering he'd promised Jake he would tally the JV and freshman end-of-the-year stats for the spring sports banquet, Brandon started digging under the piles of papers, looking for the two different score books. With a quiet "Ah-ha," he pulled them out from under his planner and shuffled them, deciding to start with JV and work his way down. The varsity stats were already figured and trophies ordered; Jake was out picking them up now in Atlanta proper.

He pulled out a memo pad and started tallying, shifting some haphazardly folded papers out of the way, his curiosity caught when he saw one page with a dark circle around some text. He unfolded it, gave it a glance, and abruptly straightened in the chair. It was an e-mail to Jake at his school address. What was circled was a long-distance phone number.

Hello Coach Campbell,

On the reference of Coach Chester at Fresno State, I wanted to send you this job listing. We're really looking for someone to turn our Varsity Football program around, and after some research, I can see that you're highly qualified. You'd definitely top out the salary range. Congratulations on your run at the Georgia state title in baseball, by the way.

I hope you'll give this position due consideration. Give me a call anytime if you have questions.

Thanks,

Sam Weatherby

Athletic Director

Theodore Roosevelt High School

559-555-0134

What followed was what looked to be a job listing clipped from a paper, detailing a call for a head football coach at a school in Fresno, California. The school, the clipping said, had not won in over 40 years and was desperate for a football coach with a proven record of winning and running a program. The salary was generous if the applicant had a degree, and Jake certainly did, and the classes he would have to teach consisted of weightlifting and football. No P.E., just two whole planning blocks for what was apparently a major football program; a mere step down from a college program. The job was marketed as a challenge, something that would certainly pique the interest of a competitor like Jake.

Brandon sat there staring at the letter for two extra-long minutes, floored. It was dated two weeks ago. Jake hadn't said a thing.

Slowly, mechanically, he refolded the e-mail and dropped it back with the other papers into the opened book. Telling himself sharply not to overreact, he decided a long, hard run was in order so he could think his way out of this sudden upset. Shifting the chair back and leaving the mess strewn across the desk, he went to change clothes. He'd drive home to run in the park. Peace and quiet would help him settle down.

Surely it was nothing. His jaw clenched as he packed a duffel bag.

The front door slammed and banged and Jake thumped into the house, loaded down with a heavy box of trophies. "Look at this shit!" he shouted irately, "They fucking have women on the goddamned trophies!"

In the bedroom, Brandon stood up from tying his running shoes. He'd half-hoped he'd get out of the house before Jake got back so he'd have some time to remind himself that Jake wouldn't do anything rash. Right? He grabbed a tank top and pulled it over his head with one hand, the duffle in the other as he walked down the hall to stop and look at his lover questioningly. "Women?" he asked mildly, proud that his voice was normal.

Jake yanked the trophy out of the box he had opened on the way home and thrust it at Brandon petulantly. "Ponytails and everything," he grumbled with another disgusted look at the little statue. He looked back up at Brandon and blinked in surprise when he noticed the bag. "You going somewhere?" he asked.

"A run," Brandon said, setting the duffel on the counter as he went to the fridge for a Gatorade. "Thought I'd drive over to Mountain Park and get some stuff at the house, run around the lake." It was easier to stay casual not looking at him.

"All righty," Jake responded in slight confusion. Something was off, but he couldn't quite figure out what. "You okay?"

Brandon couldn't help but smile. Jake seemed to worry about him a lot, especially since the burnout episode over spring break. "Yeah, just got grades on the brain, you know?" He turned around and grabbed the duffle and then stopped in front of Jake for a slow, sweet kiss that belied the elephants stampeding in his stomach.

Jake stood blinking as Brandon moved away. "'kay," he muttered, still confused and completely unashamed of showing it.

Milking the distracted daze for all it was worth, Brandon tossed a "See you at the banquet" over his shoulder before fleeing the house with some dignity intact. Once in the car, he got to the stoplight and had to wait. He noticed his hands were shaking. In a moment of unusual pique, he slammed his fist against the steering wheel.

Jake stood rooted to the spot, head cocked and upper lip curled in confusion, the box of trophies still tucked under his arm as he stared at the door. Finally he looked around the house as if there were some clue as to what had upset Brandon, because he was definitely upset about something, but Jake could see nothing unusual. He sighed heavily and walked to the kitchen, set down the box, and went to his cupboard of pills.

Even as he drove, Brandon couldn't stop thinking about the damn e-mail. He turned on the radio, loud. He rolled down the windows. He tried to focus on happy plans for vacation, which just got him to thinking. How far was Fresno from San Francisco or San Diego? He felt faintly ill and wished he could shut his brain off. A near miss rear-ending a car at the next stoplight forced him to concentrate on driving.

It wasn't until roughly an hour after Brandon left that Jake sat down at the desk and the scorebooks to see if Brandon had managed to finish the tallying. The first thing he saw when he opened the book was that damn e-mail staring at him. He hopped up with a curse and headed for the phone, hoping to catch Brandon at the house.

But he hadn't even gone inside. Brandon just tossed his keys onto the back porch and set out for the lake. Although he'd calmed down quite a bit, he needed the mind wipe a long run would give him. He'd even almost managed to convince himself the e-mail didn't mean anything. Jake loved him. He wouldn't leave him. But as he picked up speed around the lake, that one little niggle of fear continued to eat at him.

The phone rang and rang in Jake's ear and finally he hung it up with a clank, cursing inventively. What the fuck was Brandon thinking, running away like this? He hadn't even *asked* about it. Jake prowled around his house, kicking at inanimate objects and muttering to himself. The fuck. He'd just run away. Jake had thought Brandon a lot of things, but a coward had never been one of them.

Brandon ran until he thought he might collapse, but he at least made it back to the porch before flopping on the steps and lying back on the wood. He'd managed to zone out for a little while, but it was a testament to how wrapped up he was in Jake that he just couldn't shake the scare. Groaning, he rubbed his eyes with the heels of his hands. He'd have to ask about it. It would drive him crazy until he knew. Sighing, he dragged himself up and went back to the car for the duffle, then headed inside.

The more time that passed, the angrier Jake found himself. It didn't help that he had an infamous temper. It didn't help that he was terrified their carefully hewn relationship might be falling apart out there on a trail somewhere with no way for him to fix it. That was just adding to the anger. When the phone began to ring, Jake rounded on it and grabbed it, yanked it out of the wall and tossed it across the kitchen. He snorted at it and then walked out of the house into the back yard and disappeared into the grove of trees.

Brandon stopped still and stood looking at the phone. Calmer now, he felt not a little ashamed of himself. He'd never backed down from Jake, even when the other man was mad as hell. He'd never lied to him, either. And he didn't think Jake had ever kept anything from him. Taking a breath, he set his hand on the phone for a long moment, then picked it up and dialed. The more the phone rang, the more resigned he felt. Finally he hung up and laid his forehead against the wall. He hoped Jake was in the shower or something. He glanced at the clock. Four hours to the banquet. More than enough time to head back to the house and talk to Jake. He headed to the shower and cleaned up, thoughts buzzing the whole time and on the drive back as well. When he pulled into the driveway, he knew what he was going to say.

Heading into the house, he called Jake's name. No response came. The remains of the shattered phone met him in the foyer, and one of the little gold trophies sat on the corner of the bar, the bat pointing toward the cupboard of pills with the little pony-tailed head ripped off and hanging on the end of it.

Brandon stared at the mess for a long moment, then turned his chin to look at the desk. The score book lay open, the e-mail exposed. *Christ. I really fucked this one up*. Taking a deep breath, he started cleaning up the mess, figuring Jake had to come back sometime, if only to get the scorebooks and tallies for the banquet.

Jake spent an hour roaming the little clearing out back where he had grown up hitting rocks as a kid. He walked in circles, picking up bits of loose gravel and sticks. He would take a rock, toss it up, and swing. Over and over, for hours on end. He still had the ruined nub of the bat he'd used as a kid mounted on a plaque in his old bedroom.

He stood there, thinking about the last twenty years and where they had gone different from what he had wanted. Not wrong. Just different. Slowly his breathing calmed, his temper ebbed, and he was left standing in the middle of the clearing with a tight throat and chest, thinking about where he had left to go and what he would have were he to leave.

Lowering his head, Jake turned and walked slowly back to the house.

Brandon leaned against the wall facing the door, just waiting. The time dragged and dragged, until he heard footsteps. Jake walked slowly to the door, opened it, and once inside looked up at him. The look on his face about broke Brandon's heart. "Jake," he started, voice thick.

"I need a shower," Jake responded as he headed for the hall.

Brandon set his jaw and stepped in front of him, hands touching each wall, blocking the way. "I want to go with you," he said steadily.

Jake stopped and blinked at him. "What?" he asked flatly.

Tilting his head with a stern look, Brandon's expression showed that *he* knew that *Jake* knew what he was talking about. "If you leave, I want to go with you," he said.

"Why would you think I'm going anywhere?" Jake asked in a tired voice. He'd walked the anger out, and now he just felt flat and exhausted. "Why would you think I would even consider leaving and never mention it to you?"

"It scared the hell out of me, Jake," Brandon said starkly. "I know I overreacted. Except for that vacation, when have we ever talked about the future beyond this weekend or the next game?" He dropped both arms, looking truly upset. "It just made me realize that I wouldn't have anything if you left," he said miserably.

Jake gave a pained wince and looked down at the floor. "*I* wouldn't have anything if I left, either," he murmured.

Brandon's throat ached as he slowly stepped forward, closer to his lover, reaching out to lightly touch his cheek. "I'm sorry I scared you," he said. "I scared the hell out of myself, too."

"You just fucking left," Jake whispered roughly.

Brandon let his hand fall back to his side. He deserved that. "Yeah," he said, voice full of self-recrimination. "I'm too good at running, I guess. But I am sorry. Please believe me. I know I fucked up royally."

"Yeah, you did," Jake answered with a nod of his head. "So did I."

Nodding, Brandon's shoulders slumped a little. "Are we – are we going to be okay?" he asked weakly.

Jake met Brandon's eyes and his lips twitched. "You're willing to move to California with me," he murmured.

"Jake, I'd move to Antarctica with you," Brandon replied honestly. Jake replied by stepping closer and pulling Brandon to him for a passionate kiss. He wrapped his arms around him and turned them both, pushing Brandon against the wall as he kissed him harder.

Brandon's arms flew around Jake's neck, and he held on tight, joining the kiss desperately, inside chanting *Thank you God, thank you God, thank you God, thank you God...*

"Don't ever run from me again," Jake pleaded.

Brandon nodded his head earnestly. "I promise," he said. "Fuck, Jake. I love you so much it hurts."

"I'm sorry," Jake responded as he pressed his forehead to Brandon's and held the other man's face between his hands.

"Just please, don't ever leave me behind," Brandon asked,

voice cracking.

"You're mine," Jake answered with a shake of his head. "You won't be left behind."

Brandon tilted his head to kiss him again, one arm around his neck, one around his waist as Jake kept him smashed against the wall. It felt perfect, but that didn't stop him from flinching and choking in surprise when the screen door opened and someone walked in.

"Hey, Jake, I came to help with the... tro... phies..." Troy's voice trailed off as his eyes got big, blinking at what he saw as if he couldn't believe it.

Jake didn't move, closing his eyes as he kept his forehead pressed to Brandon's. "The trophies are fucked," he answered calmly. He was shocked, actually, by how calm he was. But he had no intention of acting guilty for kissing his lover in his own house.

Troy blinked again, hard, and then tilted his head. He looked startled. "*Brandon*?" he asked, voice rising at the end. The man was practically hidden under Jake's body, they were so close.

Jake finally pushed away from the wall, meeting Brandon's eyes with something like fear. The changeable eyes looking back at him glimmered with emotion and a promise. Jake turned and looked at Troy silently, waiting for him to say something else.

The blond man looked back and forth between them for a long moment before suddenly breaking into a huge grin. "Jonathan owes me fifty bucks!" he crowed.

Brandon's jaw dropped. For once Jake was stunned, and it showed. "What?" he asked in a hoarse voice.

"Heh heh heh," Troy chortled. "I told him. I told him you two had to be together. Had to be. He was like *'no way'* – kid's too straight for his own good." His eyes were dancing. "This is so great." Jake was struck speechless. He just shook his head and let his mouth fall open.

"What?" Troy asked. "You've been in too damn good of a mood since spring break. That was when I first knew *something* was up, when you didn't take Brandon's head off after that shitstorm with Misty." Troy looked awfully proud of himself.

Brandon shifted off the wall to stand behind Jake, looking over his shoulder at the gleeful man. "He seems inordinately happy about this," he murmured.

"I think he's high," Jake responded in a stage whisper. "Maybe he won't remember this tomorrow."

Troy snickered. "Dream on, butterfingers." He shoved his hands in his pockets and rolled back on his heels. "So, I'm right, right? You're a couple? I mean, not just fucking around, but *together*."

"Awful lucid for being high," Brandon said doubtfully relaxing, though he still looked at Troy like he was off his rocker. It surely wasn't the kind of response he'd expected if one of their fellow coaches discovered his relationship with Jake.

"Are you okay with this?" Jake asked his oldest friend, hope and disbelief warring in his voice.

"Hell, Jake. I'm just glad to see you happy and with someone, man," Troy said seriously. Then his eyes twinkled as he glanced up at Brandon. "Even if it is with a nerd."

Brandon choked on a curse and moved to come around Jake. "I'll show you nerd!" he threatened. Jake reached out and snagged Brandon's collar with a muttered, "Down, boy." Troy just cackled when Brandon struggled a little only to get pulled back into Jake's arms.

"Jake, I'll just hurt him a *little* bit," Brandon whined, his eyes shooting daggers at the blond.

The bigger man held him close and petted his head distractedly as he met Troy's eyes. This was one outcome Jake had never even considered a possibility. He was shocked and touched, and it showed in his dark eyes as he smiled and mouthed a silent 'Thank you.'

Although Troy was outwardly ragging on Brandon, his eyes were full of warmth and acceptance, and he nodded to his longtime friend and smiled.

Brandon huffed and leaned back against Jake to pout, which made Troy break into laughter again. "Do you find that look gets you anything you want from Jake?" he asked. Brandon stuck his tongue out at him. Jake's hand soon followed, clapping over Brandon's mouth. Brandon retaliated by licking Jake's palm.

Troy grinned. "Well. I suppose being a friend and all, I don't need to collect that money from Jonathan. I'll just expect a favor sometime down the road. We *will* be seeing you two at the banquet tonight?"

"Ugh," Jake answered with a roll of his eyes, thinking about the trophies as he wiped his hand absently on Brandon's shirt. "Come look at these damn things," he muttered as he pointed at the kitchen.

The science teacher chuckled and stepped aside to let Jake past him, and they all walked into the kitchen to look. "Jake, why the hell did you even bring these home? You should have chucked them back at them at the store," Brandon said, making a face at one of the pony-tailed statuettes.

"They were boxed," Jake answered defensively. "I only opened one 'cause I got stuck in traffic and needed something shiny to look at."

Troy looked between the two, another silly smile forming on his face.

"Never leave a store without checking that you get what you paid for, Jake. Now you'll have to drive them back and either get them redone or get a refund," Brandon replied. He glanced up to see Troy practically snickering. "What's so funny?"

"You two. You're like a damn old married couple," Troy said. Jake picked up the head of the defaced trophy and chucked it at him. Brandon grinned when Troy howled and stomped his foot. "Fine. I'll just be buzzing off in my cart, and you two can go back to necking. Or whatever you were going to do." He winked and headed out the door, whistling.

"Jackass," Jake muttered after him.

Now that Troy was gone, a bit of the daze was creeping back. "Did you expect that?" Brandon asked.

"No," Jake answered immediately. "No, I figured... I figured I'd lose him."

"If you can't depend on your best friend, then who?" Brandon said quietly. "I never had that. You're lucky."

Jake slid his eyes sideways to look at Brandon thoughtfully. "You do now," he responded softly .

Brandon's lips pulled into a happy smile, and he nodded, moving to slide his arms around Jake's waist. "So," he started, needing to nudge a little, "think we'll be that damn old married couple someday?"

"Not in Georgia," Jake answered with a laugh as he wrapped his arms around Brandon.

"Wherever. Don't care as long as you're there."

"Sap," Jake accused with a small smile and a stolen kiss.

Brandon rolled his eyes. "So lug me off to your bed, caveman," he teased.

"Mm," Jake responded with a shake of his head, "We don't have time for what I want to do to you," he declared.

"Oh really?" Brandon said as he raised a curious eyebrow. "And what would it be that you couldn't do in..." he leaned back to look at the clock, "about an hour and a half?"

"Everything," Jake answered smugly.

Brandon laughed as Jake pulled him closer. "Everything? Wow. Uh ... that's ... quite a bit," he commented. "When are you going to start on that?"

"Tonight," Jake answered. "I've got some steam to let off because of you, y'know."

"I'm looking forward to it, Thundercat," Brandon purred as he nipped at Jake's lower lip. Jake jabbed him in the ribs. Hard. Brandon squawked and tried to jerk away, turning to protect his sides as he laughed.

"Bastard," Jake snarled playfully as he held onto Brandon and finally dragged him to the ground to pin him there.

Brandon cackled and kept struggling, though he knew full well there was no way he'd get away from Jake – he was caught. And he didn't want to run any more.

Madeleine Urban is a down-home Kentucky girl who's been writing since she could hold a crayon. A longtime science fiction and fantasy fan, she loves to mix those genres with romance to get explosive, satisfying results. She lives with a partner and two canine kids, visits Disney World twice a year, and still believes dreams can come true.

Visit Madeleine's Blog at http://madeleineurban.livejournal.com

⌘

Abigail Roux is a whimsical girl who likes her beer cold and her sex hot. A past volleyball star and current rabid Braves fan, Abigail has a husband, one dog, six cats, a crazyass family, and a cast of thousands in her head. Her stories often feature love, lust and manly men.

Visit Abigail's Blog at http://abigail-roux.livejournal.com

Printed in the United Kingdom
by Lightning Source UK Ltd.
132691UK00001B/641/A

9 780980 101881